6/6/18

#2

OUTRAGE

Other Titles by T.R. Ragan

Faith McMann Trilogy

Furious

Lizzy Gardner Series

Abducted
Dead Weight
A Dark Mind
Obsessed
Almost Dead
Evil Never Dies

Writing as Theresa Ragan

Return of the Rose
A Knight in Central Park
Taming Mad Max
Finding Kate Huntley
Having My Baby
An Offer He Can't Refuse
Here Comes the Bride
I Will Wait for You: A Novella
Dead Man Running

OUTRAGE

FAITH MCMANN NO. 2

T.R. RAGAN

⊤THOMAS & MERCER

This is a work of fiction. Names, characters, organizations, places, events, and incidents are either products of the author's imagination or are used fictitiously.

Published by Thomas & Mercer, Seattle

www.apub.com

Amazon, the Amazon logo, and Thomas & Mercer are trademarks of Amazon.com, Inc., or its affiliates.

ISBN-13: 9781503938809
ISBN-10: 1503938808

Cover art by melteddashboard.com

Cover design by Rex Bonomelli

Printed in the United States of America

*The Faith McMann trilogy is dedicated to people,
including Holly Austin Smith, who work tirelessly
to raise awareness and increase understanding of
human trafficking and who struggle endlessly to
supply services and help to survivors.*
You are all heroes.
For information about trafficking:
www.traffickingresourcecenter.org.

Today, two cultural forces are converging to make America's youth easy targets for sex traffickers. Primed by the media, their self-worth often negatively affected by the images they are bombarded with, younger and younger girls are adopting adult sexual attitudes and practices. At the same time, thanks to social media, texting, and chat rooms, predators are able to ferret out their victims more easily than ever before.

—Holly Austin Smith, *Walking Prey:*
How America's Youth Are Vulnerable to Sex Slavery

ONE

Huddled beneath a wool blanket, shivering and cold with brittle leaves and twigs digging into his back, Hudson McMann opened his eyes. Through a makeshift shelter of branches leaning against the biggest tree he'd been able to find, he saw the sun just beginning to peek over the mountain ridge, splashing oranges and reds across the sky.

He felt grateful for the sun this morning as he tried to rub some warmth into his arms. If it had been raining or snowing, he wasn't sure he and Joey would still be alive. They had spent the past two nights in the mountains. During the first night, they'd heard dogs in the distance, the same dogs the drug dealers used to find runaways.

The higher up the mountain he and Joey had gone, the colder it had gotten. Although they hadn't heard the bark of a dog in the past twenty-four hours, he'd never been more afraid in his life. If they were found, they would probably be shot and killed like their friend Sean.

He was certain of it.

Being here in the woods reminded him of Grandpa's war stories. Grandpa had talked about how important it was to keep the men moving, reminding Hudson that they needed to do the same.

He shook Joey awake. "Get up. We need to start walking."

"I'm hungry," Joey said.

"Me, too."

Joey was older than Hudson, but he was small for his age, whereas Hudson was taller and bigger in the shoulders. From what he knew about the boy, Joey had had a tough childhood. He'd also never gone camping or hunting. He'd never once slept in the woods under the stars, but instead had spent more than a few nights curled up in a ball on the cold floor of a rundown warehouse.

Joey had worried about the cries of coyotes on their first night in the woods. Hudson had been more afraid of the bad men finding them than he'd been of wild animals.

With one blanket between them, a pocketknife, and not much else, they were hungry and thirsty. Joey didn't look too good. His eyes were bloodshot and rimmed with red. His skin was ghostly pale.

Yesterday Hudson had tried to catch a squirrel for them to eat, but he'd settled for eating bugs and earthworms. Grandpa had taught him that most worms were high in protein and iron. Joey wouldn't have anything to do with eating bugs. Not yet. Sooner or later, he would have to give in if he wanted to live.

Once Joey was on his feet, Hudson folded the blanket, tucked it under his arm, and started off. "We'll head east for the next mile and then make our way downward. We need to find some water—a creek or maybe a river." Grandpa always told Hudson that if he was ever lost in the woods, he needed to find a water source.

"What about Denver and Aiden? Do you think they got away?"

Hudson glanced over the vast forest of fir and pine and rugged canyon. He'd never felt so alone in his life, but if Joey had any idea of how scared he was, it would only make matters worse. "Denver is big and strong," Hudson said. "I'm sure they got away, and we will, too."

"You think so?"

He swallowed a lump lodged in his throat. "Yeah," Hudson said. "I know so."

For hours they trudged onward. It wasn't easy walking down a steep incline. They both slid over rocks and damp leaves. Every so often Hudson stopped to look over his shoulder to make sure Joey was close by. Twice he thought he'd lost him. But both times he waited until Joey staggered forward. The first time he appeared through a dense area of trees; this time Joey stumbled around a bend.

Joey was slow on his feet. Too slow.

About to walk back toward him to see if Joey needed help, Hudson heard a familiar sound—trickling water. "Water!" he said under his breath as he ran back toward Joey. "We're almost there!"

Despite the cold, Joey's forehead was slick with sweat. Hudson used the back of his hand to touch the boy's head, just like his mom did when he wasn't feeling well. "You're burning up."

The kid was paler than the moon. Worried, Hudson heaved Joey's arm over his shoulder and helped him walk down the steep slope. It took them a while to find the creek. He brought Joey to the edge, and for the next few minutes they drank their fill. He knew they were at risk drinking the water without boiling it. *But beggars can't be choosers,* he thought.

"Have you ever tasted anything so good?" Hudson asked as he slurped water from his cupped hands.

After a long moment of silence, Hudson looked over his shoulder. Joey had pushed himself a foot away from the creek and was now leaning against a boulder. His eyes were closed, and every breath sounded ragged. His lips and the tips of his fingers were bluish. Joey was sicker than he'd first thought.

TWO

The bottom of Faith McMann's shoes squeaked as she walked. It was early in the morning—early enough that the hospital corridor was devoid of people, free of the usual hustle and bustle of nurses and staff.

Faith walked with confidence, doing her best to appear as if she belonged there.

The floors were newly mopped. The overwhelming smell of antiseptics wasn't the reason she felt sick to her stomach. It was the thought of her daughter being trapped in that house for all those days, only hours away, and yet she'd failed to find Lara in time.

They had been so damn close.

Her stomach turned to knots every time she thought about it.

The man who'd called to threaten her family had told her Lara and Hudson were dead. Obviously he'd lied, since more than one of the girls who'd been held by the sex traffickers saw Lara alive and well only days before. But where was her daughter now? Who had taken her from the farmhouse? And why take Lara and not the others? Diane Weaver, the woman in charge of the girls, had refused to give Faith the answers she needed after she'd raided the place. She should have dragged the woman's ass out into the woods while she'd had the chance.

But maybe Corrie Perelman's daughter could shed light on where Lara might be. Samantha Perelman had been missing for the past eighteen months. During the raid, Faith had found the poor girl locked in a small, dark space, hidden away at the back of the kitchen pantry.

And that's why she was here at the hospital. She needed to talk to the girl and find out what she knew.

Faith waited in the shadows until the nurse was preoccupied, then hurried past to Samantha's room. The door was open, and she quickly stepped inside. A curtain divided the room in half. The first bed was empty. Lying in the other bed was Samantha Perelman.

She slept faceup, arms at her side, body rigid. If not for the faint sound of her breathing, Faith might have thought the worst. Samantha's hair had been chopped off at blunt angles around her ears—as if someone had used a dull knife to cut it. Her face was puffy, the left side badly bruised. Purplish shadows framed her eyes. She hardly resembled the seventeen-year-old girl who'd been abducted from a grocery store a year earlier while her mother shopped nearby.

A sharp pain pierced Faith's heart. The thought of all Samantha had been through tore her apart. Samantha needed her rest. Faith never should have come. She turned toward the door.

"Faith McMann?"

At the sound of the girl's voice, Faith swiveled back around.

Samantha was awake.

Faith stepped closer, stopping at the metal railing on the side of the bed. "I'm sorry. I didn't mean to wake you."

"Is Mom here?"

Faith shook her head. "It's still early."

Samantha licked her lips. "Is it true? Did those bastards take your kids?"

The strength in Samantha's voice contrasted greatly with her fragile appearance. "They took my son and my daughter," Faith said.

"It was Miranda, wasn't it? She escaped the farmhouse, didn't she? She's the reason we were found."

"Yes," Faith said. "Miranda got away and told us everything she knew."

"Where is she?"

"She's safe."

"You're the one who found me. You saved my life," Samantha said next, peering into her eyes. "You saved us all."

"If not for Miranda, we never would have located the farmhouse to begin with."

"What happened to Mother?" Samantha asked next. "She's evil. She's ruined so many lives."

The girl's mouth was dry, her voice raspy. Faith looked around for water but didn't see any. "She's in jail," Faith said. "She won't ever hurt you again."

"What about the others?" Samantha asked, flittering from one thought to another. "Are they OK?"

"The other girls who were in the house with you are safe," Faith said. Outside the room, she heard voices, which prompted her to get to the point of why she'd come. "I have something I need to ask you."

"What is it?"

"I'm trying to find my daughter. Miranda told me she was at the farmhouse and that they changed her name to Jean. I was wondering if you'd met her?"

She gasped. "That's your daughter? I like Jean. She was new to the house. Mother didn't like to see the two of us talking, so she locked me up in that cubbyhole in the pantry. Do you have a picture of your daughter?" Samantha clicked a button attached to a thick cord hanging over the metal railing. The bedside light came on.

Faith dug through her purse, pulled out one of her flyers, and handed it to Samantha.

"Yeah, that's her."

"I was hoping you might know something about where she is now."

"Jean wasn't there with the other girls?"

Faith shook her head.

Samantha appeared visibly shaken by the news, and Faith didn't like that she'd upset the girl. But then Samantha's eyes widened and she said, "You know, now that I'm thinking about it, I heard Mother talking on the phone that same morning before you arrived. Sometimes I think Mother would forget I was hidden away." Samantha scratched her arm close to where the IV needle was taped.

"Do you remember who she was talking to?"

Samantha shook her head at first, but then her eyes widened as a thought came to her. "I don't know who she was talking to, but I do think the conversation had something to do with moving Jean. They do that sometimes, you know. Move certain girls from one house to another, especially if they believe a girl is too much trouble for one reason or another." She licked her lips again. "I wish the bitch had moved me. That never would have happened, though. Mother didn't like me. She wanted me to suffer for refusing to obey her rules." More scratching.

"Do you have any idea at all where Diane Weaver might have been sending Jean off to?"

"Is that Mother's name?" Samantha asked. "Diane Weaver?"

Faith nodded.

Knowing Mother's name appeared to upset her. Samantha's eyes watered, and Faith reached for her hand and gave it a squeeze.

"I hate her," Samantha whispered.

Faith understood all too well. Her heart went out to the girl.

It was quiet for a long moment before Samantha spoke again. "I'm sorry I'm not much help. I only know that Mother sounded as if she were in a rush because she told the person on the phone to hurry up or she'd call someone else."

"You have nothing to be sorry for," Faith told her. "You're a brave young woman, and you've been a tremendous help."

Diane Weaver, Faith thought as she stood still, holding the girl's hand, trying to comfort her. All the answers were locked up in prison with her. She needed to talk to Detective Yuhasz and convince him to pay Diane a visit. Maybe he could get her to talk.

The main light came on, fluorescent and bright. Faith squinted.

A nurse walked inside and yanked open the curtain. "What's going on? These are not visiting hours."

"This is the lady who saved my life," Samantha said to the nurse. "I invited her here. She can stay."

"I'm sorry," the nurse told Faith, "but you'll have to come back during visiting hours. You shouldn't be here. I could lose my job."

Faith lifted her hands in surrender. "It's OK. I'm going." She leaned over the railing, took hold of Samantha's hand, and gave it a squeeze. "Your mom has my number. Let me know if there's anything I can do for you, anything at all."

Samantha clasped both her hands around Faith's. Her eyes welled.

"What is it?" Faith asked. "Do you need help?"

She shook her head. It took a moment for the deep furrow in her brow to disappear. "I just want to say thank you for what you did for me and wish you luck with finding your kids."

Faith realized then how fragile Samantha Perelman was. She'd been through hell, probably learned pretty quickly how to talk tough and act tougher in order to survive. Samantha, no doubt, had a long road to recovery ahead of her.

Faith smiled at the girl, praying she'd find a way to overcome and wishing her nothing but happiness in her future. More determined than ever to find Lara and Hudson, she released her hold on Samantha and turned toward the nurse. "She needs something for her arm to stop the itching."

"I'll take care of it."

"She also needs a glass of water." Without glancing back, Faith left the room, afraid she'd fall apart before she made it out the door.

With counseling and lots of understanding and love, Samantha would surely find her way back. She thought of Lara then, wondered what she was doing at that very moment. If she could stay strong until they found her, Faith would do everything in her power to help her cope in the aftermath. "Hang in there, Lara," she said under her breath. "I'm going to find you and your brother and make those bastards pay."

THREE

Diane Weaver didn't make eye contact with the other prisoners as she headed for the phones. She didn't have to look at them to feel their eyes assessing, judging, sizing her up.

Don't let them see you sweat, she thought.

Every step reverberated off the urine-colored walls, biting chunks out of the stifling silence as she continued down the corridor.

She'd arrived two days ago. If not for the chained fences topped off with barbed wire, the squat brick building would have looked more like a college campus than a prison. But that was only when she was looking at the place from the outside. The inside of the prison was another story. The air was stale, the inmates sour, and the building suffocating.

She had denied any wrongdoing, telling anyone who would listen that she was no less a victim than any of the girls being held at the farmhouse. Unfortunately the police were able to arrest her since they had found a single crack rock and pipe in her purse. She was being held on possession charges. According to one of the investigators who had interviewed her, she could end up serving life without parole, but she was pretty sure they were just trying to scare her into giving a confession.

She remained tight-lipped, and her state-appointed lawyer confirmed that her assessment of the situation was correct.

Desperate to talk to her brother, she picked up her pace. She needed to tell Eric to keep the McMann girl safe until she could figure out how the hell she was going to get out of this place.

Up ahead, two women wearing the same orange prison garb as she was mopped the floor. One of them stopped working and nudged the other. The two women watched her closely as she approached. Diane's face was bruised and battered from the beating she'd taken at the hands of Faith McMann. Dumb bitch was as good as dead if she ever saw her again.

Diane fixed her one good eye on the inmates, refusing to show weakness as she passed them by. The woman on the left was big-boned and more than six feet tall. She had white, spiky punk-rocker hair and two teardrops tattooed below her left eye. The other woman was half her friend's size. Wide-set eyes and a small mouth were framed by a bad case of acne and scabs. She looked familiar. Had they met before?

According to her lawyer, 30 percent of the inmates had been convicted of a capital offense—murder, conspiracy to murder, and kidnapping were the most common. At this point in time, she had no idea how long she would be staying.

Shoulders set back, she passed the women without incident.

The phone line stretched all the way around the corner. Standing at the back of the line, she crossed her arms and waited with everyone else. If not for the McMann bitch, she wouldn't be here. Her eye wouldn't be swollen shut, and her front tooth would still be intact.

But Faith McMann wasn't the only person she blamed.

Aster Williams never should have let it come to this. He was in charge of one of the biggest trafficking rings in Sacramento. He knew every recruiter in the business. Aster saw to it that his pimps used lies and threats to train the victims to become perpetrators in the ever-growing world of trafficking.

Aster had all the power, and yet he'd merely stood by and watched as Faith McMann gathered strength in numbers, spreading the word through the media, storming the farmhouse, and wreaking havoc. Aster should have taken care of the schoolteacher right from the start.

After Phoenix, the boy who worked for her, told Diane that a suspicious-looking woman had been on the road asking for directions, her instincts had kicked in, telling her it was time to move the girl, especially with all the public interest and intense media scrutiny over the McMann case.

Looking back, if Diane had had more time to process her next move, she would have taken the truck and left town. Sweet little innocent Jean would have been returned to her mother, and maybe they all could have moved on.

Instead Diane had seen dollar signs. The McMann kid was young and blonde and untouched. She was worth a lot of money, which prompted Diane to call her idiot brother Eric and ask him to take the girl for a while, figuring she could make a quick sale and pocket the money herself. After sending the girl off, she'd hired a couple of extra men to guard the farmhouse. Even so, she'd never truly expected Faith McMann to come charging onto her property with a half-dozen misfits loaded down with firing power.

Who the hell was this Faith McMann anyhow?

Diane had been recruiting young girls for years. She couldn't remember one time when the parents of a child had decided to grab a pitchfork and take matters into their own hands. The McMann woman was insane. She obviously had no regard for her own life.

For the next thirty minutes, as she shuffled an inch forward in line at a time, she thought about her life and how it kept going from bad to worse.

The youngest of eleven children, eight of those boys, she'd had to work hard to garner attention. The best way to do that seemed to be getting in trouble. And trouble was easy to find. Hanging out with the bad boys at school and then experimenting with drugs got her attention all right. She'd spiraled downhill fast, and it was all a blur. Her family disowned her, and it wasn't long before she found herself in Aster Williams's bed. Young and pretty at the time, she'd become his mistress. He'd treated her well until the crow's feet around her eyes deepened and no amount of makeup could hide her disappointment and age. A younger woman took over from there, a newer and younger version of herself.

Out with the old; in with the new.

By the time it was Diane's turn to make a call, she was seething with anger. She was angry with her family, with Aster, and mostly with herself for making so many bad choices. Her hands shook as she dialed her brother's number. The phone rang. Once. Twice. Three times. "Come on," she muttered. "Answer your damn phone."

There was a click and then an automated message from the California Correctional Facility letting whoever answered the call know that it was a collect call from Diane Weaver.

"Hello?"

She recognized her brother's voice. "Eric, it's me, Diane."

"You're in jail?"

She rolled her eyes. "It's a long story, but it could be a while before I can get to your house and pick up what I left with you." She closed her eyes and prayed he'd understand. The calls were recorded, and therefore she couldn't say Jean's name.

"Trista can't handle this. The animal you left with us hasn't stopped making a racket. I think it wants to be with its other family."

"Jesus. Smack it across the mouth and teach the damn dog a lesson. It's not that difficult."

"You know Trista would never hurt a fly."

Diane looked around to make sure nobody was listening before she growled into the receiver, "Grow a fucking pair, Eric. Knock some sense into that wife of yours. Do you have any idea how much that dog is worth on the outside market? It's like a fucking pedigree."

"I get it. I get it. But Trista isn't like you. She's sensitive. She doesn't want any part of this."

She closed her eyes as she attempted to summon some control over her emotions. She'd never liked Trista. *Sensitive, my foot.* The woman was dumber than mud, the kind of female who needed to be hit across the head to make her understand. "Listen closely, little brother. Trista might be sensitive, but she likes money. Money makes her happy. That little bitch you have is worth a lot of money."

"How much?"

"Close to a million. She's young, blonde, white, and she hasn't been touched."

She could hear him breathing as the wheels turned slowly inside that tiny brain of his. "Tell Trista you'll both be rewarded for helping me out. I just need the two of you to hang in there for a few more days until I get things in order."

"What about the police?"

"What about them? The trailer isn't in your name, right?"

Silence.

"You have nothing to worry about."

He sighed.

"Did you hear me?"

A guard used his wooden stick to tap the wall next to the phone. "Time's up."

"Eric! Did you hear me?"

"I heard you. Just hurry it up, sis. I don't know how much longer either one of us can take this."

She hung up the phone and headed back to her cell. She needed to think, needed to find somewhere other than her brother's place to hide the girl away. Lost in thought, she forgot all about her precarious surroundings.

"Where's the girl?" the woman with the mop whispered close to her ear.

The inmates she'd passed earlier had been waiting for her. She kept on walking. Said nothing. They were on both sides of her now, their elbows locked around hers.

She struggled to get loose.

"Don't worry," the woman with Billy Idol hair said. "We're not going to hurt you. Just want to have a little chat."

They ushered her to a closet door half-hidden beneath the stairs.

The smaller one pulled out a key on a chain from around her neck and unlocked the door.

They pushed her inside and locked the door behind them. It was a small area, musty and dank. There were brooms, mops, and a couple of garbage cans. With all three of them inside the tiny room, it was a tight squeeze. The bigger woman reached up and pulled a chain, filling the room with light.

Diane looked around for a way out, but there wasn't any. No windows. Nowhere to run.

"Name's Frisco," the big girl said, "and this is Oreo. We're not going to hurt you."

"What do you want?"

"Aster asked me to find you."

Shit! Diane's stomach dropped. She lifted a brow, tried to play it cool. "Why?"

"He's my cousin. He asked me to personally thank you."

"For what?"

"He told me he owes you for helping him hide the girl away. Obviously my cousin has a soft spot in his heart when it comes to you. The problem is, he can't help you unless you help him."

She tried to think, but didn't know what to say. "Help him how?"

"He wants to know where you hid the girl."

Ah, so that's what this is all about. Of course. Aster thought she'd moved the McMann girl on his behalf. Maybe if she played along, she could get out of here in one piece. "I didn't have time to talk to Aster about the situation," Diane said. "Everything happened fast. I knew I had to move the girl before it was too late."

"Brilliant thinking on your part." Frisco looked at her friend. "Don't you agree?"

"Yeah, sure. Makes perfect sense."

Aster might be her one chance at getting out of this place. But she didn't want to risk her brother being harmed. As far as she was concerned, he was all the family she had left. "The McMann girl is staying with a friend of mine," Diane lied. "Robert Arias. He lives in Vacaville."

Frisco smiled, revealing two rows of small, yellow teeth. "My cousin is going to be pleased."

"How soon can he get me out of here?"

The younger one, Oreo, clamped a hand over Diane's shoulder. Diane tried to shrug her off, but the ugly bitch held tight and said, "You don't remember me, do you?"

Her grimy fingernails dug through her uniform and into her skin. Diane jerked away, pivoted on her heels, and grabbed hold of the doorknob, but it was locked. Oreo jabbed a bony knee into her spine, then kicked her hard in the side.

"I was your first recruit, *Mother*." The toe of her boot connected with Diane's ribs, again and again, sending jolts of excruciating pain through her entire body until she let go of the doorknob and sank to the floor.

"You changed my name to Bella. Remember me now?"

Diane did remember her. How could she forget? She should have seen through the scabs and sores and tormented sneer. Diane hadn't wanted to be Aster's recruiter, but she hadn't been given a choice. Within a week's time she'd gone from wearing furs and diamonds to befriending young girls like Bella. She'd taken out all her frustrations on the girl, making sure the princess understood her new role as a whore. Sixteen-year-old Bella had been a quick learner, eager to please, and Diane didn't like it one bit. She preferred to see the girls squirm and cower. If Diane wasn't happy, nobody was going to be happy, which was why she'd been quick to offer Bella to every denizen of the night who had a few extra coins in his pocket.

Oreo bent down, jabbed a skinny but sharp elbow to her throat, then left her lying there.

Diane's head pounded, and her lungs burned. Black dots blurred her vision as she clutched at her throat, grasping for breath.

The light went out. The door opened and closed.

She gasped as air filled her lungs. She closed her eyes then and concentrated on breathing. Moments passed before she was able to struggle to her knees and reach for the doorknob.

Four

The first thing Faith noticed when she walked into Detective Yuhasz's office was how exhausted he looked. The lines in his brow appeared deeper, and dark shadows framed his eyes. He gestured for her to have a seat in one of the wood chairs in front of his desk. "What's going on, Faith?"

He sounded as tired as he looked. She took a seat. "I can't get Diane Weaver out of my mind."

He said nothing, merely waited patiently for her to continue.

"Is there any way you can set something up so I can talk to her?"

"No, not likely, not while she's in prison. She was arrested on drug possession charges. Her bail was set high, and it'll be weeks before formal charges are filed against her."

Before she could protest further, he shook his head. "I do know she's pressing charges against you. She said you're the one responsible for messing up her pretty face."

"Ridiculous. I never touched her," Faith lied. "Ask anyone who was at the farmhouse."

"Your word against hers."

"That's right," Faith said with a shrug before she put both hands on the top of his desk and leaned closer. "Talk to her. Please. She knows where Lara is. All the answers are right there in prison with that woman."

"It's not that easy."

Her insides twisted. She couldn't let it go. "Please. I'm begging you to find a way."

Silence hovered between them, stifling and thick as her gaze settled on a framed picture on his desk.

Yuhasz rubbed the back of his neck. "I'll talk to a few people and see what I can do."

"Thank you," she said as she stood.

She turned toward the door and then stopped and walked back to his desk. Her brow furrowed as she pointed at the picture. "I've seen him before."

Yuhasz followed her gaze. "That's Holly, my youngest daughter, her husband, David Hofberg, and their two children."

She felt the blood rush from her head as she recalled where she'd seen him.

"What is it?"

She swallowed. "It's nothing. Never mind."

"Faith," he said, prompting her to say whatever was on her mind.

"Remember the nail salon?" Faith asked. "The place where Rage and I found those young girls being sexually abused?"

He nodded.

"He was there."

Yuhasz picked up the picture and handed it to her. "Take a closer look. Are you absolutely positive it was him?"

"I'm certain. That's the man I saw exit the back door. The same door I snuck through before I found the pervert on top of that young girl."

"OK," he said, rubbing his jaw. "Thanks."

"What are you going to do?"

"I don't know. I need to think on it a bit."

She wanted to tell him she was sorry, but sorry didn't seem adequate, so she said nothing. She just walked out the door, leaving him standing motionless and looking more than a little concerned.

———

Prior to raiding the farmhouse, Faith had received a phone call. The caller had described both of her children in detail, down to the mole on her son's right ear, before threatening to kill her family if she didn't back off. Because of those threats, Faith was determined to do all she could to fortify her parents' house.

Her friend Beast, a monstrous-size man with meaty hands and a neck as thick as the trunk of a large oak tree, had agreed to help her. The wires they were installing would alert them by beeping if anyone came within three yards of the house.

"I talked to Samantha Perelman this morning," Faith told him as she secured wire around the top of the metal post he'd just hammered into the ground.

Beast stopped what he was doing and looked at her. Sweat trickled down the side of his face. "I thought Samantha's parents asked everyone for patience and understanding."

"Time is not on my side," she told him. "You know that. I had to try. She didn't look well, it's true, and I was about to leave when she awakened and called out my name."

"And?"

"She heard Diane Weaver talking on the phone the same morning we attacked the farmhouse. She said it sounded as if the woman was trying to move Lara to another location. So I went to see Detective Yuhasz about the matter, hoping he could pay Diane a visit. He said he'd do what he could, but he didn't sound hopeful. After I left his office, though, I thought it would be a good idea to do some investigating of my own—find out everything I can about Diane Weaver. Does she have family? What about close friends? Anyone at all who might have an idea of what she's done with Lara."

Beast was about to say something when loud voices emanated from inside the house. They both turned and watched Rage come rushing through the back door. She gestured toward Faith.

She'd met Rage the same day she'd met Beast. Everyone who attended anger management was asked to choose a nickname. Rage had chosen her name because she was one pissed-off young woman. Faith didn't know her exact age, but she guessed her to be in her late twenties. Rage had been dealt a bad hand when it came to life. It was Beast who'd found her in a ditch on the side of the road and taken her to the house in Roseville where he lived with his dad. Although Beast and Rage were merely friends, they were inseparable.

"You might want to get in there before someone gets hurt," Rage warned. "Your sister-in-law is threatening to take the kids and leave before your brother gets back from his latest haul. Jana and your mom are not happy about it."

Faith left the gloves and pliers on the ground and headed that way. From where she stood, she could hear more than one raised voice. What the heck was going on?

Bri stood in the living room, holding her two daughters, one on each side, close to her hips, as she smoothed their hair in an attempt to comfort them.

"What's going on?" Faith asked.

Mom lifted her arms, clearly frustrated by the sudden turn of events.

"Bri came to pick up a few things and say goodbye," Jana told Faith. "She's going to Florida to live with her parents."

"Does Colton know?" Faith asked.

"No," Bri said. "I've tried to do things your brother's way—but I can't do this any longer. I'm sorry."

"Why now? Did something happen?"

"I awoke in the middle of the night to a strange noise. I called the police. When they arrived, they took a look around. The back door looked as if it might have been tampered with, but the lock still worked and no one had broken in, so they left. I can't simply wait for these men, whoever they are, to get to us. Every shadow, every noise is cause for panic. I won't live like this."

"I'm scared," Kimberly said, her eyes rimmed with tears.

Bri held her daughter tight.

"All I'm asking," Lilly said to Bri, "is that you and the girls stay here with us for two nights until Colton returns. Talk to your husband before you run off."

Bri's face reddened. "I don't see how you can possibly look upon your granddaughters, knowing what those men are capable of, and expect me to stay one more minute than is absolutely necessary," she said. "You obviously want the same thing that happened to Faith's kids to happen to mine. You don't care about anyone but yourself."

Mom's hands were shaking now.

Dad stepped close to Mom and put a hand on her shoulder to calm her, but she would have none of it. "How could you say such a thing, Bri? I love all my grandchildren equally, and I would never wish harm to come to any of them."

"You've always been controlling, but telling me to stay in California, where my children will be in danger, is too much."

"Mom wasn't telling you what to do," Jana chimed in. "She was asking." She put a hand on her stomach and waddled over to a chair to have a seat.

"Wait until your child is born," Bri told Jana. "I can guarantee you'll be singing a different tune after he or she comes into the world. I love my kids too much to risk their lives." Bri looked directly at Faith. "We've all been threatened. Colton told me about the phone call you received before all of you took up arms and went marching into unfamiliar territory with guns blazing. How you can allow your loved ones to risk their lives, I do not know. Jana's husband is in the hospital with a knife wound, for God's sake. Your brother was shot, and yet he acts as if nothing has changed. You're all crazy."

Bri was obviously scared, but that was taking it too far. Faith opened her mouth to protest, but Bri raised a hand to stop her, and said, "I'm not like the rest of you. I can't do this—walk around with my eyes wide-open, afraid of every shadow, wondering when those horrible men will show up next. I won't do it. I won't allow you all to continue to put my family in danger. I'm leaving."

Faith's mom sighed, and her shoulders fell as if heavy weights had settled there.

"Mom, it's OK," Faith said. "Bri should do what she feels is best."

Faith's dad, Russell, spoke for the first time since she'd stepped inside. "If Bri will feel safer living in Florida for a while," he said, "I don't think that's such a horrible idea. I'm going to take Bri and the kids to the airport." He went to his granddaughters, dropped to his knees, and took them into his arms. "You two take care of your mother while you're gone. We're going to miss you, but we know you're in good hands." Kimberly and Dacotah wrapped their small arms around his neck. Both of the girls were crying, visibly confused and scared.

Faith went to the girls and said her goodbyes, too.

Mom hugged both of her granddaughters. "I hope you girls know I love you with all my heart."

After their goodbyes, everyone stood together outside the front entry and watched them drive off.

Faith understood her mom's wish for Bri to talk to Colton before she left for Florida, but she also understood Bri's determination to keep her children safe by whatever means possible. She was frightened. They all were. She wondered what she would do in the same situation. The truth was, she didn't know.

FIVE

Detective Dillon Yuhasz kept a tight grip on the steering wheel as he drove along East Natomas. His thoughts were on Faith McMann, which wasn't unusual of late. The poor woman had been forced to watch her husband die as her two children were taken from their home. But Faith refused to sit idly by while authorities worked her case.

In the beginning he'd thought of McMann as an annoyance since she expected to be a part of every aspect of the investigation. But somehow, God help him, she'd grown on him, and now he found himself admiring her determination and perseverance. Nothing was going to stop her from finding her children. And to hell with anyone who got in her way.

Overall Faith's plight made him think about his own two daughters. They were in their early forties, two years apart. One was in a relationship. The other was married with two children. Although his daughters hadn't been taken from him, he felt as if he'd somehow lost them over the years.

As a father, he already knew he was a failure. But seeing the certainty in Faith's eyes when she'd pointed at his son-in-law, David, as one of the men she'd seen at the salon worried him beyond measure. He'd called his daughter and left a message, but she had yet to return his call.

He kept trying to come up with a good reason as to why David might have been at the nail salon, but nothing made sense. The salon had been nothing more than a cover-up. It was a brothel run by the women who sat on stools all day clipping and trimming and taking money from the sleazy backroom clientele.

It didn't look good, but he couldn't help but hope David had a reason for being there that day.

Keeping his eyes on the road, Yuhasz stepped on the gas. Trees swayed, and thunder sounded in the distance. According to last night's weather forecast, record winds were expected over the next few days.

Lightning lit up the sky. Thunder crackled, echoing off walls of dark clouds.

Since leaving his home in Auburn, he'd seen fallen tree limbs scattered across the road. If the weatherman was to be believed, it was only going to get worse.

He made a left onto Finchley Lane and then a right onto a cul-de-sac, where his youngest daughter, Holly, lived with David and their two children. They had lived in the quiet Folsom neighborhood for only three months. The two-story house was a great place for his grandkids. He'd taken time to check it out when he'd first heard she was moving here. Good schools and neighbors who looked after one another. Although his daughter didn't care one way or another about his opinion on the matter, he approved.

Detective Yuhasz parked at the curb, climbed out of his vehicle, and followed the stone path toward the front entry. A gust of wind hit him with enough force to throw him off balance. He looked at the sky and saw dark, billowy clouds huddling together to make more mischief.

He knocked on the door, waited a few minutes, then knocked again.

Holly answered.

She wore thick foundation and oversize sunglasses. The strap of her purse hung over her shoulder. She feigned surprise at seeing him. "Dad! What are you doing here? I was just about to leave to go pick up the kids."

"They don't get out for another forty-five minutes. I checked."

Her shoulders fell.

He stepped inside, walked right past her, making his way to the living room. Everything was perfect. Two young children lived here, and yet there were no fingerprints on the table, no shoes or toys scattered about or piled in a corner. There wasn't one stain on the light-colored carpet or any sign that children lived within these walls.

The door clicked shut. "Dad," she said. "What are you doing?"

"What's going on, Holly?"

"What are you talking about? What's wrong with you?"

"Why haven't you returned my calls?"

She shrugged.

The left side of her face had a yellow tint to it. Her cheekbone was swollen. He didn't like where his thoughts were headed. "Take off your sunglasses," he told her.

"No," she said. "Quit acting so weird. I have to go. I don't want to be late."

"Take them off, Holly, or I'll pick up the phone and give your mother a call right now."

"Really, Dad? You're threatening your forty-year-old daughter with a call to Mother?"

He pulled his cell phone from his pocket.

"OK, OK." She slid off her glasses and lifted her chin, her blue eyes blazing. "Is this what you wanted to see?"

Her left eye was swollen and shadowed in purple hues. He'd given his rat bastard son-in-law recommendations, convinced Narcotics to hire him. His fingers curled into a fist at his side as he turned and headed for the door.

She ran after him, grabbed hold of his arm. "Where are you going?"

"Where do you think? To have a talk with that goddamn husband of yours."

"Don't do it."

He was already halfway down the path nearing his car when she said, "Please. It will only make things worse."

His youngest daughter had always been a warrior, strong-minded, the sort of woman who didn't take shit from anyone, but her voice sounded soft, fragile, scared. He turned to face her. "How long has this been going on, Holly?" A muscle in his jaw quivered. "Tell me the truth."

She looked to the ground, as a child being punished would. "A few years."

"Three? Five? How many?"

"At least ten."

His heart skipped a beat and then wilted. This explained so much. They used to be close. She'd always been Daddy's little girl. He'd never understood why she'd begun to push him away. Over the years, she'd come up with a million excuses as to why it was best if he didn't come to his grandkid's soccer game or stop by for a quick visit after work. He'd thought it was his ex-wife's doing, convincing his daughter he wasn't fit to be part of her life.

But that wasn't it at all. Not even close. He was an idiot. A blind fool for not checking up on her before today. His wife had always said he wasn't good at communicating, and for the first time, he realized she was right.

David Fucking Hofberg was beating Holly. Had been for a while now. And Holly was doing what so many abused wives did—trying to hide the truth along with the bruises.

When she finally gathered the courage to look at him, he said, "So what do you expect me to do—nothing?"

She nodded, a movement so subtle he nearly missed it. A tear ran down the side of her face.

He stepped forward and took her into his arms. If she thought for a millisecond that he would simply walk away without teaching the scumbag a lesson he wouldn't soon forget, she didn't know her dad very well.

Hell, she didn't know him at all. "Listen, Holly." He let go of her and looked at his watch. "I'm going to send a car to pick you and the girls up in an hour."

"No," she said. "I won't go."

"You will go. You know why?"

She crossed her arms and said nothing.

"Because you love your kids. I know you do. And the last thing you want is for them to grow up in an abusive home." He paused. "I want you to go live with Uncle Bob for a while. He and Stella have been nagging me for years to bring the grandkids for a visit. Remember Uncle Bob's house? The place right on the beach in San Diego? The kids will love it there. Go pick them up and tell them you're taking them on a little vacation. Disneyland, the whole works. You don't need to worry about a thing. Just get into that car when it comes. Got it?"

She had the good sense to nod her agreement.

He had so much more he wanted to say to her. Telling her he was sorry would have been a good start, but the words stuck in his throat. Instead he rested a hand on her shoulder and said, "Everything's going to be fine. Just go back inside and pack. I'll talk to you tonight."

Despite all the horrible thoughts swirling around inside his head on the way over here, the last thing he'd expected was to learn that his daughter was being physically abused. After watching her walk back into the house, he went to his cruiser and climbed in. His hands were shaking, and he was breathing hard. His fingers curled tightly around the steering wheel. He wanted to hit something, preferably smash a fist through David Hofberg's skull. He never thought of himself as a violent man. Not until this very moment.

Shit. Shit. Shit.

He looked toward the house and saw Holly's silhouette behind the curtain covering the large-paned window. He started the engine and headed off. Everything else he'd come to talk to his daughter about would have to wait for now. Holly had enough problems without him asking her about any of her husband's extramarital affairs.

Six

Lara looked at the wall clock for the hundredth time since Eric had left the trailer home. He'd been gone for thirty-two minutes already, and Trista had yet to go to the bathroom or wander into the kitchen for a snack. If Trista would just leave the room for half a minute, Lara could make a run for it.

When Eric was home, he used a chain and a combination lock on the front door, the only door that led to the outside. But his wife, Trista, never bothered with the locks. Maybe she trusted Lara to stay put. Or maybe she was just lazy.

Lara didn't like Eric or Trista, but living with them was way better than being at the ranch with Mother. Nobody had been happy at the ranch. All the girls were afraid of being dragged off by a strange man. Lara didn't like to think about what happened to them when they were gone. She didn't like to think about the farmhouse at all.

Lara was still scared, but it was different now. Eric and Trista were kind of dumb. Eric was a horrible slob, too. No matter how many times Trista asked him nicely to leave his boots at the door, he wouldn't do it. He just trudged through the place, leaving muddy footprints from one end to the other. But other than that, he wasn't too bad. He didn't raise his voice, and he never hit her or pulled her hair. He never looked at her in the same way those other guys at the ranch used to look at her, all crazy-eyed and creepy.

When Eric first brought her here, he and Trista had spent every minute trying to convince her everything would be OK. They said if she stopped crying and did as she was told, she would be taken home. The problem, Trista insisted, was that her mom was in jail. She'd hit a policeman in the head, and now she had to spend time locked up like all the other bad people in the world.

That was a lie, though. Lara's mom would never hurt a flea. Everybody loved her. All the kids at Lara's school wanted to be in her class every year, which was why she knew Eric and Trista were lying. Ginger, the old lady who lived next door, probably didn't believe a word they told her, either, but Eric and Trista offered to pay her a lot of money if she kept a close eye on Lara. So whenever they left her with Ginger, the old woman watched her like a hawk.

The last time she'd been left with Ginger, she'd almost gotten away. If only she'd been able to escape five minutes earlier, she would have succeeded. She could have made it to the main street and shouted for help. But she'd hardly made it past the next trailer before Eric and Trista drove up, stopped the car, and yanked her inside.

She looked at the clock again, an ugly plastic thing with a picture of an octopus and a giant crack running through the middle of it.

He'd been gone for forty-one minutes.

Unable to sit still for another second, she was about to ask Trista if she could run over to Ginger's house, make up a lie and tell her she'd forgotten something there, when Trista stood, tossed the remote on the couch, and headed for the bathroom. She was so upset about something the man had done to his girlfriend on her favorite afternoon show she hadn't even spared Lara a glance.

It was now or never.

Without bothering to grab her shoes from the room down the hall or grab one of Eric's or Trista's dirty sweatshirts lying around, she raced to the door, turned the knob ever so quietly, and then peeked outside.

Nobody was there.

The gravel driveway was empty.

Ginger's blinds were shut tight.

Lara stepped out into the cold and shut the door as quietly as possible.

And then she ran as fast as she could.

SEVEN

Faith no longer remembered what her life had been like before the attack.

Another world. Another time.

Her heart ached. Every moment of every day was like reliving a nightmare. Sleep deprivation wasn't helping matters, but how could she sleep when her children were out there somewhere, alone and scared? The thought of either one of them being harmed made it difficult to breathe at times. She wasn't the first parent to have her children taken from their home, and, sadly, she wouldn't be the last.

But one thing was clear—she would find her children.

Nobody could convince her otherwise.

She would find them, and the people responsible would pay.

Her cell phone rang. She picked up the call when she saw it was Detective Yuhasz.

"Bad news," he said after she said hello. "Diane Weaver is out of jail."

Her anger sparked and sizzled, spreading through her insides like wildfire. "How is that possible?"

"Bail was posted. Apparently she was released and then allowed to drive off in a taxi. O'Sullivan is working on locating the cab number and driver so we can find out where she might have gone."

"Who paid her bail?"

"Someone by the name of Thomas Keen."

"Has he been located?"

"No. We believe he might have used a fake ID. They're checking it out."

Faith did her best to stay calm, but it wasn't easy. "I can't believe she would be allowed to simply walk away."

"I've got a man stationed near the farmhouse to watch out for her."

"I thought the place was boarded up."

"It is, but we're hoping she'll head back there to retrieve personal items."

Faith moved her head from side to side, trying to get the kink out of her neck.

"The good news is," Yuhasz continued, "we've learned a few things about Diane Weaver. She comes from a large family, including a brother Eric, who has spent a few years in the area."

"Have you talked to him?"

"So far all known Sacramento addresses for Eric Weaver have turned out to be dead ends."

"You call that good news?"

"We're working on it," he said, his tone much more serious. "From what we've gathered so far, Diane and her brother have been bad news since they were in their teens. We were able to get in touch with her parents, but they weren't much help. They haven't seen Diane or Eric in over a decade, and they have no idea where either of them is living."

"If she does have a brother in the area, it makes perfect sense, doesn't it, that he would be the one to help her by taking Lara—"

"Like I said, we're working on it. When I have more information for you, I'll let you know."

"Thank you," she said. "I appreciate it."

"There's one more thing."

Faith waited.

"Divers believe they might have found your husband's SUV."

"Where?"

"In the canal in Central Valley. They'll be pulling the vehicle out in the morning."

"Were they able to see inside?"

"No. The water's murky. Zero visibility."

Faith held her breath. She knew Lara was alive. More than one person had seen her. But Hudson . . . she hadn't heard a word about Hudson. "I want to be there when they pull it out of the water."

"Are you sure? I can call you as soon as it's pulled out."

"No," she blurted, then paused to catch her breath. "What if he's in there?" she asked, her voice cracking. "What if they left my son in the car before they dumped it in the canal?"

"I'll pick you up in the morning on my way. Does eight o'clock work for you?"

"I'll be ready."

Faith hung up the phone. She stood in silence for a moment, did her best to collect herself before she walked into the kitchen, where she found Rage, Jana, and Mom. Dad and Beast were outside, where they had been all day, finishing the final touches on the alarm system. Beast's father, Little Vinnie, had left a few minutes ago. Mom filled the teakettle with water from the faucet and put it on the stove.

"That was Detective Yuhasz," Faith said. "They think they might have found Craig's car in the canal in the Central Valley a few hours away."

Mom's eyes widened, but before she could ask the question, Faith shook her head. "They won't be able to see inside until they pull the car from the water. I want to be there when they do. Detective Yuhasz is picking me up in the morning."

Nobody said a word, everyone lost in their own thoughts.

"Where's Miranda?" Faith asked in hopes of stopping her mind from wandering too far into a black abyss of worry and fear.

"She's upstairs watching TV," Jana said. "I'm worried about her. For months she was held captive, traumatized in who knows how many ways, only to escape a perverted lunatic and then learn that her mother is dead. We need to get her help."

"What do you suggest?"

"She needs to talk to someone," Rage said.

"My friend, Kirsten Reich, is a therapist," Jana said. "I'll see if I can set up an appointment for her, OK?"

Faith nodded. "It couldn't hurt."

"I thjnk it would be a good idea for you to talk to her, too."

Faith said nothing.

"Looks like they're getting ready for the apocalypse," Mom said as she stared out the window and watched the men at work.

"That's exactly what they're doing," Jana said.

For a moment they all watched Beast and Faith's dad dig holes for posts and then mix cement, working hard to finish the perimeter fencing that would alert them to anyone moving around the house.

Rage gestured that way. "I think I'll go see if they need any help."

As soon as she shut the door behind her, Jana looked at Faith and said, "She doesn't look well."

"I do worry about that one," Mom added.

A few months ago, Rage had been diagnosed with inoperable brain cancer—stage four astrocytoma. Her days were numbered. "I wish there was something I could do for her," Faith said.

They continued to stare out the window.

"Did you know she has a son whom she gave up for adoption?" Jana asked.

Faith looked at her sister. "Are you sure?"

36

She nodded. "I overheard Rage and Beast talking about him when we were in the command post. They've been trying to locate the adoptive parents for years with no luck."

The teakettle screeched, sending Mom running.

"My good friend Dee Dee was adopted," Jana went on. "After spending years looking for her biological parents, she was able to find and meet them. Her mother and father both had families of their own by then, but she got the closure she wanted, needed. Do you want me to ask her if she can point me in the right direction to help Rage find her son?"

"Would you?" Faith asked. "That would be wonderful. I'll pay for it. Whatever it costs."

"OK then. I'll see what she says." Jana leaned in close and said in a low voice so Mom wouldn't overhear, "How are finances? With Craig's business being shut down and you not working right now, I'm worried about you and the whole money situation."

Faith wasn't ready to tell her about the $2 million she'd found stuffed in the pool equipment at the house where her family was attacked. That money was now stashed right outside her parents' home, way up high in the tree fort where she and her siblings used to play. The less her sister knew, the better. "We had life insurance," Faith said. "The kids and I will be fine."

Mom didn't pay them any mind. She quietly set the teacups she'd gathered on the table. Ever since Bri and the kids had left for Florida, Mom had been on edge. Colton had yet to return from his latest delivery, and she and Dad had hardly talked since he'd returned from taking Bri to the airport.

Jana grabbed cream from the refrigerator and sugar from the pantry.

Faith couldn't stand to see her mom look so tense. "Maybe it would be best if you and Dad went to Florida, too," Faith said. "Aunt Valerie has a big enough house. She would love having visitors. And you, too,

Jana. You could have the baby without worrying about looking over your shoulder every minute."

"You're not the only one who carries a gun these days," Jana said. "I'm not going anywhere, but nice try."

"Your father would never leave while his kids were in danger," Mom said. "And despite the fact that your father can be an old fool at times, I would never leave his side." She looked into Faith's eyes. "We're in this together, every one of us." She pointed a finger at Faith for good measure. "And don't think for a minute that we're doing any of this for you. There's not one of us who could simply move on without doing everything possible to find Lara and Hudson. Let's finish what we started, and then get on with things."

The second Lara saw a car turn into the trailer park and realized it was Eric, she cut to the right, hurried past the front of a trailer home, and hid behind an oak tree. Her heart thumped hard against her chest. The palms of her hands felt sweaty.

There was no way he'd seen her. She'd been plenty fast, she was sure of it, but then she heard the car come to a screeching halt, followed by the slamming of a car door.

The tree trunk was wider than she was. She held perfectly still, hardly breathed. Just as she was beginning to think he'd gone the other way, she heard the sound of rubber boots crunching against gravel.

He was coming this way.

If only she could run as fast as her brother. Hudson could easily reach the road. He would have been able to get away for sure. If she took off running now, she decided, instead of waiting for him to find her, she might have a chance.

She drew in a deep breath and then went for it. She ran fast, used her arms the way Hudson always told her to. Small rocks and sharp twigs dug into her bare feet as she ran deeper into the wooded area surrounding the park, but she felt hardly any pain. Her only thought was of escaping.

The harder she pumped her arms, the faster her legs went. She weaved through trees and thick brush, hopped over a trickling creek. The thought of seeing her family again kept her going and filled her with hope.

She could do this.

Pain ripped through her shoulder as his fingers dug through her T-shirt and into her skin.

Her screams were muffled by his other hand now clamped over her mouth. He didn't bother to drag her to the car. Instead he picked her up and held her tight against him as he walked back to the trailer, where Trista sat quietly, focused on her daytime TV show. From the looks of things, she hadn't noticed Lara was gone.

Eric didn't say a word to Trista. He just kicked his boot right through the TV, putting an end to her show. Trista jumped to her feet, but she knew better than to say anything. Judging by the look in her eyes, she knew she was in big trouble.

Lara kicked and tried to bite the palm of his hand, which wasn't helping his temper, but she didn't care.

"Grab the fucking duct tape, you dumb bitch!"

Trista looked frantically about before rushing into the tiny kitchen, where she opened a drawer and found what Eric had asked for.

He then shoved Lara into one of the two chairs in the kitchen area and told Trista to tape the brat to the chair while he held her in place. Lara kicked him in the shin, and he whacked her across the face with the back of his hand.

Her eyes welled with tears, but she didn't want to cry. "I want my mom. I want to go home!"

He took a step back once Trista finished taping her waist and chest to the top of the chair and each ankle to one of the wooden legs and said, "There. How do you like that, kid?"

"I hate you both."

"The feeling is mutual."

"They're going to get you, and you'll both spend the rest of your lives in jail. Bad guys worse than you don't like people who hurt kids. They'll beat you up and pull out your teeth with pliers."

Eric laughed. "Someone's been watching too many movies."

Trista wrung her hands. "What if she's right?"

Eric shook his head. "Don't be stupid." Then he leaned over and rubbed the leg Lara had kicked earlier and said, "I'm going to go get my car, and I don't want either of you to move. Not one inch." He looked right at Trista. "Do you hear me?"

She crossed her arms over her chest but didn't say a word.

Lara tried to wriggle free, but Trista had done a good job with the tape.

When Eric opened the door to make his exit, a man wearing a dark suit stood just outside. Car keys dangled from the stranger's fingers.

Eric snatched his keys from the man. "Who are you?"

"My name isn't important. What is important," he said as he stepped inside and wagged his finger at Lara, "is that you have something that doesn't belong to you."

At first glance, Lara thought the man at the door might be there to save her, but then he pulled out a gun and looked her square in the eyes. That's when she knew it wasn't a friendly face she was looking at. He wasn't there to help her at all. His eyes were dark and cold, and goose bumps suddenly covered her arms and legs.

He pointed the gun at Eric and told him he wanted to have a talk. With the gun jabbed into Eric's back, he used his other hand to shut the door, and then he pushed Eric, making him stumble into the middle of the room.

Lara was surprised Eric wasn't fighting back. He looked scared.

The stranger took the duct tape from Trista and told her to come with them. Together, the three of them headed for the bedroom at the end of the hallway.

As soon as the door to the bedroom clicked shut, Lara looked around, eyes wide. Trista's cell phone was on the couch. She lowered her head and tried gnawing on the tape around her arm. Her heart hammered against her chest, and tears streamed down her face as she heard Trista pleading for her life.

She wriggled her arms and twisted her ankles to try to loosen the tape, but it was no use. She started using her toes, pushing off the floor and hopping instead. The chair moved a little bit at a time. *You can do this,* she told herself. *You can do this.*

If she could reach the phone, she could call 911.

She tried to block out the sounds coming from the other room. Moaning and groaning and all sorts of weird squeaking. She didn't have far to go. Just a few more feet. She filled her head with thoughts of Mom, Dad, and her brother, Hudson. How happy they would be to see her when she finally got away.

EIGHT

Hudson used the wool blanket as a stretcher and pulled Joey along, trying to take the easiest path, doing his best to avoid rocks and fallen branches. The blanket had holes in it now, and he knew they wouldn't be able to go on like this for too much longer. Not because of the makeshift stretcher, but because every muscle in his arms ached, and his legs were beginning to wobble.

Staying close to the creek, he made sure to drink as much water as possible. Using the pocketknife, he cut a piece of blanket and used it as a sponge to squeeze water into Joey's mouth. The sun would be going down soon, and he knew he'd have to stay far enough from the creek so as not to attract the attention of a bobcat or a mountain lion. He'd seen black-tailed deer, coyote, and gray squirrel, but no bears. And for that he was thankful. He'd eaten a few more worms, but he'd heard enough stories from his grandfather and Dad to know that a handful of earthworms wouldn't be enough to sustain him for long.

He also knew there was a good chance they would die in the forest, and yet he couldn't help but think it was better to die near a fresh stream surrounded by wildlife than in the hands of horrible men who cared only about making a few dollars off the suffering of others.

Over the past few weeks he hadn't had time to wonder about Mom, Dad, or Lara. But he wondered now. What had they done with his sister? If he did get out of here alive, would his family still be there? The bad guys had been hovering over his parents when he and Lara were taken from the house. It was all a blur. Sometimes in his nightmares, he saw blood. But he didn't know if the images were real. Nothing made sense any longer. One minute he was singing in the car with his sister, and in the next, men he'd never seen before were dragging him from his home. He kept hoping he would wake up and realize it was all a bad dream.

His bones ached as he pulled Joey through dirt and leaves. Every muscle throbbed. It was his will to live that kept his legs moving. He knew from all the stories he'd heard from Dad and Grandpa that patience and determination were important if anyone lost in the woods had any hope of surviving.

But he could feel the cold seeping into his bones, and that worried him because he felt as if he were being frozen alive from the inside out.

Every once in a while Joey would start wheezing uncontrollably, as he was doing now. *Patience and determination*, Hudson thought, *might not see us through another night*. He used all his strength to pull Joey to the biggest tree trunk he could find. He propped him up, high enough so Joey would hopefully be able to breathe easier, and then Hudson went in search of wood to make a shelter.

With his arms filled to the brim with long branches, he was about to trek back to where he'd left Joey when he saw a dark shadow in the distance. His heart pounded in his chest as he stared ahead, past crooked rows of trees and undergrowth.

He dropped the wood at his feet and began to run toward the shadow. He couldn't help but wonder if lack of food and sleep was causing him to see things that weren't there, but he kept running just the same.

Weaving through the pines, he jumped over a narrow part of the creek until he was absolutely sure of what he was seeing—a small cabin made of rough logs and half-covered with vines. The roof was nothing more than a metal sheet with a crumbling stone chimney.

He headed that way, his breathing heavy.

And then a thought struck him. *What if the bad guys are inside? What then?*

He slowed his pace as he drew closer, careful not to attract any unwanted attention in case they were waiting for him.

Not only was he afraid of what he might find in the cabin, he also worried about leaving Joey behind, even if for only a short time. He stopped and looked back the way he'd come, memorizing the path he'd taken from where he'd left Joey. If the cabin were empty, he would go back and drag him this way. Although his legs and arms felt weaker than ever, there was no way he could leave Joey out there to die, cold and alone.

Leaves crunched beneath his shoes as he moved closer. The cabin was ancient, made of old rough-wood timber. It had a pointed roof and a chimney made out of stone. There was no porch, which made it easy to peek through the grimy window. Nobody was inside. There was an old wood-burning stove and bunk beds in the corner. He tried the door. It creaked in protest. When he put some muscle into it, the door opened.

Instead of entering right away, he walked around the outside of the cabin to make sure nobody was hiding out. The cabin was small with a tiny outhouse at the back. He peeked inside. It was cold and drafty. It was also empty—nothing more than a wooden platform with a hole in the middle.

He walked back around to the front of the cabin and went inside. The place had a damp, moldy smell, but not too bad considering it looked as if no one had inhabited the place for years. The kitchen area was no bigger than the size of his dresser back home. There was an old pot inside a dented metal sink, but no water hookup. There were six drawers. He opened them, one after another, and nearly cried with joy when he found a box of matches and two fat candles, both burned down to the halfway mark. He laughed when he found three cans of black beans. There was no can opener to be found, though.

Finished searching through the drawers, he walked across the warped wooden planks. Each step left a footprint in a fine layer of dirt. Thin, dirty mattresses covered the bunk beds. No blankets or pillows. A neat stack of wood was piled high against the wall next to the wood-burning stove. He went that way and got a whiff of stale burned wood when he kneeled down to take a look inside the stove. His eyes grew wide at the sight of a small-handled ax leaning against the stone section of wall behind the stove. He picked up the ax and examined it closer. The blade was still fairly sharp.

He didn't like the idea of starting a fire and possibly alerting the men who had shot Sean. But after dark came, he would need to warm the place up for Joey's sake. If they came, he'd use the ax on them if he had to.

The long, eerie howl of a coyote made him pick up his pace. He needed to hurry back to the creek where he'd left Joey and drag him up the hill. He went to the kitchen and grabbed the tin pot from the sink. After he hauled Joey back to the cabin, he'd return to the stream and gather water to make bean soup.

Through the window he saw darks clouds moving this way. He went to the door and opened it wide. A gust of cold air smacked him in the face.

That wasn't a coyote after all. It was the wind. The trees looked as if they were sword fighting, their branches whipping back and forth.

Darkness was coming fast. He'd been inside the cabin longer than he thought. With his gaze fixed on the path he'd taken, he ran as fast as he could, hoping it wasn't too late and Joey was still alive.

NINE

Aster Williams parked at the back of the building. He'd found a new place in Sacramento to do business—a warehouse off Riverside Boulevard. There was too much crime in the area for the police to stay ahead of the game. If an officer found himself on this particular road, mostly he tended to take a bribe in the form of drugs or cash, or he simply looked the other way.

Although Aster occasionally used his home in El Dorado Hills to do business, he preferred not to. He had a wife and kids. No reason to bring his work home when he owned a half-dozen buildings in the region. As the youngest child born to a handyman and a mother who never worked a day in her life, he'd learned early on how to work the streets to make a few bucks. He worked from the bottom up, and he'd worked hard to get where he was today.

Much too hard to see everything ruined by a fucking schoolteacher with a big mouth. It was bad enough Faith McMann had survived. But that wasn't good enough for the bitch. She'd gone out of her way to make a spectacle of herself. A fucking fourth grade teacher gathering arms and going after his men. The notion left a bitter taste in his mouth.

She needed to be taught a lesson, made an example of.

Women were put on this earth to serve men. Nothing more. Nothing less.

His dad and his uncles had taught him at a young age that all women—young, old, black, white, or yellow—were not to be seen or heard. Every time his mother tried to stand up to his dad or Aster's older brothers, she'd get the shit kicked out of her. It got to the point where he couldn't wait for her to open her big, blubbery mouth just so he could see her get her teeth kicked in.

By the age of twelve, Aster could hardly look at his mother without feeling sick to his stomach, which was why he'd strategically placed one of his brother's tiny race cars along with a few drops of vegetable oil on the stairs leading down to the basement. He'd then hidden in his room for an hour waiting for good ol' Mom to get the laundry.

And then crash, bang, boom!

Down she'd gone. Thunk, thunk, thunk each time her head hit another step.

When he'd checked on her, saw her twisted body lying in a heap at the bottom of the stairs, he'd thought for sure she'd broken her neck, so he left her where she was. His mom hadn't known he was home. His brothers had gone to a friend's house after school that day. As soon as the school bell rang, Aster had raced home, climbed the old oak tree, and snuck in through his brother's bedroom window.

After she'd fallen down the stairs as planned, he'd grabbed the toy car and cleaned up the oil as best he could. Then he watched TV until he heard Dad's car pull into the driveway.

Nobody had been more shocked than he was to find out his mother had survived the fall. To this day, though, he didn't understand why his father had made him and his brothers go to the hospital every day to watch over her.

What was the point? Up until then, Dad spent every moment either berating her or slapping her. So why ruin a perfectly good weekend watching over the vegetable?

Dad died of a heart attack a few months later, and Aster and his brothers had been divided among the uncles. He got stuck with the meanest of the bunch. Turned out his uncle had a fondness for leather belts. He had a collection of them. He'd used them often—mostly on Aster. Six months after burying his dad, they buried his uncle, too. Everyone, including the doctors, figured he'd had a weak heart like his brother. Only Aster knew the truth: a little hydrofluoric acid goes a long way.

And the irony of it all was that Mom was still alive, and he was the one who saw to her every need. Go figure.

Women. The bane of his existence. Aster had never planned to marry, but he'd wanted kids of his own. Unlike his mother, his wife caught on quickly. For the most part, she knew her place.

But Faith McMann was another story—the bitch couldn't just stay home and comfort her elderly parents and let the cops do their jobs. No, she had to throw herself into the limelight. And for that she would pay.

He straightened his tie as he strolled across the parking lot. On the street corner he spotted a couple of losers selling drugs. His phone vibrated before he could shoo them away. He picked up the call.

"The farmhouse is being watched," the caller said. "Dark sedan. Feds. Thought you might want to know."

"Keep me updated." Aster disconnected the call as he came around the other side of the warehouse.

The steel rollup door at the loading dock was open. His number one man, Patrick, met him at the entrance. "What's with the hair?" Aster asked with a laugh.

Patrick's eyes narrowed. "What do you mean?"

"Is that gel?"

The kid's jaw tightened. It was easy to push his buttons. Patrick had been with him for a few years now. He was thirty-five, just a kid as far as Aster was concerned. He wore expensive suits and always stank of cologne. Everything about him was a little too perfect. Funny that the kid's appearance never bothered him one way or another before now.

They walked side by side through the wide-open space. Every foot-fall smacked against the cement floor as they headed for a small, semi-dark room in the back. The steel door clanged shut behind him.

Six men of various heights and sizes stood with their backs to the wall, their hands clasped in front of them as they waited for his arrival.

"Where are the table and the chairs?" he asked Patrick. "I thought you were going to have the place fixed up."

"Jimmy's working on it," Patrick said.

Aster watched the kid snap his fingers and signal for one of the boys to get him a chair. Judging by the way the men jumped to do his bidding, he realized Patrick had been pushing his weight around to gain some clout. He admired the kid's gumption. There was something about Patrick that reminded Aster of himself when he was that age. And that worried him.

"Fucking incompetence," Aster said as he took a good long look at each man in the room, ignoring the chair that had been placed behind him. "Are you all fucking idiots?"

Nobody moved. Not one muscle twitched.

"I've already questioned them," Patrick said. "There seems to have been a miscommunication."

"A miscommunication?" Aster scowled. "By who exactly? What part of 'keep your fucking eyes on Diane Weaver and follow her after she's released' didn't make sense?"

One of the men stepped forward and said, "My name is Curtis. Nobody told me she was being held in a different facility due to injuries sustained in prison. I was told to park at the back gate where prisoners are released. Following the instructions I was given, I sat in my car from sunup until sundown, but she never showed."

Curtis looked and sounded as if he'd graduated from some ritzy-ass college. Who the fuck was this guy? Aster pulled a pack of gum from his pocket, retrieved a single stick, unwrapped the silver foil, and popped the gum into his mouth. After a moment, he said, "It cost me a hundred thousand dollars to post bail, and yet nobody knows where she is?"

Silence.

Aster looked from Curtis to Patrick. "Is this the guy you put in charge of keeping an eye on Diane Weaver?"

Patrick nodded.

"I did exactly what I was told to do," Curtis said, his voice suddenly squeaking like a mouse. "Nobody told me she was being looked after at another facility."

"Whose job was it to figure out the nitty-gritty details?" Aster asked Patrick.

Patrick scratched the back of his neck but said nothing.

"Where's your gun?"

Despite his look of confusion, Patrick pulled his 9mm from his waistband.

Aster removed a latex glove from his inside jacket pocket and took his time slipping it on his right hand. Then he held out his gloved hand toward Patrick and wriggled his fingers.

Patrick handed over his gun, his nostrils flaring as Aster placed the barrel up against the side of his head.

"Should I shoot you or Curtis? It's your call."

"I didn't do anything wrong," Curtis said. "I followed the instructions given me. I did exactly as I was told and never—"

"Curtis," Patrick said.

Aster pivoted on his heels, turned the gun on Curtis, and fired three shots into the man's chest before he could say another word.

Aster handed the gun to Patrick, removed the glove, and shoved it back into his pocket. "Let this be a lesson to you all. Do your fucking job, and do it right the first time." He looked at Patrick and said, "Walk with me."

Before they reached the docking bay, Aster put a beefy arm around Patrick's neck. "I'm worried about you."

"Why is that?"

"I think maybe you're getting too big for your britches."

The kid's jaw hardened just like before.

"No more second chances—do you hear me?"

Patrick nodded, his face turning red as Aster squeezed.

"Find those McMann kids and bring them to me," Aster ground out. "I'm running out of patience." He tightened his hold on Patrick's neck until the kid began to turn a light shade of blue, then he let go, watched him fall to his knees, and walked away.

TEN

Diane Weaver bolted upright. She looked around, her eyes wide, her teeth chattering. It took her a moment to remember she'd fallen asleep on a bench in the middle of the park. After she'd been let out of prison, she'd been surprised when she realized no one had followed her. Having nowhere to go, she'd asked the driver to take her to Curtis Park in Midtown. There was a house on Sixth Avenue that belonged to the mother of an old friend—a stripper who had brought her home years ago. But she'd spent most of the day yesterday knocking on doors, and no one had ever heard of Laurie Carrico.

She pushed herself up from the bench and then took a moment to find her bearings. Every bone in her body ached from all the beatings she'd taken lately. She had the king of all headaches, her mouth felt as if it were full of marbles, and her stomach grumbled from hunger.

Back on Second Street, she got halfway down the block before a car pulled to a stop next to her. She recognized the driver as one of the people she'd talked to recently.

"Hello," the woman said. "You knocked on my door yesterday asking about Laurie Carrico. It turns out my husband knew exactly who you were talking about. Laurie has long since moved away, but her mom lives on Eighth Avenue, not Sixth."

The woman sped off before Diane could ask her for a ride or a dollar to get a cup of coffee.

It took her ten minutes to get to Eighth Avenue, but the good news was she recognized the house right away. She knocked on the door of the small bungalow and waited.

Before she knocked a second time, she heard someone working his or her way to the door, so she held off.

The door creaked open. It was Laurie's mother all right. The old hag had aged.

"Hi there," Diane said. "Your daughter, Laurie, sent me to check on you."

"Sort of early, don't you think?"

"Nah. Mind if I come in?" Diane didn't wait for permission. She stepped inside and headed for the main room. All the curtains were shut, making it hard to see anything. She pushed open the curtains and let some light in. She looked around and then sighed. The place was a dump. Nothing of any value decorated the walls or the tables. She headed for the kitchen next, and the woman followed her.

"Who are you?" the woman asked.

"My name's Diane. Surely you remember me! I stayed here with your daughter for months. I made all the meals and kept the place clean."

The woman shuffled her feet as she walked across the linoleum. When she reached for the phone, Diane panicked. Her gaze settled on the butcher knife sticking out of the knife block on the counter. "Who are you calling?" she asked.

"My daughter. I don't appreciate you barging in like this. I need to check with her and make sure you're telling the truth about her sending you here."

"Listen, I don't have much time," Diane blurted out. "I just wanted to offer you money for that old station wagon you used to keep in your garage. Maybe you don't even have it any longer, but I thought I'd just come by and check with you." She held up her hands as if she were surrendering. "I didn't mean to frighten you."

The woman put the phone down. "How much were you thinking of offering?"

"Two thousand dollars," Diane said.

"Make it three thousand dollars in cash, and the car is all yours."

"Well, I don't have cash, but I'll write you a check, which is practically the same thing. I have three times that much in my bank account, but I need to make it last. And you can cash it as soon as the bank opens."

Silence stretched between them as the woman thought about it.

Diane remembered the bronzed Buddha she'd seen sitting on the table in the living room. She didn't want to kill the old bat, but if her hand was forced, she'd knock her over the head with the figurine on her way out, then take the car anyhow.

"Write the check, and you have yourself a deal."

Diane smiled. *Smart move.*

Fifteen minutes later, she was driving the musty old car onto the highway. Diane had nothing but the clothes on her back, but she didn't dare return to the farmhouse for anything. Too risky. She needed to get to her brother's place before Aster figured out what she was up to. The warden wouldn't tell her who had posted her bail, but she wasn't born yesterday. Aster Williams was responsible for her release. He was the only one she knew with enough money and the motive to set her free. If she'd believed for one minute that Aster would allow her to hand over the McMann girl and then go on her merry way, she might have used the old lady's phone and called him already.

But she knew Aster better than most.

He was not a trusting or forgiving man.

And despite what the two prison bitches had told her, she knew Aster didn't give a rat's ass about her or anyone else. He knew exactly what she was up to. More than likely, he also knew she meant to find a buyer for the McMann girl and take the money for herself. He had a sixth sense about those sorts of things.

Aster had a big house, a well-trained, pretty wife, two kids, and all the finely tailored suits he could possibly want. He didn't need the girl any more than he needed another luxury car. But Aster was all about principles and teaching people lessons.

He would come after Diane just as she knew he would go after Faith McMann and her team of misfits. Every woman in his life needed to know her place, or else.

His mother was a good example of his cruelty.

Diane had gone with him once when he'd visited the old broad in one of those ritzy homes for the elderly. He'd told Diane to wait in the car, but she'd grown bored. And besides, she'd been curious, wanted to see what he and his mother talked about when he came to visit. She'd snuck inside, made her way down the hall, and peeked inside, shocked to see him pinching and poking his mom's fleshy skin and then flicking her in the head with his fingers every time she whimpered. Horrified, she'd rushed back to the car. Praying Aster hadn't seen her, she'd sat quietly, pale and unmoving, until he returned twenty minutes later looking quite satisfied, if not downright happy. She'd seen him kick a dog out of his way before, but witnessing him torturing his elderly mother had frightened her in a way that nothing else did. She never asked him about his mother again.

Never told anyone what she'd seen.

Never would.

Keeping her eyes on the road, Diane hoped a quarter tank of gas would get her to Lodi. Her brother Eric and his wife lived in a mobile home off Rio Vista Drive. Eric was the youngest of her eight brothers. He'd been a decent brother, if not a little slow.

She pressed her foot a little harder on the gas pedal, but whenever she tried to go much more than fifty miles per hour, the underbelly of the car rattled. Staying at a steady forty-five, she ignored the honks and dirty looks she got along the way. When she took exit 267A, she breathed a sigh of relief.

Diane turned on to Rio Vista and then entered the mobile park. Her brother's place was at the very end, which was sort of nice because his tiny home actually had a view of a woodsy area. When she used to visit, she and her brother would sit out back and enjoy a cold beer and watch the deer mosey on by.

She got out of the car and stretched her arms over her head. Just that small movement caused her pain. The bruises on her arms were turning a dark purple. She leaned over and took a peek in the side mirror. It was hard to believe she was looking at the girl who'd won her first beauty pageant in elementary school. She frowned. Her face would never be the same.

As she stood there looking at her brother's home, a gust of wind blew her hair to one side. *Strange,* she thought, when she noticed the door was ajar.

A prickly unease swept up her spine. Back in the day, Eric would have come outside the moment he heard a car pull up. Where was he? If she'd had her cell phone, she would have called him and told him she was on her way.

Gravel crunched beneath her feet as she walked. It was too quiet.

Making her way up the wooden ramp, she bent down to take a closer look at the stain she saw there.

Was that blood?

She brushed her finger through a splatter of red. Her pulse accelerated. Up ahead she saw a bloody footprint.

"Eric? Trista?"

There was no answer. She used her sleeve to open the door wide enough so she could see inside. Stepping over the threshold, she followed the bloody trail of footprints to the back room, where she found her brother tied to a chair, his throat slit open. Trista lay naked on top of the bed, blood everywhere.

Diane stood there for a moment, taking it all in. A small part of her knew she should be horrified. At the very least, overwhelmed by her brother's demise. But her only thought was, *Shit*. Where was the girl? The McMann girl was her chip, her ace in the hole, her way out of this shit hole of a town.

She hurried to the other room. Checked the closet and under the beds. It didn't take her long to realize the girl wasn't there. That didn't surprise her, but the fact that someone had taken the time to rape her sister-in-law did. For years she'd watched Aster and his men at work. "Get in and get out" was Aster's mantra.

She went back to the bedroom, careful not to leave her fingerprints behind.

On top of the dresser she found her brother's wallet. Using the sleeve of her shirt, she took his credit card and what little cash he had, then opened drawers and went through his things, taking anything of value. As she walked to the corner of the room, where her brother sat in a chair, his head slumped to one side, she felt a pang in her chest at the thought that it was her fault he was dead. That one small emotion made her feel better about herself. She wasn't heartless. She would miss her brother.

Whoever had done this had come for the girl.

She knelt down and used the tips of her fingers to close her brother's eyes so his glossy orbs weren't staring at her as she slid the gold band off his finger. With that done, she went through the closet and grabbed some of his wife's clothes and anything else she might need while she figured out what to do next.

ELEVEN

It was way past midnight by the time Lilly Gray entered the bedroom and climbed under the covers. Her first and last thoughts every single day were of her grandchildren, Lara and Hudson. A worrier by nature, she'd never once imagined anything like this happening to her family. Lara was such a quiet little girl. How would she ever stand up to those monsters? And yet she worried about Hudson for the opposite reasons. He was bold, sometimes fearless. Would those traits get him into more trouble than he could handle?

Disturbed by her thoughts, she had a difficult time settling in for the night. But then Russell reached for her. Although she and her husband hadn't said two words to each other since his return from taking Bri and the girls to the airport, she didn't pull away when his hand settled gently on her arm.

"It's easy for families and people in general to stay together when things are good," he said. "But when things are bad—with everything going on right now—I don't know if I can handle this without you by my side. I need you with me, Lilly."

Silence hovered between them before he tried again. "Bri needed space—I could see it in her eyes. Think about it. What would have happened if I hadn't helped her get away? She would have been a cancer to this family right now. She was freaking out. We needed to let her go. She needs time."

"What about Colton?" she asked, her voice not much more than a whisper.

"Colton will understand. I'll talk with him."

"Bri should have called him."

"She knew he would have tried to stop her, and what could he have done about it while he was hundreds of miles away?"

Her back was to him, but she turned so she was facing the ceiling. They had been married long enough for him to take it as a truce. He leaned closer and kissed her cheek. "Not every decision I make will be the right one," he said. "But for the sake of our family, the two of us have to stick together and be as one. We need to be strong for everyone."

After a quiet moment stretched between them she asked, "What do we do about Faith? I don't know if you're seeing what I'm seeing, but she's not the same girl she used to be. She's not the same girl she was before you all raided the farmhouse and came home without Lara. If we don't find those kids, I don't know if she'll get through this in one piece."

"You're right. She's not the same girl." He sighed. "We've both got to come to grips with that and do our best to help her through this as well as we can so hopefully there are still pieces of our daughter left when all is said and done."

"If we find our grandkids, they'll never be the same, either."

"No, I don't suppose they will be. I guess none of us will ever be the same. We could lie here each night and pretend and wish, but it still won't be so."

"You're an old fool," she said, turning to him, "but I love you."

He reached for her and pulled her close. "I love you, too. Don't you ever forget it."

Beast followed Rage out of the house, not at all surprised by her refusal to let the strong winds and cold air stop her from taking her morning run. As always, he kept his distance. She didn't like anyone hovering or watching her too closely.

About five minutes into their run, he noticed her form was off. Leaning too far forward, Rage appeared to be putting too much force into each step, and she wasn't using her arms to drive her legs.

Less than a minute later, she went down fast, using both hands to break her fall before rolling to her side.

He could hear her cursing as he rushed to her side. Her knees were scraped. "You're hurt," he said as he leaned over to pick her up.

She slapped his hands away. "I don't need your help! I'm not an invalid."

He straightened but didn't move, merely waited out the storm continuously brewing inside that head of hers.

She scowled up at him. "Why do you do this?"

"Do what?"

"Why do you watch over me like you do? It's annoying. I'm not your lover, your sister, or your child. I'm nothing to you."

It wasn't often she took her frustrations out on him, but when she did he knew it was best if he let her use him as a jousting post. "We've been over this a million times."

She tried to push herself to her feet, but her legs wouldn't hold.

Day by day she grew weaker. His heart wilted.

"What's happening to me?"

"I don't know, but you're going to the doctor." He leaned over again, scooped her into his arms, and marched back toward home as she pummeled his chest with her fists.

"I won't go. There's nothing they can do."

"They can help you with the pain."

"I told you I don't need help. Put me down."

Ignoring her, Beast walked the half mile or so back home. He didn't put her down until they were in the house where they lived with his father, Little Vinnie. The man had no business being called little anything, but he'd picked up the name in high school after he'd sprouted from five feet to six foot four by his senior year.

Little Vinnie liked to cook. When they came through the door, he was cooking up some eggs and sausage.

Beast set Rage on the couch.

She tried to kick him but was too weak to do any damage.

Little Vinnie turned off the stove, opened a cupboard, and found the ointment he'd made from honey, turmeric, ginger, and olive oil. He then made his way to the couch and took a seat next to Rage.

Beast had no idea how Little Vinnie had come up with the concoction, but he'd been rubbing it on her arms and legs since she was first diagnosed and given six months to live. His dad had read somewhere that her muscles would grow weak and sore and thus massaging the ointment into her skin would relieve some of the pain. It had become one of their daily routines, and she never tried to stop him.

But she did continue to bitch, muttering under her breath, as Little Vinnie massaged the ointment into her limbs starting with her left shoulder and working his way downward to her elbow. She succumbed quicker than usual, her head falling back into the cushions as he worked his magic.

After taking a shower, Beast dressed and then headed out the door without saying a word to either of them. He didn't know where he was headed, but he needed to get away. He needed to breathe.

They were losing her.

Rage had refused treatment since it would not save her life. She was fond of saying she preferred to live while she died. She'd suffered through a seizure but had developed no verbal, cognitive, or motor loss until today.

The reality that she was dying right before his eyes, slowly but surely, struck him in that moment. He climbed into his truck, his hands wrapped tightly around the wheel. He thought back to the day when he'd received a call that his daughter and wife had been killed in a car accident.

It happened so fast. A kid texting and driving hit them head-on. Wham. Bam.

But with Rage it was happening so slowly.

There were so many things he wished he'd had the time to tell his wife and child before they were taken from him. And here was his chance to tell Rage how much she meant to him. She was like the daughter he'd never had the chance to raise, and yet the words always stuck in his throat like old, crusty bread. A slow death was not easier. Either way, losing someone you loved sucked.

How could he ever tell Rage that he loved her as a father loves a daughter? It would only come out sounding like a goodbye, and he wasn't ready for that, didn't know if he'd ever be ready.

Twelve

Faith stood off to the side as a dozen men worked the scene. She'd made the two-hour drive to the Central Valley with Detective Yuhasz. He'd seemed deep in thought for most of the ride, so she'd let him be. Now she stood looking over the ribbon of canal water that ran next to grazing lands and almond orchards.

Agents Burnett and Jensen of the FBI were there, too. Agent Burnett was a tall woman, easy to spot in a crowd. She looked over at Faith and tipped her chin in acknowledgment.

The valley's infamous fog made the hills look pale and the sky gray. The canal water the men were searching through was brown and murky, impossible to see to the bottom. They had been looking in this particular area for a girl who recently went missing. A farmworker had reportedly seen a car go into the canal shortly after the child was taken. And that's when a diver had brought up the license plate that ended up being registered to Craig McMann. Detective Yuhasz was contacted, and here they were.

Yuhasz had mentioned on the drive that the canal was often referred to as an "underwater junkyard," stretching nearly 117 miles through the valley. The canal authority pulled out fifty to one hundred cars every year. The waters also held weapons, remnants of meth labs, and the bodies of murder victims.

Since arriving early this morning, they had pulled out a motorcycle, two sedans, a pickup truck, a Ford Explorer, and finally her husband's SUV.

After hook and chain were attached, the familiar car was pulled slowly from the canal. A wave of sickness swept through her. She struggled to breathe normally as the car was dragged from its watery grave. Rust-brown water seeped from every crevice, leaking onto the ground around the men's feet.

She kept her distance, even found herself taking a few steps backward.

Why had she come?

A surge of anxiety and fear set in as she turned about and walked back to Detective Yuhasz's car. She no longer wanted to see or know what they found inside. She didn't want to be here at all. Her legs felt heavy as she walked. Sharp pains sliced through her as she continued onward. She couldn't breathe, and her heart felt as if it might burst.

When she reached the car, she stopped, hands on hips, and bent over until she managed to fill her lungs with air. After a moment she climbed into the passenger seat, closed her eyes, and concentrated on breathing. Minutes stretched into eternity until Yuhasz opened the door and got behind the wheel. "Nothing inside," he said.

"Nothing at all? Are you sure?"

"Nothing we can see with the naked eye. They'll dry the vehicle, tow it our way, and then forensics can do the rest." He turned on the engine, waited for her to buckle up, and then drove around the other vehicles before merging onto the main road back toward home.

Thank you, God, she said inwardly as the news slowly seeped into her consciousness. Hudson wasn't in the car. Hudson was out there in the world somewhere. He was the bravest kid she knew. He would be fine. Lara and Hudson would be fine.

After a while, when she was calm again, she looked at Detective Yuhasz and said, "Thank you for bringing me here today. I appreciate it."

"Not a problem," he said. "How's the rest of the family holding up?"

"We've been better. Colton's wife took the kids and went to live with her parents in Florida. My brother's on the road and doesn't have a clue."

"Why didn't she tell him?"

"I think she was afraid he would talk her into staying, and that was the last thing she wanted to do."

"Family is a fragile thing."

"You have a daughter and a son?"

"Two daughters. One is married with two kids of her own. The other has a girlfriend. They're talking about adopting."

"What about you, Detective?"

He raised a questioning brow. "What about me?"

"What do you do for fun in your spare time?"

"Fun? Never heard of it. What is that?"

She smiled. "Stupid question. Sorry."

"Not a stupid question. I've been known to hit a few dives in Sacramento and show off my karaoke skills. My daughters have accused me of being stuck in the 1990s, but who cares as long as I'm enjoying myself, right?"

Faith had a difficult time imagining the detective singing onstage, but she nodded just the same.

"I enjoy a cold beer every once in a while," he added, "and I used to win a few bucks playing billiards."

"I'll have to dig out my cue stick," Faith said, "and play you sometime."

"You've got yourself a deal."

It was quiet for a moment before Faith said, "I used to think the world was filled with rainbows and unicorns, and, sadly, I'm not joking."

He said nothing.

"How blind can one person be?"

Keeping his eyes on the road, Yuhasz said, "Ignorance is bliss for a reason. There's something to be said for not being born in the middle of a war zone or being lucky enough to escape the grittier parts of life."

"Yeah, I guess so. Out of sight, out of mind." She thought about Craig and tried to recall what their last words had been the morning of his death. Nothing came to her. Death could be a fickle fellow. "All those people out there struggling to survive," she said, speaking her thoughts, "and yet in the end there's no getting around the inevitable. The grim reaper will come. Guaranteed."

"When death will come," Yuhasz said, "he won't go away empty." He glanced at Faith. "An old proverb."

"I'm not afraid of death," Faith shot back. "I just don't want to be there when it happens. Woody Allen."

There was a long pause before Yuhasz added, "Inside each of us, there is the seed of both good and evil. Eric Burdon."

"There are a thousand hacking at the branches of evil to the one who is striking at the root. Henry David Thoreau."

"Nice."

"Agreed."

━━━━━━

Beth Tanner took her plate to the kitchen and stared out the window as she rinsed. The wind, she noticed, had knocked one of her good chairs into the pool in the backyard. She wiped her hands on a cloth before making her way through the sliding glass door leading to the pool. At closer view she realized she wouldn't be able to save the chair without using the aluminum pole with pool brush stored in the garage.

She cut across the side yard, surprised by the strength of the wind. Overhead, tree limbs crackled and snapped as the squall blew through the branches. Careful to shut the gate behind her, she considered leaving the chair where it was until the weather calmed. Before heading inside, though, something in the distance caught her eye.

As her hair whipped about her face, she stood motionless, her gaze fixed on Faith McMann's house across the street. Most would say it would be silly of her to believe it could have been anything more than a shadow playing tricks on her, especially during a sudden windstorm. But nonetheless, she didn't move. She'd learned long ago to trust her instincts, feel the energy around her, the ground beneath her feet.

There it was again.

The dark shadow was actually a person. He or she was inside Faith McMann's house, walking one way and then the other. Looking for something perhaps?

Chair forgotten, she entered her house through the garage, went to the kitchen, and grabbed the phone. She was about to dial the police, but she stopped herself. "Screw that," she said aloud as she smacked the receiver back in place. What good had the police done Faith other than throw her in jail and cause her more grief?

Beth had been home watering plants in the front yard the day Faith's husband was killed. After hearing a scream, she'd put her dog inside the house, and when she'd rushed outside again she'd seen Craig McMann's car take off down the road between their houses. She found Faith choking on her own blood. Being an ER nurse, she'd known it was too late for Craig, so she'd worked on Faith. It was a miracle she was able to save her.

Faith might have recovered, but if she was ever going to find those kids, she needed all the help she could get.

And damn it all if Beth wasn't going to protect her little corner of the world.

She pulled open a bottom drawer and grabbed a handful of zip ties she used for trash bags; then she rushed to her bedroom. Working fast, she slipped into a lightweight jacket and then crammed the zip ties inside the pocket. Next she tied her hair back to keep the wind from blowing hair into her face, and then headed for the closet. She unlocked the gun case and grabbed the Marlin lever-action rifle because it was already loaded and it could shoot a cartridge powerful enough to knock down any species of game in North America.

It wasn't yet noon. Any other day and she would have been in the ER assessing and stabilizing patients with life-threatening ailments. But this was her day off. Most of her neighbors were at work.

Her best bet, if she didn't want the intruder to see her coming, was to head for Mr. Hawkins's house and then cut across his yard and crawl under the fence to get to the McMann house.

She exited her house and walked at a clipped pace as she cut across the field of persimmon trees instead of merely walking down the neighbor's driveway. After entering Hawkins's backyard through his side gate, she weaved through backyard furniture that had toppled over and then trekked through the tall grass separating Hawkins's house from the McMann house. All went as planned. Crawling under the fence was a tighter squeeze than she'd imagined, but she managed. A silver Subaru was parked outside Faith's house.

One man or two? Her adrenaline soared.

Maybe more. Perhaps the same three who'd murdered Craig McMann were inside.

If there were three men, things could get a bit hairy. But two men she could handle. Standing at the hood of the Subaru, she peeked around the garage toward the pool area. Nobody there.

She couldn't walk to the front door because there were too many windows. Whoever was inside would see her. If he were smart, he'd get in and out in a hurry. This house had a bad history. Why would he linger? What sort of fool or fools was she dealing with?

She didn't have to wonder for long. The intruder came around the corner as if he didn't have a care in the world. If he weren't wearing a dark cap over his head and gloves, she might have asked questions first and knocked him in the head second. But as things stood, good old-fashioned instinct took over, and she struck him with the butt of her rifle.

He went down, crumbling to his knees in slow motion. She hit him again just in case, then retrieved the zip ties and secured his hands and legs.

THIRTEEN

No sooner had Faith said goodbye to the detective from the front steps of her parents' house than her cell phone rang. Caller ID told her it was her neighbor Beth Tanner, the woman who had saved her life after the attack. She picked up the call and said hello.

"Faith, it's Beth. I can't explain over the phone, but I need you to meet me at your house on Rolling Greens Lane."

"When?"

"Right now. There's something you need to see."

Faith turned around and headed for her car parked in the driveway. "I'm on my way." She got as far as Auburn-Folsom when she spotted Miranda walking on the side of the road with her hand out and her thumb raised to the sky.

Faith passed her by, then pulled to the side of the road, rolled down the passenger side window, and waited for her to catch up.

Miranda leaned her head into the car. "What's up?"

"Where are you going?"

She shrugged. "I just needed to get out for a bit."

"This is a dangerous road to walk on. Why don't you get in and come with me? I'm going to stop by my house to talk to a neighbor."

Miranda hesitated before she climbed in. After Faith merged back onto the road, Miranda said, "Why did you move?"

"To my parents' house?"

Miranda nodded.

"The truth is, after my family was attacked, I became frustrated with the police. In the heat of the moment, I made a bad decision that ended up getting me thrown in jail. The judge let me out on two conditions. One, I must live with my parents for ninety days, and, two, I have to attend anger management classes twice a week."

Miranda chuckled.

"What's so funny?"

"I've met some mean people in my lifetime, and you're not one of them. Not even close."

"I didn't have an angry bone in my body until those men took everything from me." She spared a quick glance at Miranda before setting her gaze back on the road. The girl had been through so much, and yet she kept her hardships to herself. "I'm sorry I haven't been able to spend more time with you since you've been staying with us."

Miranda swished a hand through the air. "I'm the last person you need to worry about. Besides, I can't stay with you and your parents forever."

"Oh, yes, you can," Faith countered. "I'm serious. You've already met Lara, and you'll love Hudson."

"You're that certain you'll find them?"

"I am," Faith answered without hesitation.

"Do the police have any idea where your son might be?"

"No. Not at this point."

"I wasn't really just off for a walk," Miranda said.

"No?" Faith asked, feigning surprise. "Where were you going?"

"I thought I would hitchhike my way to the hotel I told you about. The one in San Francisco, the place I escaped from. I'm going to find that disgusting john they call Mr. Smith, whose face I can't get out of my mind, and I'm going to confront him."

"What makes you think he'd still be there?"

She shrugged. "That man, whoever he is, practically owns the place. He had people in the salon, at the front desk, and guards at the door. He could own the hotel for all I know. Either way, it's not like I have anything better to do. I'll sleep in the park like I used to do, and then I'll watch the entrance of the hotel every day and night until he returns."

"That's much too dangerous," Faith said.

"I'll be prepared."

Faith sucked in a breath. "I'm glad I found you before you got too far."

"Whether I go there today or next week, I'll go eventually. I won't allow that man or those people to keep on hurting young girls."

"How do you plan on stopping them?"

"I have some money. I know where I can get my hands on a fake ID. I'll buy a gun, and then if he dares return to the hotel, I'll wait for him. And I'll take him out."

Faith sighed. "Why don't we talk to Detective Yuhasz and see what he can do to help?"

"I'm not eighteen. He'd have no choice but to shove me into a foster home or some sort of shelter. I've been trapped for too long. I couldn't handle it. I would run away first chance I got. I'm tired of people telling me what I can and cannot do."

"Shooting the man who hurt you might not be the answer. You'll be the one who ends up behind bars."

"That's sort of calling the kettle black, isn't it?"

"Touché."

"I'm not going to let wealthy pricks like Mr. Smith pay to rape girls like me who have no way of fighting back. I'd rather take him down and then live behind bars knowing I stopped him from doing to someone else what he did to me."

Sadly, she couldn't argue with that. Faith stopped at the red light on Douglas Boulevard. "I think we need to do some planning before we go."

"Before we go where?"

"To San Francisco."

"You're going with me?"

"It's obvious your mind is made up, and I'm certainly not going to let you go alone." The light turned green. Faith stepped on the gas.

"Why would you bother," Miranda asked, "when you have so much to do already?"

"We never would have found the farmhouse if it weren't for you," Faith reminded her.

"But we were too late."

"Maybe so, but Mr. Smith paid Diane Weaver—isn't that right?"

Miranda nodded.

"Then he must have contacts. Maybe he's the one who can lead us to where they're hiding Lara and Hudson."

"I didn't think of that. You might be right."

Faith made a left onto Rolling Greens Lane. Her house was the third on the right. She parked next to a silver Subaru she didn't recognize, then looked at Miranda. "We both want to stop people like Mr. Smith from hurting anyone else. Promise me you won't make the trip to San Francisco without me?"

"I promise."

Faith reached out and put a hand over hers. "You're not alone, Miranda. No matter what happens, you're not alone."

"Thanks," Miranda said before Beth Tanner appeared and they both exited the vehicle.

Beth gave Miranda a quick once-over. "Who's this?"

"This is Miranda. I'll explain later, but you don't need to worry about her seeing whatever it is you want to show me."

"That's fine," Beth said. "Come with me. He's in the garage."

"He?" Faith asked.

"The man I found rummaging through your house. A black knit cap and gloves was my first clue he wasn't a door-to-door salesman."

"What's he doing in the garage?"

"He's tied up, and I do mean literally."

Faith's pulse began to race. "Take me to him."

"This way."

Faith and Miranda followed Beth to the side of the house and through the door leading into the garage. At the far corner, hunkered down between stacks of plastic bins and metal shelving, was a man.

His arms were pulled behind his back, his wrists zip-tied to a built-in shelving unit.

She'd tied his ankles, too, and duct taped his mouth and legs, just above his knees. His eyes were wide-open. He was trying to talk, but the words were muffled.

Faith walked over to him, her heart beating rapidly inside her chest as she stared at him.

"After I tied him up, he wouldn't stop kicking his legs, so I had to pull out the tape. He wouldn't shut up, either," Beth explained.

"Do we know who he is?"

"He had a gun tucked in his waistband, and I found a wallet in his coat pocket. His name is Martin Hoyt. He's twenty-nine years old and one hundred and sixty pounds of scrawny."

Faith examined him closely, her gaze fixed on his eyes.

He didn't look away, didn't blink. She didn't recognize him as one of the three men who had broken into her house and killed her husband. But what if he'd cut his hair since then or lost a few pounds? She tried to imagine him with curly hair and a birdlike nose, but it was no use.

He wasn't one of the three attackers. Or was he? A dark shadow on the curve of his neck caught her eye. She bent down on one knee, grabbed a fistful of hair, and jerked his head to the left. The tattoo on this man's neck was the same tattoo she'd seen on the intruder when he bent over and slit her husband's throat. This particular man might not be the one who did the deed, but he had to be connected somehow. The hate she felt for him and his thug friends rushed through her body. She stood up and kicked him in the gut, and then again in the side.

He grunted, looking to the others for help.

The blood in her veins sizzled and popped as she looked around the garage. She went to the area where Craig kept his tools, dug around until she found a crowbar. It was solid, heavy, perfect.

"Don't do it," Beth said as she stepped in front of the man, keeping Faith from coming any closer.

"It's OK," Faith said, although that was far from the truth. Nothing was OK. She wanted to bash the man's head in, would have no qualms doing so. "Move aside," she said calmly. "I just want to ask him a few questions."

"Do you recognize him?" Beth asked.

"No."

"I do," Miranda said.

They both turned to face the girl.

"I know him as Fin. That's the name he used when he came to the farmhouse to brand the girls."

Beth sighed as she stepped out of the way.

Faith knelt down again, and this time she ripped the tape from his mouth. "Where's my daughter, Lara McMann?"

"I've never heard of her."

"Bullshit! You're the tattoo artist I've heard so much about."

"I have no idea what you're talking about."

"He's lying," Miranda said.

"Did you give my daughter a tattoo?"

"They called her Jean," Miranda reminded him. "And you took your time with her. You liked her. I know you did."

He frantically shook his head. "It wasn't me!"

"He's lying," Miranda said. "I watched him do it."

Faith stood and whacked him across the knee with the crowbar.

He let out a bloodcurdling scream.

"Where's my daughter?"

"I don't know."

Faith smacked him again.

He screamed again, louder this time.

"Last chance," Faith ground out. "Where is she?"

"I don't know. Nobody knows, I swear." He cowered. "Mother sent her away, but nobody knows where she is!"

"What were you doing inside my house?"

"I heard there was millions of dollars hidden around here somewhere. I was looking for the cash."

She lifted the crowbar high above his head.

"Faith!" Beth shouted. "I called you here so you could question him, not so you could get yourself thrown back in jail."

Arms trembling, Faith lowered the weapon. Beth was right. She needed to think about Lara and Hudson. She needed to be smart. "What should we do?"

"He doesn't deserve to live," Miranda said. "He enjoys tattooing the girls and making them suffer. He knows things."

Faith wasn't ready to call the police. Not yet. She didn't want to make any hasty decisions. "We'll keep him here until I figure out what to do with him."

"What about his car?" Miranda asked. "Someone might see it."

"I'll hide it in my garage," Beth offered.

Fin squirmed. "You can't leave me here."

"We can do anything we want with you," Faith told him. "If you tell me the name of your boss, I'll let you go right now. Nobody will know you were ever here," she lied.

Silence.

Faith grabbed the roll of duct tape and ripped off enough to wrap around his mouth.

"I need water."

"I need a name."

When he refused to answer, Faith slapped the tape over his mouth.

"What now?" Miranda asked.

"Beast would love to have a talk with this man," Faith said. "Beast doesn't like people who hurt children." She looked at Fin and shook her head. "You had your chance, buddy."

FOURTEEN

Between watching Craig's car being pulled from the canal, finding Miranda on the side of the road, and then discovering the man who had branded her daughter tied up in her garage, it had been a long day.

It bothered her to think she'd wanted so badly to kill the man. And yet she knew he was scum. He'd refused to give them the name of the man or woman he and Diane Weaver worked for, but he had appeared to be baffled as to Lara's whereabouts.

After leaving her house, she'd called Beast to tell him what was going on and asked him to pay Fin a visit. Hopefully he would have better luck getting the tattoo man to talk.

Faith and Miranda had returned to her parents' house a few hours ago. After doing her own search of the Internet for anything about Diane Weaver and coming up with nothing, Faith took a quick shower before joining Mom, Dad, and Miranda at the kitchen table.

Mom had made pork chops and green beans.

Faith pushed her food around her plate, trying to figure out what her next step would be. Diane Weaver was out there somewhere, and she had all the answers. But if the police couldn't find her or locate her brother, how the hell was she going to find them?

And what about Richard Price?

Richard Price was a client who had used her husband's business to launder money—the instigating factor that ended up turning her world upside down. After her husband's business partner stole $2 million from Richard Price's account, then hid it in the pool equipment at Faith's house and pointed the finger at her husband, three men had come looking for that money and ended up taking her kids instead.

According to the FBI, weeks after Craig's death, Richard Price was found murdered in his car on the side of the road.

Who had killed him, and why?

Too many questions without any answers.

The alarm beeped, alerting them to the fact that someone was nearing the house. The front door opened and then slammed shut.

"Where is she?" her brother's voice boomed as he came charging through the house.

Faith and Dad came to their feet at the same time.

Miranda and Mom remained seated.

"Where are they?" Colton asked.

Dad stopped Colton in the living room before he got as far as the kitchen. "Bri and the kids are in Florida with her parents," Dad said. "She was frightened, Colton. Not only for herself but for your daughters. She couldn't handle the stress. She needed to go."

Colton paced the living room, back and forth in front of the fireplace, before plunking himself down on the couch. With his elbows propped on his knees, he rubbed both sides of his head. "She promised me she wouldn't make any decisions until I returned."

Faith's brother's eyes were bloodshot, his face pale. He looked like hell, and Faith's heart went out to him. Her family was falling apart, and there wasn't anything she could do about it. How would any of them ever manage to carry on?

"I'm so sorry," she told Colton, her hand on his shoulder.

"It's not your fault," he said, his shoulders slumped forward. "The only people at fault are the nameless bastards who decided to enter your house and take Lara and Hudson in the first place." He looked at Dad. "They have to pay for what they've done to our family. We can't let them get away with this."

The phone rang. Mom picked up the call after two rings. "Yes. OK," she said. "We'll be here."

Mom walked into the living room. "Detective Yuhasz needs to talk to us. He said it's important. He's on his way now."

FIFTEEN

Faith was standing outside when Detective Yuhasz arrived at her parents' house in Loomis. Jana and Beast had arrived separately two minutes earlier and were inside.

She'd already spent the morning with the detective. He wouldn't have come all this way if it wasn't important. The thought made her nervous. If he'd located Lara or Hudson, he would have told Mom on the phone. Instead he'd felt the need to drive the forty minutes from Auburn to talk to all of them together.

He parked his car, climbed out, and walked her way. Six feet tall and broad-shouldered, he kept his silver hair cropped short. His jaw was bristly today. He looked worn-out. She and Detective Yuhasz didn't always see eye to eye, but she had a newfound respect for the man. People had high expectations when it came to the police force, herself included. But they were only human, and sometimes there was only so much they could do when it came to protecting the citizens in their communities.

"Everyone else is in the house waiting," she told him.

He nodded, his expression grim, which made her all the more nervous.

He followed her inside. Mom, Dad, Colton, Jana, and Beast were seated in the living room.

Miranda had gone upstairs to the guest room. Although Detective Yuhasz had seen Miranda before, he had yet to question Faith about who she was or why she was there. It was best if he didn't know, since protocol might force him to question her and possibly have her processed through children's services, as Miranda feared. Faith didn't have the time or patience for bureaucracy. And, besides, she knew Miranda would run away before she would be taken into foster care.

Mom jumped to her feet the moment the detective walked inside. "You must be chilly. I'll get you some tea."

Detective Yuhasz waved her off. "I'm fine."

"It's no bother." Mom went to the kitchen and set about filling the teakettle and putting it on the stove. When Mom was nervous, she tended to flit around and try to find ways to keep busy.

Dad gestured for the detective to take a seat.

As soon as he did, Faith said, "We're all here. What's going on?"

"I received a call from authorities in Mendocino County and learned that a few days ago there were reports of shots fired within the national forest," Detective Yuhasz began. "Officers in the region have been going door-to-door. During their questioning," he went on, "they discovered that Nicholas Quintero, one of the top wanted drug lords in the country, has been spotted in the area." He took a breath. "Needless to say, a response team was sent out to canvass the woods. Late yesterday, a group of heavily armed team members found and raided a marijuana-growing operation. Quintero, it turned out, was using child laborers to trim and care for the marijuana."

"And you wouldn't be telling us this," Faith said, "unless there was reason to believe Hudson was one of the children. Is that right?"

Mom stood nearby, her hands entwined in front of her, the tea forgotten.

Without answering Faith's question, Yuhasz continued. "So far they've been able to verify that somewhere between three and four dozen boys were being forced to work for Quintero. Twelve of those boys had been brought to the area in the past month. According to one of the men arrested, five boys escaped the premises only a few days ago and have been missing since that time."

Faith sat up taller. "What about the other boys? The boys they found? Do we know if—"

Yuhasz shook his head. "Hudson was not among the children found."

"How do you know?"

"The Mendocino police had taken a couple of group pictures of the boys at the time of the raid. Hudson was not in the photograph. Detective O'Sullivan scanned a recent photograph of Hudson and sent it to the sheriff's office."

He rubbed his prickly head.

Faith leaned forward and waited for him to continue.

"More than a few of the boys rescued," Yuhasz said as he looked at Faith, "recognized Hudson as one of the boys who escaped."

She smiled. "This is huge!"

He nodded.

She felt suddenly breathless. Her son was alive. Faith looked at her father. "Hudson is alive. We have to find him."

"Let's hear the rest of what the detective has to say. Then we'll talk."

"So what now?" Jana asked impatiently, both hands splayed against her pregnant belly.

"Search parties are out there looking now," Yuhasz went on. "But officials in charge have warned they believe at least two of the men in charge of the marijuana operation are also out in the woods, and these men are armed and dangerous."

Everyone remained silent until Dad looked at Yuhasz and said, "Anything else?"

"That pretty much sums it up."

"I need to help in the search for Hudson," Dad said. "That's all there is to it."

Colton nodded. "I'm going, too."

Yuhasz released a ponderous breath. "I had a feeling this would be your response, which is why I called the sheriff's office. They said there's not much they can do to stop you, but if you do decide to go, you'll need to check in with them and fill out some paperwork. The sheriff also said you should be aware that the people living in the neighborhoods bordering the forest are nervous. They've been trapped in their homes for days now, and most, if not all, have guns loaded and ready to shoot first and ask questions later."

"So no stopping to ask for directions," Colton said. "Got it."

Yuhasz frowned. "As you get higher into the mountains, you'll have to keep your eye out for black bears and mountain lions and, of course, any other predators out there."

"From the sound of it," Colton said, "wildlife is the least of our worries."

"If Hudson has been in the woods for two nights already," Faith asked, her pulse still racing, "what are his chances of survival?"

He shook his head. "I don't think anyone knows the answer to that, Faith. There are so many variables, you know, possible obstacles to consider."

"Like what?"

"Besides wild animals and dangerous criminals?" Colton asked.

She nodded.

"Hypothermia, dehydration, and exhaustion, for starters," Colton said flatly.

"The good news," Beast chimed in, "is that Hudson could live on the inner bark of some trees and eat bugs if he had to. From what your dad has told me about Hudson, the boy has spent a good amount of time in the woods, and he's been taught the basic survival skills."

She knew what Beast was trying to do, and she appreciated it. She'd known him for such a short time, and yet he was a true friend and solid as a rock.

"He's only nine years old," Mom said, her voice quivering.

"Most forests are dotted with cabins," Yuhasz told her. "There are plenty of hardships for those boys out there, but there's hope."

After Yuhasz left, Beast volunteered to go with Colton and Dad in search of Hudson, but Dad pulled him aside and asked him to keep an eye on Faith and the rest of the women, reminding him that Jana's husband, Steve, wouldn't be released from the hospital until the next day and would be on crutches.

Faith hated the idea of being left behind, but she needed to continue her search for Lara. And, as Colton had pointed out, she would only slow them down. She'd been running in the mornings and practicing at the shooting range, but she wasn't a trained hunter like her brother and father, and she couldn't remember the last time she'd hiked over rough terrain.

Although Beast had told them Rage was busy with Little Vinnie at home, she showed up around ten with detailed maps of the Mendocino forest. Since receiving a call from Beast to let her know what was going on, she'd spent some time doing her own research before she headed over. She had highlighted paths she and Little Vinnie believed might be the shortest route through the forest.

They all brainstormed, throwing out possibilities of things that could go wrong. They talked about the ground being wet, which could make it difficult to detect footsteps if the thugs were hiding out.

As Dad collected his fatigues, heavy vest, and sidearms, everyone else gathered any and all gear they believed the men might need during their trek through the forest.

Everyone tossed in opinions as they worked. They talked about contaminated water, cold temperatures, and wild animals. Dad showed them his handheld filter and chemical tablets that would purify water. For every problem, he had a solution.

"Judging by the maps I saw, the woods are thick with brush," Rage said. "Someone could be hiding out, and you won't be able to see them. And Little Vinnie mentioned all the mud you'll have to deal with."

"How do you know so much about surviving in the woods?" Dad asked Rage.

"These days all you need is an hour on the Internet to learn a little about most things." She shrugged. "If I were going, I'd probably make sure to keep my eyes and ears open and always be ready for the unexpected."

Dad chuckled. "Maybe I should take you with me instead of Colton."

"It's probably the best idea I've heard so far," Rage said, "but Beast and Little Vinnie wouldn't know what to do without me around to harass them all day."

Beast nodded, agreeing with her assessment.

By the time everyone in the room put in their two cents, and after they plotted and planned for the worst, it was midnight. Yuhasz had called to give them the name of the commander with whom Colton and Dad would have to check in to ensure they weren't mistaken for the criminals hiding in the area. Chances were there wouldn't be any phone service after they set off. If that were the case, Colton and Dad would use the two-way radios to communicate if they lost track of each other in the forest.

Faith didn't like how quiet her brother had become. She went to him now, talked to him while he organized and packed his gear. "I know you're upset with Bri, but I don't want you to set out in search of Hudson if you don't have a clear head. Beast is willing to go in your place. He's a good man, and he won't let Dad down."

"Faith. Stop. I'm fine. I only wish Bri had waited until I returned home. Other than that, I understand why she had to go. I miss my girls.

And the truth is, for the first time since Lara and Hudson were taken, I've realized I don't have a clue as to what you're going through. Because I can't imagine what I would do or who I would become if I were standing in your shoes." He put a finger on Faith's chin and lifted her head so she had no choice but to look at him. "I'm going to find Hudson, and I'm going to bring him back home to his mother. Do you hear me?"

Her eyes welled. "Thank you."

SIXTEEN

Hudson tossed the last of the wood scraps into the wood-burning stove and then stood and listened. For the first time in what felt like forever, it was quiet. No thunder or lightning. No rain drumming against the rooftop.

No raspy death rattle coming from the bottom bunk.

Joey was awake. His first words were, "Where are we?"

Hudson had been feeding him mashed beans. Even watered down to a soupy mixture it hadn't been easy getting him to swallow between fits of coughing. Throughout their first night inside the cabin, Hudson wasn't sure if Joey would make it. But at the moment, Joey actually had some color, which gave him hope that the boy might live.

"After you passed out in the woods," Hudson explained, "I went to gather wood and found a cabin. It's kept us out of the rain and wind. How are you feeling?"

"Like death."

Joey's voice was hoarse from coughing so much.

Hudson brought him the pan of water from atop the woodstove. "Thirsty?"

It took him a minute, but Joey managed to push himself upward until his back was against the cabin wall. He took the pan and drank, then wiped his mouth with his sleeve. "You saved my life."

"I did what anyone would do."

"Nobody I know would have bothered to drag me through the woods. How old are you?"

"Nine." He noticed the way Joey was looking at him. As if he didn't believe him. "I've always been big for my age. Every year one parent or another petitions for my birth certificate when I play football with their sons."

One corner of Joey's mouth turned up. "We're opposites," he said. "I'm the runt of the family."

"Where are you from?"

"Los Angeles."

Although they had been rooming together for a few weeks now, they had never talked about personal stuff before. "How did you end up here?"

"My parents were . . . are field-workers. They sold me and my brothers to those assholes we ran from when I was seven."

Hudson didn't know what to say, so he kept quiet.

"How did you get dragged into this shit hole of a place?" Joey asked.

"Three men came into my house, attacked my parents, and then took my sister and me."

"Where is she?"

Hudson shook his head. "I have no idea. The last time I saw her, she was crying and struggling to get away." He swallowed, didn't like thinking about what might have happened to her.

"If I get out of this alive," Joey said, "I'm going to kill every single man who ever touched me. And then I'm going to find a way back to LA to pay my mother and father a visit."

Joey's nostrils flared as he described what he would say and possibly do to his parents if and when he ever saw them again. The anger and resentment he saw in Joey's eyes caused chills to crawl up the back of Hudson's neck. Joey might be small, but Hudson had seen him in action when he fought the older boy, Denver, for a half loaf of bread. The men in charge had thought it was amusing and let them go at it for a good fifteen minutes. They finally had to pull Joey off the other boy, leaving Denver bruised and bleeding.

It took some doing, but Joey sat up and then inhaled before pushing himself to his feet. He reeked of his own stench. "Is there a bathroom in this place?"

"Outside," Hudson said. "Behind the cabin. It's not much, but it does the job. There's also an old barrel filled with water to wash yourself." Hudson looked out the window. "It's cold out there, but it's not raining. Do you need help walking?"

Joey waved a hand through the air. "I'm wobbly, but I'll get there."

"I'll get a fire going and then open the last can of beans and fry up some fish."

Joey gestured toward the fish in the sink. "You caught those with your bare hands?"

"It just takes patience, and having a spear helps, too," Hudson said, pointing to the long, thin piece of wood leaning by the door. One end had been whittled down to a sharp point.

"Clever. Glad I followed you instead of Denver," Joey said.

"Here—take this with you." Hudson handed Joey the ax. "If the door to the outhouse gets stuck, you're going to need this."

After Joey left the cabin, Hudson made quick work of using dry leaves to clean up Joey's mattress, dirty and damp from fever and urine. He tossed the leaves outside and then went back to the bed and turned the mattress over. He gulped the last of the water and then headed down the hill to the creek to gather more. On his way back up the now-familiar trail, he collected wood for kindling.

Joey was still inside the outhouse when he returned.

Figuring it would take him a while to get cleaned up, Hudson made a fire and then started cleaning the last two fish. Grandpa would be proud, he thought. As soon as Joey got his strength back, they needed to get off the mountain before the next storm swept in. He had no idea how far away they were from the men who had held them captive, but it made sense that they would have found him and Joey by now if they'd been looking.

He opened the door to toss the fish bones outside and found himself looking into the beady eyes of one of the men he'd just been thinking about. Every muscle in his body froze.

Derek had found them after all.

With a pistol pointed at Hudson's chest, he said, "You stupid boy. And here I'd thought you were the smart one in your little group. You never should have run."

It took Hudson a second to calm himself and think of what to do. Without looking away from the man, Hudson slowly reached for the spear leaning against the wall only inches away.

Derek looked into the cabin and said, "Where's our little friend Joey?"

"I'm right here."

The ax landed on the top of Derek's head with a sickening thud. Blood spurted in every direction.

Joey stepped aside as Derek fell backward like a newly sawed tree.

Hudson thought he might be sick as he watched blood gush from the man's head. His hands clutched his middle as if that might stop him from losing his last meal.

"There," Joey said. "We're even. You saved my life, and I saved yours."

Hudson couldn't take his eyes off the dead man now stretched out on the soggy ground in front of him. Derek's eyes were wide-open, his mouth agape.

Joey followed Hudson's gaze. "Never seen a dead man before, I take it."

Hudson thought of Sean, one of the boys who had escaped only to be shot in the back, but he didn't say anything. He just stood there and watched Joey kneel down and yank the ax from Derek's skull. Joey struggled to remove his backpack. Derek was a good-size man, and he was deadweight. When Joey tried to push the body to one side, he was suddenly overcome with a coughing attack.

"You better get back in the cabin and get warm," Hudson said as he came forward. "I'll do the rest."

Joey looked white as a ghost, his eyes cloudy with sickness. He coughed some more, spit into the dirt, and then pushed himself to his feet. "Yeah, I think I need to rest for a minute."

Hudson tried to convince himself that the man was only sleeping. He started with Derek's boots, untying the laces, then pulling them off. He kept finding himself staring at Derek's face. He didn't like the way his eyes seemed to be looking straight at him, so he glanced away.

Joey had yet to go inside. He stood under the door frame and stared out toward the woods. "I wonder if they'll come looking for him."

"I think they will," Hudson said. "That's why you need to get inside and get some rest before we head off."

"Head off? Today?"

Hudson nodded. "Even if no one ever comes looking for Derek, it's January. We've been lucky so far that the weather's been good to us, but see the sky?" He didn't wait for Joey to answer before he added, "There's a storm coming, and we don't want to be trapped here when it starts to snow."

Joey walked inside and shut the door behind him.

Hudson did his best to concentrate on what he was doing. The boots might be too big for either one of them, but the wool socks, pants, shirt, down jacket, and heavy knit cap would help keep both of them warm. As he stripped the man bare, he felt himself becoming calmer. He was undressing a dead man, and yet his heart was beating at a normal rate.

Is this what war had been like for Grandpa?

Had he been so set on escaping that he'd become desensitized to everything around him? Did the will to live take over all other emotions?

The pistol was lying on the ground. Hudson added it to the growing pile of gear and clothes they would take with them. He then worked on removing Derek's backpack, jacket, and shirt. Inside the backpack he found a bag of cannabis, a pipe, a lighter, beef jerky, corn nuts, sunflower seeds, a soft water bottle that his dad called a hydration bladder when they went hiking, and a box of ammunition.

He stood, looked around, then leaned over and picked up the gun. As an afterthought, he headed down the hill toward the stream to make sure no one else was hiding out. Before he got to the halfway mark, he found camping gear stacked at the base of a tree. There were only two items: a small tent and a sleeping bag rolled to the size of a pineapple.

Derek hadn't wanted them to know he was alone. Why else would he have left only these two items here? Hudson picked up the tent and the bag and headed back to the cabin. As he passed the body, he thought about moving the corpse to the side of the cabin, but he decided it wasn't worth the bother. Besides, he wanted to get out of the cold. There was a lot to do before they headed out for the long trek down the mountain.

SEVENTEEN

The night sky was pitch-black and stars were few by the time Faith said goodbye to Colton and Dad and then headed upstairs for bed.

She pulled off her jeans, crawled under the covers, and stared at the ceiling. She was running on adrenaline, the beat of her heart racing along with her thoughts. In twenty-four hours Dad and Colton would no longer have phone contact. The idea of being cut off from her brother and father and not knowing what was happening drove her crazy. She couldn't stop thinking about Hudson and what he might be going through.

Was he lost in the wilderness alone? Was he cold and scared? Was he hurt?

If she continued to allow herself to imagine the worst, she'd never make it through the next hour, let alone another day.

Instead she decided to focus on Hudson's strengths—the things he was good at that might help him through his ordeal until Colton and Dad could get to him. For starters, Hudson did extremely well in football and track. He was big for his age and quite strong.

Faith felt her nerves calming as she continued down this path of thinking. Hudson was fast, and he was clever. He wasn't afraid of the dark. In fact, Craig had gone on and on about their first father-and-son fishing trip after they'd returned home. "Our boy is a natural outdoorsman," he'd said proudly.

Those were the moments Faith chose to think about.

She needed to stay positive.

She imagined Hudson sticking with the other boys. Maybe they'd found a cave or another place where they could keep warm. Hudson was still alive, she told herself over and over, and he would be home soon.

As expected, they all got little sleep, and when morning came Mom wasn't the only one who needed to keep busy. After Mom and Jana left for the hospital to pick up Steve, Faith and Miranda headed for San Francisco. Neither one of them had a solid plan. They weren't supersleuths, but Faith figured it couldn't hurt to check the place out, especially since Miranda was going to do just that with or without her.

Faith had reserved a room at the hotel. The chances of them seeing the same man who had raped Miranda were probably slim to none, but Miranda was convinced the hotel staff was in on the sex-trafficking gig. Although her plans did not include spending the night, she also thought they might need a key card to ride the elevator. If they could get to the top floor, they could see who, if anyone, was staying in the suite.

If Miranda did happen to recognize one of the people who had played a part in helping that man bind and rape her, Faith had already decided to follow that person or get a name at the very least.

Before they reached the hotel, Faith pulled to the side of the road. She put the car in Park, then gestured to the glove box. "There's a Taser in there. Put it inside your purse. It's easy to work. If you need to use it, just turn it on. It's charged and ready to go. There are also sunglasses in there. You should put them on. Once we're inside the hotel, if you recognize anyone, don't confront him or her. I think it would be best, at least for now, if we get descriptions and their names if they work for the hotel and are wearing name tags."

"Sounds good," Miranda said. She pulled a cell phone from her purse. "Your sister said to take pictures, too."

Faith frowned. "My sister knows what we're up to?"

"Yeah. She asked me what we were doing today, and I told her. I thought you two were close."

Faith smiled. "We are. It's fine." She hadn't wanted to worry her sister, but no harm done.

"I'll just pretend I'm taking a selfie," Miranda told her. "From what I've seen online, everyone's doing it."

"We should go," Faith said. "Are you ready for this?"

"I've been ready for a while now. Thanks for bringing me here today, you know, and for everything you've done."

It sounded to Faith as if she was saying goodbye. The idea of Miranda spending the rest of her life on her own didn't sit well with her. "I'm the one who should be thanking you. There aren't too many people I know who would have gone out of their way to help me and my children as you have done. You're very brave."

Miranda looked the other way, staring out the window.

"You won't run off without letting me know where you're going, will you?"

She turned back to look at Faith. Her eyes glistened. "I won't go anywhere without telling you first. I promise."

The wind had picked up by the time Faith drove through the roundabout in front of the hotel. Men were holding on to their hats, and women were strapping their coats tighter around their waists as they waited for a car or a taxi in front of the hotel.

Faith and Miranda climbed out, leaving her car with the valet. She tucked the ticket inside her purse and then followed Miranda into the hotel lobby. With her hair pulled back into a bun, sunglasses, and red lipstick, Miranda looked much older.

The inside of the lobby was teaming with people, an eclectic group made up of many ethnicities. They weaved through the crowd, both of them looking around as they waited in line to check in.

It was a beautiful hotel. Crystal chandeliers, plush furniture, and marble floors.

Miranda tapped her on the arm. "Back in the corner you'll see the salon I told you about."

Miranda didn't appear to be nervous. Judging by the stiffness of her spine and the tautness of her jaw, she was angry.

After checking in, they went to the salon. As Faith asked questions about facials and massages, Miranda took a look around. By the time Faith finished, Miranda was nowhere to be seen. The seconds ticked by. Her pulse accelerated. She should have called Detective Yuhasz, told him what her plan was. Coming here without help was a mistake.

She was about to charge through the glass door she assumed would take her to the changing rooms when Miranda appeared. She was talking to a woman about a body treatment she'd had the last time she was here. Her last question had to do with whether or not they provided in-room treatments. When the woman said that they did, she thanked her and walked away.

"What was that about?"

"Let's keep walking."

Faith looked over her shoulder. The woman, a tall and striking blonde, was staring at them. They headed for the elevators. Once inside, Faith pushed the button for the top floor. The doors slowly closed. The interior of the elevator was made up of floor-to-ceiling mirrors. She didn't like the expression on Miranda's face.

"That was her," Miranda whispered.

"Who?"

"Cecelia. The woman who made sure I received a thorough body scrub before escorting me to the old man's suite."

Faith had no idea what had happened to Miranda inside this hotel, but she knew it had affected her deeply. For eighteen months the girl had been trapped inside the farmhouse, forced to have sex with a number of men, and yet the one night spent in this hotel was the night she couldn't get out of her mind.

When they got to their room, Faith locked the door, then turned and rested gentle hands on Miranda's shoulders. "What happened here, Miranda?"

Miranda shrugged her hands away. She went to the minifridge, took a look inside, then shut the door without getting anything to eat or drink. Next she went outside to the balcony overlooking the city.

Faith followed her.

The wind whipped her hair to one side. "The day I was brought to his suite," Miranda told her, "I thought about jumping off a balcony just like this. I wanted to end it all. Just be done with it."

A long pause ensued before she continued. "That shriveled old man got his rocks off by tying me to the bed and ramming assorted objects inside of me."

Faith stood behind her. She closed her eyes.

"Naked boys wearing nothing but strips of leather kept me from screaming out while two women in matching bra and panties licked his wrinkled body before he climbed on top of me and raped me. All night long it went on like this."

Faith shook her head. "I'm so sorry."

"Yeah," Miranda said. "Me, too." She sighed, her gaze on the swarm of people below.

"When I was in the lobby, you know, before I was taken to his room, there were so many people," Miranda said. "Just like today. I remember peering into all the different people's faces, praying someone, anyone, would look at me and see that something was wrong. I tried to gather the courage to ask for help, but I knew it wouldn't do me any good. People are afraid to get involved. People are afraid, period. And I can't blame them. I can only put blame on the recruiters and the pimps and the johns who collect girls and boys and use them and abuse them as if we mean nothing—as if we don't count. All for money. Anything for money."

Miranda turned to Faith then and said, "What's wrong with this world? Have people always been so cruel? Is it just me? Is it everyone?"

"I don't know," Faith said. "I really don't know."

"That woman in the salon," Miranda went on. "The one named Cecelia. She could have helped me the day I was brought here, but she didn't."

"She works for the hotel, doesn't she?"

Miranda nodded. "Do you think people like Diane Weaver or whoever she works for have some sort of deal with the hotel?"

"I wish I had answers for you, but I don't." It was the blind leading the blind, but what else could they do? Detective Yuhasz didn't have men to spare or time to drive to San Francisco on a wild-goose chase. "Come on," Faith said. "Why don't you show me which room you were held captive in?"

"What if no one answers?"

"Then we'll keep an eye on the woman in the salon instead, follow her home if we have to."

EIGHTEEN

"So, what's the plan?" Rage asked after Beast parked in front of Faith McMann's two-car garage on Rolling Greens Lane and turned off the engine.

"We need to find a way to make this guy talk."

While Faith and Miranda spent the day in San Francisco, she and Beast had done a little research. Faith had told them that the name of the guy tied up in her garage was Martin Hoyt, but he was known in the trafficking business as Fin. They also knew that Fin once worked for Mother, also known as Diane Weaver, and that someone had posted her bail and she'd ended up with a get-out-of-jail-free card.

They needed to find her.

And their man Fin might be just the guy to lead them to her.

Rage climbed out of the car and followed Beast to the side of the house. Beast opened the door leading into the garage and stepped inside. He whistled through his teeth and screwed up his face. "Christ almighty, it stinks in here!"

Rage found a switch and turned on the light. She waved her hands around to get the air flowing. From the looks of things, or should she say, smell of things, the man sitting in the far corner of the garage had taken a crap in his pants. He was looking at them through half-squinted eyes.

Rage groaned. "This is disgusting."

"Hey, buddy," Beast said as he walked over to the man. He didn't hesitate to lean forward and rip the tape from the guy's mouth.

Fin squealed.

Beast ignored him. "I heard from my friend Faith McMann that the cat got your tongue."

"Fuck you."

Beast looked over his shoulder at Rage. "I guess Faith was wrong. He can talk!"

A trail of urine had made its way across the cement, seeping into a crack near the rollup door.

"This is just too gross," Rage said. "I can't handle this." She knew she needed to get things moving along. She pulled her gun from her waistband, walked forward, and pushed the barrel against the side of Fin's head. "My name is Rage. I'm terminally ill, and there's only one reason you should care—I have absolutely nothing to lose after I kill you. So listen closely. If you give us the name of the man or woman you're working for, we'll let your little boy live."

He chuckled, and Rage could tell it was forced.

"I don't have any kids."

"Nice try. My friend here uploaded your license plate number and your real name into his database. Guess what we found?"

He said nothing.

"A faded picture of an adorable little boy. It took an extra hour or so of research, but we got a name. Franklin. Of course I would never hurt a little kid. And neither would my friend here. But if you don't tell us everything you know about Diane Fucking Weaver, including where she's hiding out, I'll have no choice but to make sure the press gets the entire scoop on you when you're arrested, including the name of the child living with his mother in Elk Grove. I'm sure they'll want to talk to her. And you and me both know, the media hounds won't be the only ones paying the mother of your child a visit, don't we?"

His head slumped forward.

"That boss of yours, the one you're so afraid of, will go after everyone you know." Rage knelt down so he had no choice but to look her in the eyes. "Start talking. We don't have all day."

———

Forty-five minutes later, Beast had his phone pressed to his ear as he watched the road like a hawk. Rage sat in the passenger seat next to him, chewing on her thumbnail. They were in his truck, parked on the side of a narrow street off Eureka Road. He thanked his friend and then disconnected the call. Getting two names out of Fin hadn't been easy. The tattoo man was scared. That much was clear.

"What did your friend have to say?" Rage asked. "Any luck?"

"Both names were bogus." He continued to stare straight ahead, pissed off that he'd let the tattoo man go. And yet he'd had a feeling the guy was lying, which was why he'd ended up going with plan B. He got Fin's car from the neighbor's garage, put it back where Fin had left it, and then knocked him out cold before cutting him loose. It was only a matter of time before Fin woke up and realized he'd been set free.

"There he goes," Rage said when Fin's car sped by as planned.

Beast made a right onto the main road. They followed him a few miles down Eureka until they merged onto the freeway heading down I-80 West toward Sacramento.

Rage sighed.

"What is it?" Beast asked. "Are you feeling all right?"

"Yeah, I'm good. I've just been thinking a lot about Little Vinnie lately."

"What about him?"

"Have you noticed how he's been repeating himself lately? Asking the same question two minutes after he asked it the first time?"

"No," Beast said. "Can't say that I have."

"Bullshit. You're just in denial like you are with everything."

He kept his eyes on the road, didn't say a word. Mostly because he figured she was probably right. He had noticed his dad slowing down lately. He'd also noticed Dad no longer bothered with crossword puzzles.

"Well, you better start paying attention," Rage went on lecturing. "Because when I'm gone, Little Vinnie is going to need someone to help him out."

"Don't say that."

"Oh, stop it," she said. "We're all going to die sometime."

He grunted. Lately, Rage always seemed to be trying to get him to talk about things he had no desire to talk about. But the least he could do, he figured, was try and offer a little conversation. "We fight to survive because what else can we do?" he asked. "There will always be good, evil, and those who fall somewhere in between."

"Well, in case you didn't know," Rage said, "you're one of the good ones."

He spared a quick glance her way. "You're not getting all mushy on me again, are you?"

"Not me. I don't have a mushy bone in my body."

He chuckled.

Rage was staring straight ahead when, a few seconds later, she asked, "Why do you think guys like Fin do what they do?"

Beast was glad to change the subject. "Who knows what might trigger the evil living inside someone. Look at Hitler, for instance. He was rejected by the Vienna Academy of Fine Arts. What would have happened if he'd become an artist?"

"I wonder," she said quietly before pointing ahead. "Looks like Fin is taking the next exit."

They got off on Truxel and continued to follow the silver Subaru for a few miles until the car slowed and pulled into the drive of an apartment building.

Beast continued a few yards before making a U-turn. He parked across the street from the building, where he could still see the silver car.

He shut off the engine.

"There he is," Rage said. "Second floor, last apartment on the corner."

Beast could see Fin from where he sat. He was looking around nervously, seemingly scouting the place out as he dug around inside his pocket for his key.

Rage reached for the door handle.

"Where are you going?"

"I want to take a quick look around, see if there's anyone hanging out at the front office who might be able to tell me more about our boy Fin."

He sighed.

"I'll be right back. I promise."

As he watched her go, he felt sad for failing her. She'd tried on many occasions to open up to him about life, her sickness, and her feelings. He didn't do feelings. His wife used to beg him to open up, but nobody really understood. Every time he said more than a few words, he only made things worse. He never knew the right thing to say. It was much easier to keep quiet and observe.

He released a ponderous sigh as he watched her jog across the two-lane road. The moment her foot landed on the sidewalk, a deafening boom sounded, leaving his ears humming as he ducked for cover.

Debris dropped from the sky, scraps of wood and paper coming down like rain. A metal pipe bounced off his windshield, leaving a crack in the middle of the glass.

Car alarms sounded.

Rage, he thought. Where was Rage?

He jumped out of the car, ran through the billowing smoke. Tires squealed as nearby traffic came to a top. A van nearly struck him as he darted across the road.

There she was, lying in a heap on the sidewalk. His heart skipped a beat.

She was on her side; blood dripped from her chin. He put his hand on her shoulder. "Rage!"

He was about to scoop her into his arms when her eyes fluttered open. "What happened?" she asked, her voice hoarse.

He caught his breath, tried to calm himself, didn't want her to know how much she'd scared him. "There was an explosion," he told her. "How badly are you hurt?" He helped her sit up, then checked her for injuries.

She nudged his hand away. "I'm fine."

Sirens sounded in the distance.

Rage wiped her chin, saw the smeared blood on her hand, and said, "It's only a scratch."

"Come on," he said, "you're going to need a couple of stitches at least. Let's get out of here." He helped her to her feet. "Can you walk?"

"Beast," she said, stopping him from worrying too much.

"I know, I know," he said. "We're all going to die sometime. I'd prefer it not be today, OK? Anything wrong with that?"

She rolled her eyes at him and then bent over and brushed dirt from her pants. Then she crossed the street, heading back for the truck.

Beast looked around.

People were running in and out of their apartments, checking on their friends and families. The apartment Fin had been about to enter was gone, along with half of the apartment next to his. Blown to smithereens. There was no way Fin had made it out alive.

What the hell was going on? Fin was a tattoo artist, a small fish in a very big pond. Did his own guys have him killed? If so, why?

Shit. Instead of getting answers, now all they had were more questions.

He looked over at his truck, where he saw Rage sitting in the passenger seat, waiting. Seeing her bleeding and unresponsive on the ground had unsettled him. How would he ever go on without her? She meant the world to him. He'd done exactly what he'd told himself he would never do again. He'd grown too attached to another human being, and now he would suffer the consequences.

Nineteen

After leaving her brother's place, Diane Weaver had found a run-down motel right off the freeway. It was a rat hole, but it would have to do. She'd just returned from the corner market where she'd bought enough food to last her a few days. On her way back to her room, two different people had tried to sell her drugs. Whatever. She wouldn't be staying here for much longer. Another night or two should be enough for her bruises to heal. She just needed a little time to figure out what her next step would be.

The clothes and other items she'd taken from her brother's place were in a pile on the floor next to the bed. A loud knock made her jump. *Shit.* She put a hand on her chest until she caught her breath. Someone was banging on the door down the hall. Her gaze darted around the room. She grabbed the cushioned chair from the corner, then dragged it across the carpet and positioned it in front of the door for extra protection.

After the racket finally stopped, she made her way to the bathroom and turned on the shower water. Ever since leaving prison, she'd felt dirty. Staying in this run-down, piece-of-shit hotel room wasn't helping matters. And being unable to get the image of her dead brother out of her brain was making her crazy.

She stripped off her clothes. Every shade of purple and blue blended together, making a colorful trail up the right side of her body. As she waited for the water to warm up, she leaned closer to the bathroom mirror. Her face was still swollen, hardly recognizable. At least she could finally see out of both eyes.

She stepped into the tub and let the water spray her face. She used the tiny bottle of shampoo to wash her hair. The water wasn't as hot as she liked, but that didn't stop her from reveling in the feel of warm water against her aching body as her thoughts returned to her brother.

He didn't deserve to die like that.

The only man mean and cruel enough to kill him was Aster Williams. She'd never told him or anyone else about her family—nobody at all. But she knew Aster well enough to know he would go to great lengths to punish those he felt had betrayed him. If Aster had found her brother and killed him, then he would kill her, too. Exactly why she needed to forget all about finding the girl and just get out of town.

The sooner the better.

But she wouldn't get far without money. As she rubbed the soap between her thighs, she thought about turning a few quick tricks. But a beat-up face and body wouldn't get her much, certainly not enough for a plane ticket out of hell.

The only person she knew with enough money to help her, other than Aster, was his sidekick, Patrick.

She'd left a message on his phone.

Patrick would help her. He hated Aster. He'd never said as much, but he didn't have to. She'd seen the way Patrick looked at Aster whenever they were all in the same room together. She'd also seen the way Patrick looked at Aster's wife. He wanted what Aster had. And, best of all, Patrick owed her a favor.

Before setting off, Hudson had let Joey sleep as long as possible. After sharing what was left of the food, Hudson filled every container he could find with water he'd boiled on top of the wood-burning stove.

The first day after leaving the cabin had been slow going.

The second day, still following the stream, they made better time, although every once in a while Hudson worried they were headed deeper into the forest. They hadn't seen a trail of any sort or another cabin since leaving. He'd made sure they rationed the jerky, nuts, and fresh water, but they were running low on everything. It wouldn't last much longer. Two days? Maybe three?

They had both lost a lot of weight. Joey was still coughing. Every once in a while he would hack up some bloody phlegm, but he never complained or asked Hudson to slow down. He wanted off the mountain as badly as Hudson did. They didn't talk much. When they did it was usually about what they would order if they could have anything they wanted to eat. Joey wanted steak and potatoes. Hudson wanted a giant chocolate-dipped vanilla ice-cream cone.

It was early in the morning when they awoke to a horrible sound—a cross between the high-pitched scream of a baby and squealing tires on the highway.

Joey poked his head outside the tent. "What was that noise?"

"I don't know, but we better pack up and get out of here."

They worked faster than usual, breaking the tent down and rolling up the sleeping bag within minutes.

Hudson had given Joey the wool socks and the heavy winter coat he'd taken from Derek. He'd also told him to sleep in the tent to keep the cold wind off his ears and face during the night. Hudson wore the knit cap and buried himself deep inside the down sleeping bag.

Packed up and ready to go, they heard the noise again. Not as loud this time, but just as eerie sounding.

They started off.

When they heard the noise for the third time, Hudson knew they were close—too close to ignore. They crept through the brush, weaving between trees, careful not to make too much noise. Hudson could hear Joey breathing close behind.

And there it was again, not as loud this time. A low whimper sounded from behind a large moss-covered boulder.

Hudson drew in a breath and headed off in the direction the sound was coming from. Joey stayed on his heels.

Neither of them said a word when they saw who'd been making the racket.

It was Denver. He was on the ground, sitting up, his back against the trunk of a tree. Blood, fresh and crimson, dripped from his face and hands. He was missing part of a leg, and a chunk of flesh had been ripped from his arm. It was obvious a wild animal had gotten a hold of him.

"Water," he managed to say.

Hudson grabbed the bladder, held it to his mouth until Denver had had his fill. He was a bloody mess, and he was shivering.

"I'm so cold."

Unable to stand seeing him suffer, Hudson dropped what he was carrying and pulled off his coat and then unzipped his sweatshirt. He then carefully slid one of Denver's arms into a sleeve and then the other. It wasn't easy maneuvering his battered limbs, but what else could he do? Hudson then pulled up the hood to cover Denver's ears and the wound on his face and neck, and he zipped the sweatshirt as high as he could. It was a tight fit, but at least Denver would be warmer than before.

"Where's Aiden?" Joey asked.

Denver could say only a few words at a time. Between gurgles, Hudson heard the words *dragged off* and *mountain lion*.

Hudson thought about sharing their food, but what good would it do? He wasn't sure Denver would even be able to chew in his condition. "What should we do?" Hudson asked as he turned to face Joey.

Joey pulled the gun from the backpack he was carrying, then walked up close to Denver and put the barrel up against the side of Denver's head. His hands were shaking, his expression one of horror.

Before Hudson could protest, Joey fired a shot.

TWENTY

It was close to noon when Colton and his dad were finally able to check in at the sheriff's office in Mendocino County. They had gotten little sleep, and Colton figured it was going to be a long day. They spent the first forty-five minutes filling out paperwork, including a waiver they both had to sign letting the world know they were heading up the mountain at their own risk.

They were also given some cold, hard facts. Mendocino National Forest covered 913,306 acres and had no paved road leading to it. There were wild animals roaming about, not to mention dangerous and wanted men. They were then given maps pinpointing the exact location of where the marijuana operation had taken place. Armed guards were watching the area. Plainly marked on the maps were cabins used by rangers and various working stations used by fire crews on an as-needed basis.

After being warned of various other dangers, they were escorted a few miles into the forest, pointed in the right direction, and then left to their own devices.

"Want me to take the lead?" Colton asked.

Dad grunted and started up the hill, leaving Colton to follow behind.

Although their fatigues and equipment were heavy and threatened to slow them down, adrenaline pushed them in record time to the area where the boys had been held captive.

Heavily armed security as well as tall redwoods and thick brush surrounded the area. Crime tape circled most of the outbuildings. Upon learning Colton and his dad were relatives of one of the missing boys, the officers allowed them inside the cabin where the five missing boys had lived. One boy, they learned, had been shot within minutes of escaping the cabin. His body had been removed the day of the raid and the boy had been identified as Sean Porter, a twelve-year-old from Los Angeles who had been reported missing at the age of seven.

According to the officer in charge, temperatures were swiftly dropping and more heavy rainfall was expected in the next forty-eight hours.

The inside of the boys' cabin was devoid of light and furniture. *A bleak existence for anyone, young or old,* Colton thought. It was tough to imagine Hudson trapped inside this room for so many nights.

Their heavy boots were the only sound as they walked around the room, examining every inch of the place. The window had been boarded up from the outside. In the corner of the room was a gaping hole. Dad bent down on one knee to get a closer look at the hole. "This is where they escaped."

The anguish in the old man's voice rang clear. Colton rested a hand on Dad's shoulder and squeezed. "I wouldn't be surprised if digging their way out of this place was Hudson's idea. We're going to find him, Dad."

Dad straightened as he walked across the room, back the way he'd come, showing no signs of slowing down after their long hike up the mountain. "We better get moving."

Colton nodded and followed him out the door. While Dad talked with the commanding officer, Colton took a look around the wooded area surrounding the cabin. The temperatures had already dropped by at least five degrees in the past hour. It would be dark soon. They wouldn't get far before they would be forced to set up camp.

Colton continued on, looking for any sign that Hudson had been there, the leaves and twigs brittle beneath his boots. He recalled all the nights he'd spent with Dad, Craig, and his nephew camping in the Sierra mountains. Hudson had been in his element, always ready for a challenge.

After Dad broke away from the officer, Colton waited for him to approach.

Dad pointed east. "This way."

Colton followed. No questions asked.

Dad gestured toward a tall redwood up ahead. When they arrived at the trunk of the tree, he knelt and brushed a gloved hand over the soil. "According to the officer, this is where one of the boys was shot. Assuming the other boys were close by, we'll use this as a starting point. As we move on, we need to think as we believe Hudson would think."

"He would have been scared."

"Yes, but if the boys had been planning their escape, they might have at least had a plan, which could mean Hudson already knew where he would go if and when he escaped."

"But if they were being shot at," Colton said, "that might have overridden everything else, including logic and planning." He pointed to his right, where trees and brush were less visible. "I say we move that way."

"Hudson is a runner," Dad said. "He's fast, but more than that he's smart. He would have run straight uphill."

Colton shook his head. "Why would he do that when he could get twice as far going downhill?"

"Didn't you ever chase the little bugger?"

"No, I can't say that I did."

"Well, I have on many occasions. And every single time the rascal did the same thing. He ran straight uphill because he knew old

Grandpa would never be able to catch up to him. I'm telling you, the kid is smarter than the average bear." Dad waved his hand toward the top of the hill, debate over, and trudged upward and onward, his legs sturdy and his gait strong, looking as if he'd traveled back in time and was once again a sergeant in the army.

As the sun began to dip out of sight, they spotted a lean-to at the base of a fallen tree. Whoever had built the shelter had made cord using fibrous bark from the dead tree. The lean-to was made up of tree branches along with a thick layer of leaves to minimize wind draft. One side had since fallen, but overall the shelter was well built.

"Two indents," Dad said, pointing to the ground. "Two people. Both small."

Colton examined the soil and layers of leaves. Sure enough, there were two indents in the dirt not yet fully concealed by the elements. Colton's chest tightened at the thought they could be close. He shut his eyes and drew in a breath.

"Let's set up our tents and then eat and get some sleep," Dad said. "We'll set off before the break of dawn."

━━━━

Parked in front of a pool hall on Fruitridge Road, Dillon Yuhasz watched the front entrance with hawkish eyes. Dressed in civilian clothes, he was off the clock. As he waited for David Hofberg to exit the place, he scolded himself for ever allowing the douche bag to get within ten feet of his daughter. He'd known from the start that something wasn't right with Hofberg, but he'd pushed his instincts aside. His daughter had met Hofberg back when Yuhasz was still happily married. His wife surprised him on his birthday by inviting the guys he worked with, including rookie Hofberg, to a Sunday barbecue. To his chagrin, his daughter Holly and Hofberg had hit it off immediately. They'd dated for only a few months before they announced their engagement.

Everything after that happened in a blur. As soon as they were married, Yuhasz's wife insisted he help his new son-in-law get a job working investigation. She bugged him about it every day until he gave in and got Hofberg a job in Narcotics.

He pulled the metal handle under his seat and pushed the chair back to give himself more room. The weather wasn't helping matters tonight. Rain and wind made it difficult to see through his windshield. For an hour now, calls had been coming over the radio. Uprooted trees and an old lady's trellis had been knocked over. Some neighborhoods were hit harder than others. The weather was turning more and more sour by the minute. Downed trees and roads littered with branches and leaves. He didn't care. Not tonight. One of the rookies could take care of that shit. He was too busy watching Hofberg.

Well, not exactly watching him, but waiting for him.

Yuhasz had talked to his brother that morning. Holly and the kids were having a good time. As far as he knew, Holly had listened to their advice and shut off her cell phone.

After sending Holly and the kids to stay with his brother, Yuhasz had kept a close eye on Hofberg and watched him escort a tall, voluptuous brunette into the Hilton on Twenty-Fourth Street. Last night it had been a Cameron Diaz look-alike, but younger.

Although his daughter had pleaded with him not to touch her husband, there was no way he would or could stand by and do nothing after seeing Holly covered in bruises. No way. It stopped tonight.

He'd sit here until morning if he had to, but just as the thought entered his mind, the door to the bar he was watching opened, and he realized he might be climbing into bed sooner than he thought. His son-in-law stumbled outside with a perky little redhead close to his side, helping him along.

Yuhasz turned on his windshield wipers so he could get a clearer view. He looked across the parking lot to the blue Honda and motioned at the two dark figures inside.

Phil was the first to exit the vehicle. In his right hand he carried a twelve-inch stick.

The other guy, the one climbing out of the passenger seat, was his old pal Ed.

Ed didn't carry a stick. He preferred to use his knuckles. Brass knuckles. Yuhasz and Ed went way back. Ed had grown up with an abusive father. After too many beers one night, Ed had told him about the time his dad came home only to learn that his wife, Ed's mom, had gone for coffee with friends. The problem was she wasn't allowed out of the house. Ever. So his dad went to the garage, found the choker collar once used on their dog, the kind with the sharp prongs, and slipped it around his wife's neck. She was forced to wear it for two months.

His mother was eighty-five years old now and still had deep scars around her neck. Less than a year after the dog collar incident, his dad died of unknown causes. Rumors that he'd been poisoned circulated for a while, but Ed's mom had his body cremated, as were his wishes.

Needless to say, Ed wasn't a fan of domestic violence.

Yuhasz kept his eye on his son-in-law as Phil walked up from behind him and looped his elbow around his left arm, leaving Ed to usher the redhead the other way, giving her the story they had rehearsed about David Hofberg being a wanted man and therefore she better hurry up and skedaddle before the police came. Without sparing Hofberg another glance, she jumped into her beat-up Corolla and sped off.

Ed looked Yuhasz's way and gave him a quick salute.

Just before his friends dragged Hofberg into the dark alley, he saw Hofberg look frantically about until his gaze fell on him. Although it was too dark and rainy for Hofberg to see him clearly, he most likely recognized his car.

Knowing the asshole couldn't see him, but not caring either way, Yuhasz smiled at the bastard right before Phil clunked him over the head with his big stick and dragged him off to teach him a lesson he wouldn't soon forget.

TWENTY-ONE

A long row of patrol cars and emergency vehicles forced FBI Agent Elaine Burnett to park across the street from the trailer park. As far as she was concerned, a lot of people had the wrong idea about trailer parks. Her grandmother lived in a nice mobile home in Sacramento. She had plenty of space and a large kitchen. The plots were small, but she and her neighbors had enough outdoor space to grow a rosebush or two.

But this particular trailer park in Lodi was not anything like her grandmother's. It was run-down, and it smelled like a dump. Broken windows were covered with plywood and patched with duct tape. Every other trailer had sheets for curtains. The entire park was littered with garbage, heaps of God knew what.

Elaine had gotten the call an hour ago telling her they'd located Eric Weaver and his wife, Trista.

Her first thought was, *Bingo!*

Eric Weaver had done a decent job covering his trail. His wife was another story, though. They were able to find Trista's sister, Danielle Ferguson, which in turn led them to their mother, Alexia. Things picked up as soon as they subpoenaed records showing assets including bank accounts and property.

The first agent to arrive at the trailer home called Elaine directly to tell her both Eric and his wife were dead. Homicide. This led to Elaine's second thought, which was one continuous string of muttered curse words.

As she approached the trailer home at the end of the park, the first thing she noticed was the blood on the pathway leading to the front door. The CSI unit had already arrived, and everyone was busy collecting evidence. It was getting dark, and industrial lights were being set up around the vicinity.

Agent Jensen greeted her at the entrance. He pointed at a bloody footprint. "Looks like one smaller bloody footprint on top of a larger one."

She knelt down for a closer look. "Someone was here after the murder took place."

He nodded.

Once they stepped inside, they both slipped into coveralls and slid cloth booties over their shoes. A young man was scraping dried blood from the wall without smearing the print. When he saw her, he told her Johnston was waiting for her in the bedroom to the right.

She left Jensen and followed the covered path across the carpeted floor.

Sam Johnston, a serious crime scene technician and full-blown workaholic, stopped working long enough to gesture toward the bed. "Thought you might be interested in a particular item I saw under the bed."

Elaine had known Sam for a while now. With years of field experience, Sam was considered to be one of the best crime scene technicians there was.

Elaine slid on her latex gloves and got down on all fours. Beneath the bed, out of reach, she saw a shoe—an ankle boot—pink and child-size. It was a tight squeeze, but she inched her way beneath the bed until she touched the boot with the tip of her finger. Another inch allowed her to grab it with two fingers.

On her feet again, she held up the ankle boot with fringe on one side, examined it carefully, and then slid it into an evidence bag. "I was told on my way over here that there was no sign of the girl."

"That's correct."

"She was obviously here at one time." There was a pause before Elaine raised an eyebrow at Sam and said, "Why would they go to so much trouble to move the girl around? First the farmhouse and now this."

Sam shrugged. "I collect the evidence. It's up to you to figure out the rest."

"It looks to me as if this case has somehow become personal," Elaine said, thinking aloud. "Or maybe it was always personal. Maybe the money Craig McMann's partner stole was just a front to throw everyone off track."

"You do realize," Sam said, "I have no idea what you're talking about."

Elaine nodded, although she wasn't listening to a word Sam said. The idea that maybe she and Jensen had been looking at this case all wrong caused her insides to thrum, something that happened whenever a case she was working on took a possible turn in a different direction. She made a mental note to talk to Jensen and then pay Faith McMann a visit.

"The good news," Sam said, breaking into her thoughts, "there's no evidence here that would lead us to believe Lara McMann was harmed, which means there's a chance she's still alive."

"True," Elaine said. They might not have found Lara McMann, but the pink ankle boot, described in detail by Faith McMann as the shoes her daughter was wearing when she was taken, was their first clue that the ten-year-old had indeed spent time inside the trailer home.

Through open blinds, she squinted at all the bright fluorescent lights surrounding the area. Now if only the weather would cooperate. The wind and rain were never helpful in homicide investigations, but her team members were doing the best they could under the circumstances.

She left Sam to go in search of Jensen. In the living area, a vacuum sweeper was being used on the couch. Soncie Lyles, a rookie, was searching for footprints and palm prints. Residue lifters were used to collect fibers, hairs, and stains. All this action made for a tight squeeze. Prior to her arrival, she'd instructed two of her team members to talk to neighbors.

Based on footprints she and Jensen had seen within congealed blood outside the door, someone had entered the crime scene prior to their arrival and then left without reporting to authorities that a double murder had taken place. Who had been here, and why hadn't he or she called the police?

It irked her that it had taken her team this long to locate the trailer. Diane Weaver's brother had been living only an hour from Sacramento, and yet it had taken them days to track him down. She wasn't happy about this turn of events. If they had located the trailer twenty-four hours earlier, they might have been able to prevent two deaths and perhaps found the McMann girl before she was swept off to another location.

She spotted Agent Jensen standing inside the other bedroom, where Eric Weaver and his wife, Trista, had been killed. Eric had been found propped in a chair in the corner of the room, his throat slit wide-open. Eric's wife was on the bed, raped and tortured from the looks of it. When they turned her over, they found bite marks on her backside. Bite marks, like fingerprints, were unique. If all went well, a forensic dentist would be able to make a cast to help them determine who the assailant might be.

Agent Jensen gestured for her to come forward. The ME's had finished collecting evidence and were packing up. The guy in the jumpsuit gave her the go-ahead to walk across the room using the pathway made out of plastic stepping plates.

"Did you see this?" Jensen asked. He used a wooden tongue depressor to lift a clump of Eric Weaver's hair.

Elaine leaned closer to get a better look. "What the hell?"

Jensen nodded. "Yep. Cut his ear clean off."

"Why would anyone go to all the trouble to cut off his ear?"

He shrugged. "Back in the day, it was called cropping."

She looked at Jensen as if he'd lost his mind.

"Just telling you what I know. Cutting off a person's ear used to be a form of punishment."

"It makes no sense," she said. "If this guy"—she motioned around the room with a wave of a hand—"came here for the girl, why would he take the time to torture these people and cut off an ear?"

"Maybe he didn't come here for the girl. Maybe he had a bone to pick with these people and the girl was an extra."

Her gaze made a clean sweep around the room. "Where is it?"

"The ear?"

"Yes, the ear," she said with less patience than before.

"No idea. Must have taken it with him."

She let out a frustrated breath. "We can't let this little tidbit get out of this room. If the guy who made this mess has the McMann kid, I don't want the media speculating as to what the maniac might be doing with the girl."

Jensen acknowledged what she was saying with a nod.

Someone called out to Elaine, letting her know that the next-door neighbor was available to talk.

She went back to the entryway, peeled off her coveralls and cloth booties, and stepped outside. The wind felt ice cold against her face as she walked to the trailer next door. Barry, a homicide detective she'd met many times before said, "Good luck," before he opened the door for her.

The woman's name was Ginger Thompson. She stood less than five feet tall, slightly hunched, with lots of thick silver hair that swept past her shoulders. "I had to call three times," she complained as Elaine followed her into the main room, which consisted of a couch, two end tables, and a large television on a tiny wooden stand. "Nobody would take me seriously."

Elaine had already been told on her way to the trailer park that Ginger had a tendency to call the police a couple of times a week. For that reason, authorities gave her a nonemergency number to call. She was likened to the boy who cried wolf, and therefore nobody had taken her seriously. "I'm sorry," Elaine said, loud enough to be heard over the television. "I'll look into the matter."

The woman scowled and took a seat on the couch.

"Mind if I turn the volume down while we talk?"

Ginger lifted her remote and lowered the volume.

Elaine then asked for permission to take a seat next to her.

"Sure."

Elaine had to stop herself from reaching into her bag and pulling out a face mask or some Vicks VapoRub at the very least. The woman's trailer didn't smell much better than the one next door with two decaying corpses inside. Instead she looked at her notes. "Can you tell me who lives next door?"

"Of course I can." Ginger used a fingernail to pick some food from her front tooth. "I might be old, but I'm not stupid. Eric Weaver and his wife, Trista, have lived next door for as long as I can remember."

"Did they have children?"

"No. Trista didn't want kids. They made her nervous."

"So, you never saw them with children?"

"Who said that? Trista might have been a twitchy, nervous little thing, but she was a good Christian woman, which is why she and Eric recently took in a little girl named Jean after the girl's mother was thrown in jail." She waved a hand through the air. "Drugs or something like that."

Stunned, Elaine leaned closer to Ginger and looked her squarely in the eyes. "Are you sure about that?"

"Why wouldn't I be?" Ginger looked at the television, and her mouth dropped open. "Hold on a minute. Oh, my God, I think that actress, Alaina Bowers, is going to call off her wedding." She turned up the volume and listened. "Holy smokes. I was right!" When a commercial came on, she turned down the volume again. "Now, what is it you want to know?"

"I'm surprised by what you told me about seeing a little girl next door because you told the investigator who was here earlier that your neighbors didn't have any children."

"That's because they don't." She pulled a face. "You people don't know how to ask the right questions. Do you want to know what she looked like? Because I can tell you."

"You met the little girl?"

"More than a few times," she said with growing frustration. "Every chance they got, those two tossed the kid into my trailer so they could run off to do errands. Not once did they offer to get me groceries or take me with them. In fact, they said they were going to pay me. They owe me a lot of money, especially since the girl wasn't easy to watch. A bit strange, I must say."

"How so?"

"She kept telling me she needed to find a telephone to call her parents. I tried explaining to her that her mom knew where she was but couldn't get to her right now, but she didn't seem convinced. The last time I babysat, I caught the kid trying to sneak out through that window over there."

Elaine reached into her bag, pulled out a picture of Lara McMann, and held it in front of Ginger. "Was this the little girl you watched over?"

Her eyes widened. "That's her, all right. Why do you have a picture of the kid?"

"Did she look OK to you?" Agent Burnett asked, ignoring her question. "I mean, did you notice any bruises, anything like that?"

"No bruises that I can remember. She was a scrawny thing—I can tell you that. And she sure likes to eat. I figured she might be trouble, though."

"Why do you say that?"

"I don't know. She couldn't seem to sit still, and she was sort of suspicious-looking. I thought she might try to steal my things if I didn't keep an eye on her. Is she wanted by the police?"

"I take it you don't watch the news."

"No. Never. It's too damn depressing. I like all the housewife shows, and sometimes I like to watch that popular dance show with all the celebrities."

"*Dancing with the Stars*?"

"That's the one. You watch it, too?"

"When I have time," she lied, hoping to get on the woman's good side. "When was the last time you saw Eric or Trista?"

She shrugged. "I don't remember."

"This is important, Ginger, so I need your full attention. Try to think. When the little girl tried to sneak out your window, could that have been the last time you saw her?"

"Yeah, yeah. That was the last time I saw any of them."

"Any of them, meaning the little girl, Eric, and Trista?"

"Yes."

"And that was when?"

"Oh, hell, I don't know, two days ago, maybe three. All the days seem to run together. Bet you can't guess how old I am?"

Elaine sighed and tossed out a lowball guess. "Seventy-nine?"

Ginger got a chuckle out of that. "I'm ninety years old. Hard to believe, I know."

Agent Burnett forced a smile. "If I think of any more questions, would you mind if I stopped by again?"

"Sure, yeah." Ginger picked up the remote and turned up the volume. "You can stay and watch TV with me if you want," she said loud enough to be heard. "I taped a few episodes of *Hoarders*. It's about crazy people who keep all sorts of junk, even trash, until their house is so full they can hardly get through the door."

"I better go, but thank you for your time."

Ginger didn't spare her another glance.

Twenty-Two

Faith came out of the bathroom at the same moment the door to the hotel room opened.

It was Miranda, and she didn't look happy.

"The ugly old man is nowhere to be seen," she said. "I watched that damn suite for over three hours before a lovely young couple glowing with happiness appeared."

"What did you do?"

"Don't worry. I just turned around and came back here."

Faith breathed a sigh of relief.

"How about you? Any luck with Cecelia?"

"Not so far. I followed her to lunch. Watched her nibble on a salad as she texted nonstop, then followed her back to the hotel. Most of my afternoon was spent reading the newspaper in the lobby." Faith grabbed her coat and bag. "It's getting late. I think it's time to head home. We can come back another time."

Miranda shook her head. "I can't leave without at least confronting Cecelia. She knew exactly what was going on when she brought me from the salon and then took me to the ugly man's room."

Faith exhaled. "OK, but don't do anything you'll regret."

"I have a few questions, that's all."

They both put on their coats.

Faith waited at the door until Miranda was ready to go. Neither of them said a word as they walked down the hall. Faith noticed a man in a suit standing off to the side near the end of the hallway. When she attempted to make eye contact, he looked the other way and walked off. Her stomach quivered. Were they being watched?

As they stepped into the elevator, Faith noticed the pained expression on Miranda's face. Her frustration was palpable during their short ride to the lobby. The elevator doors slid open, and they stepped out.

"That's her!" Miranda said. "Cecelia's leaving."

Sure enough Cecelia was exiting the salon wearing a raincoat and gloves. They stayed far enough back to keep an eye on her without being seen. Despite the cold and drizzling rain outside, the sidewalks were crowded. For a few seconds they lost sight of Cecelia. And then Miranda pointed up ahead where she saw her crossing the road.

"I don't like this," Faith said. "Something's going on."

"You don't have to come. I can follow her and call your cell when she reaches her destination. Maybe she lives around here."

That was doubtful. Living in the city wasn't cheap, but Faith kept her thoughts to herself.

The light drizzle quickly turned to raindrops. The cold nipped at Faith's nose as she quickened her pace, trying not to slip on the wet road.

Miranda was younger and faster. She hurried past Faith, refusing to let Cecelia out of her sight.

Faith inwardly scolded herself for wearing heels instead of boots. Her toes were beginning to cramp, and a blister had already formed on her left foot.

Where was Cecelia going?

The hairs on the back of her neck stood on end. First the man in the hallway and now this. It dawned on Faith then that it all seemed a bit too convenient that Cecelia happened to be leaving just as she and Miranda stepped out of the elevator. Had the man in the suit told her they were headed for the elevators?

Twice now Faith had seen Cecelia glance over her shoulder. Was she afraid she was being followed? Or was she making sure they were following her?

Miranda was getting too far ahead, nothing more than a shadow up ahead.

Faith stopped and hurriedly took off her heels. The wet cement felt good against her sore feet as she ran to catch up. Farther away from the hustle and bustle of city life surrounding the hotel, the buildings were now mostly apartments and warehouses. Faith reached the street corner just as Miranda turned right. She wanted to shout for Miranda to wait up, but she didn't want Cecelia to hear her.

Up ahead Miranda made another turn. Faith's heart pounded as she tried to keep up, her chest heaving as she gasped for breath. And then she saw her. Miranda was standing at the next street corner, gesturing for Faith to hurry. Across the street was what looked like an apartment building set between large Victorian homes.

Faith caught up to her. "Where is she? Where did she go?"

Water dripped from Miranda's chin as she pointed. "Cecelia made a left down that alleyway over there. I think she's on to us."

"I was thinking the same thing."

A light on the third floor came on. "That could be her," Miranda said. "We've come this far. Let's check it out, see if we can get the name of the apartment building."

"OK," Faith agreed. "And then we head back to the hotel, get my car, and get out of here. We can come back later in the week."

They slowed their pace, took in their surroundings, memorizing names of streets and buildings for when they returned. By the time they turned in to the alleyway where Miranda had seen Cecelia go, Faith's clothes were soaked through. They passed by a trash bin filled to the brim. The smell was rancid. It took all she had not to gag.

Voices stopped them both.

"Where are they?" a man asked.

"Shh. They'll be here any second," a woman said.

A gasp and then the woman's voice asked, "What are you doing?"

A muffled shot rang out.

Faith grabbed Miranda's arm before she could take another step, but it was too late.

"There they are!" someone shouted.

Miranda whipped about and ran back the way they came. She was out of sight by the time Faith darted out from the alleyway and onto the street. Another shot was fired, hitting the metal trash bin to Faith's left. She kept waiting to feel the sting of a bullet in her back. She took a sharp left into a darkened alcove—the entryway to a deli shut down for the night. With her back flat against the wall, she didn't dare make a sound.

The quick thump, thump, thump of running feet bounced off the wet pavement.

She held her breath.

A tall, dark shadow ran right by without a glance her way.

But judging by the voices she'd heard, there were two men, so she stayed where she was.

A throaty chuckle sounded as a dark figure appeared. This guy didn't seem to be in a hurry. She couldn't see his eyes, but she knew he was looking at her. "Come out, come out wherever you are."

She stepped out of hiding, took two steps his way, and then swung the high-heeled shoes still grasped in her hand. She swung hard and high. The three-inch heel caught him in the ear.

His high-pitched scream pierced through the night. She kneed him in the groin, then took another swing with her shoes, catching him in the back of the head, before dropping the shoes and running back the way she'd come.

If she stayed in the open, she'd be an easy target. She zigzagged across the street, then cut down the same alleyway where she and Miranda had first heard the voices. She ran past the trash bin, cut a sharp right, and nearly tripped over Cecelia's motionless body in her haste to get away.

Cecelia was on her back. A street lamp gave her enough light to see that the woman had been shot in the chest. Blood seeped through her blouse. "Help me," she said.

Faith stopped, pivoted on her feet. *Damn.*

"They'll be back," Cecelia said, her voice raspy. "My gun." Her hand was outstretched, her fingers clawing against the pavement, struggling to reach her bag.

Faith grabbed the leather purse, rifled through it, and found the gun. Holding the pistol in front of her, she turned toward the darkened alleyway just as the same man she'd hit with her shoe tore around the corner. He nearly tripped over his own feet when he saw Faith standing there with a gun aimed at him.

Her hands shook.

"Put the gun down, lady. We only want to talk to you."

"What do you want to talk about?"

He reached for the gun tucked in his waistband.

Faith fired. She'd been aiming for his heart, but the bullet struck him between the eyes. He crumpled to the ground.

With a heaviness in her stomach, she walked over to him and used her foot to knock his gun away. He didn't move. She stared at him for a long moment, unable to believe it had come to this.

She had killed a man. And for what?

Did he have a family? Young children waiting for him to come home?

Her hands shook; her knees wobbled. She thought of Lara and Hudson. And about Miranda and all the other girls being held against their will, used as sex slaves. The anger she'd been trying so hard to tamp down came swooshing through her like a tsunami. She walked back to Cecelia and put the barrel of the gun still grasped in her hand against the woman's skull. "Who do you work for?"

"Patrick," she said, her voice barely audible.

"Patrick who?"

No words came forth.

"You've got two seconds to tell me his full name before I blow your brains out."

Still nothing.

Faith felt for a pulse. She was dead. Faith's head fell forward. *Damn.*

Faith pushed herself to her feet at the same moment Miranda showed up.

Miranda looked at the dead man, then walked over and gave Cecelia a closer look. "Are they both dead?"

Relieved to see Miranda in one piece, Faith nodded. "Did you see the other man?"

"Yeah, I did."

"Where is he?"

"I Tasered him right in the face." She lifted the stun gun in the air. "This thing works great, but I'm not sure how much time we have before he's on his feet again."

Faith wiped her prints from Cecelia's gun, then knelt down low to the ground and wrapped Cecelia's fingers around the handle and rested her finger against the trigger.

Leaving the gun in the palm of Cecelia's hand, she searched through her bag and pulled out her wallet. "Her name's Cecelia Doyle. She lives in Daly City." Faith wiped her prints from the wallet and put it back in the bag.

"Why don't we take that with us?"

"No," Faith said. "We don't want to be connected to this mess. Come on. Let's get out of here."

Twenty-Three

Three knocks sounded. A pause. Another two knocks.

Diane Weaver slid off the bed, walked to the door, and peeked through the curtain. It was him. Patrick was here. *Thank God.*

He'd come just as he said he would. And he was alone. She undid the chain, unlocked the door, and let him inside. A cold wind rushed inside along with him. She shut the door behind him.

"Where have you been?" Patrick asked as he peeled off his jacket, wet from the rain. "We've been looking all over for you. Aster is in a panic. What's going on?"

"Does he have the girl?" she asked.

"What girl?"

"The fucking McMann kid," Diane ground out. "Who do you think?"

His jaw hardened. "I think you better take a good, long look at who exactly you're talking to."

She straightened her spine, tried to calm herself as she peered into his eyes. He'd changed since she'd seen him last. He seemed different somehow, more confident and cocky than before.

His eyes were narrowed, the muscles around his mouth tense. She didn't want to cower in front of Patrick, but she wasn't in a position to do anything else. "I'm sorry," she said, swallowing her pride. "It's been a stressful time—that's all."

"How so?" he asked without sympathy.

He knew damn well she'd been beat up and thrown in jail. That wasn't enough? "My brother and his wife were killed," she said with a whimper. "It wasn't pretty. They were both tortured."

Patrick didn't look impressed. In fact, he looked downright bored by her story. She wanted to shake him or slap him, anything to get a response. "It was Aster's doing," she added. "I'm sure of it."

Patrick shoved his hands deep into his pants pockets and jiggled his keys. "Aster posted your bail. So why would he bother to kill your brother?"

"He must have discovered I'd handed over the McMann girl to him. You told me to keep the girl safe, so I sent her to my brother's house. I don't know how he would have found her, though, since I never mentioned I had family in the area." She took a breath. "You're Aster's number one man these days—you must know what's going on."

"Sorry, sweetheart. I have no idea who killed your family members. Until this moment, I didn't realize you even had a brother."

"If Aster is responsible," she said, "we both know he'll come after me next."

The fact that Patrick had no response did nothing to ease her worry.

She studied his face, tried to figure out if she could trust him. When Patrick was in his early twenties, hardly a man, he'd worked for one of the big bosses in the area known as Old Man Stanton. At the time Stanton had a monopoly on most trafficking activities. Aster had watched him like a hawk, and the moment Stanton made the mistake of taking a run without his bodyguard, Aster Williams moved in quickly, taking out Stanton first and then his men, one at a time. If Diane hadn't stopped him, Aster would have killed Patrick, too.

"I saved your life," she reminded him.

"So you've said on numerous occasions."

"I need your help."

Diane had taken the time to spruce herself up today, hoping Patrick would pay her a visit since she'd left him more than a few urgent messages. She'd fixed her hair and used makeup she'd taken from her brother's house to cover the bruises. She wore her late sister-in-law's knit dress, which accentuated her curves. Although she was a little out of practice when it came to seducing a man, she made sure to sway her hips as she walked toward Patrick. With her breasts pressed against his hard chest, she purred as she stood on tiptoes and kissed his neck.

He put his hands on her shoulders and nudged her backward, away from him. "What the hell are you doing, Diane? You look like shit, and this place is a dump." He walked toward the bed and looked around, went so far as to open a few drawers as if he thought she might be hiding something.

"You owe me, Patrick. You said so yourself."

"Listen," he told her, his voice stern. "When you called me, you told me you had something I wanted." He used his foot to slam shut the bottom dresser drawer. "I don't see one goddamn thing in this shit hole that I could possibly want. You better start talking."

"OK, OK. Jesus. You used to want me. Every time you looked at me, your eyes would blaze with desire."

"Look in the mirror, honey. Age has fucked you up the ass sideways."

"I need money, Patrick. I need to get out of the country before Aster finds me."

"You're worrying too much. Aster is a busy man. If he was looking for you, I would know."

"Maybe he's not telling you everything these days. Maybe he thinks I was going to sell the girl and keep the money for myself."

"Was that your plan?"

"You're not listening to a word I'm saying! You told me to move the girl, and now my brother and his wife are dead. Maybe I should call Aster and tell him the truth—that I have no idea where that McMann kid is."

Patrick rubbed his chin. "Slow down. Give me some time to figure things out."

"Don't you get it? Aster posted bail because he doesn't want me to talk to the authorities. Letting me go was his way of assuring I wouldn't talk before I had my day in court. But killing me is the only sure way to guarantee I never tell anyone what I know."

"This is a sticky situation, Diane. Don't you dare call him. If he ever found out I helped you get away, it would be my ass buried ten feet under."

"Does that mean you're going to help me?" She moved toward him again. "A new name, a passport, and a ticket out of here. That's all I'm asking. You'll never see me again—I promise." Her fingers clung to the sleeve of his jacket.

As he pried her hand off him, she noticed a dark callousness to his eyes. She couldn't help but wonder if he knew more than he was telling her.

"I'll help you," he finally said.

Overwhelming relief flooded her senses. She wanted to wrap her arms around him and thank him, but she didn't dare touch him again after he'd made it clear he wanted nothing to do with her.

He gestured downward.

Confused, she didn't realize what he was up to until he slid his belt off and then unzipped his pants.

Humiliated and filled with hatred, she sank to her knees and stared at his nubby little cock. The palm of his hand came to rest behind her head before he pulled her to him.

TWENTY-FOUR

It was dark outside by the time Lilly Gray changed into her warm flannel pajamas, slipped on a robe and slippers, and then headed downstairs for some decaffeinated green tea.

After spending the entire day waiting for the doctors to discharge Jana's husband, and then picking up his medications and making sure Steve and Jana had everything they needed, she'd come home to an empty house. She knew Faith and Miranda had something planned, but she'd been too worried about Russell and Colton and too busy with Steve and Jana to pay close attention. She picked up the phone and called Faith for the third time in less than an hour.

No answer.

She didn't bother leaving a message.

She thought of her husband hours away in a vast forest searching for their grandson. The thought of him trudging up a mountaintop with a weak heart pushed heavily on her mind. It didn't help that the weatherman insisted heavy rains were coming, the worst of the storm headed directly toward Mendocino County.

In the kitchen, she tried to distract herself. She put the kettle on the stove, washed a few dishes, and wiped down the countertops. A noise caught her attention. Her heart skipped a beat. She stood still and listened closely.

Following the scraping noise outside, she reached slowly for the curtains above the sink. With a fistful of fabric grasped in her hand, she whipped the curtain aside.

Then let out a breath.

It was only a tree branch brushing against the side of the house.

The curtain fell back into place.

Breathing easier, she readied her cup and saucer and then double-checked the alarm her husband and Beast had set to go off if anyone came near the house. The light was red. *Good.* That meant the alarm was on.

She checked her phone for messages. There were none. She thought about calling Jana before deciding against it. Her daughter was pregnant and finally home with her husband. The last thing Jana needed right now was her mother calling her to fret over every little sound.

There it was again.

A door slamming shut? Or had another tree branch fallen?

The Fitzpatricks lived across the pond. It had to have come from that way. Although she couldn't remember ever hearing the neighbors coming and going before.

Stop it. Stop it. She was getting herself all worked up over nothing.

The teakettle whistled. Her nerves were shot. With a trembling hand, she took her time opening a tea bag and pouring hot water into her cup. She breathed in the aroma, even went to all the trouble to slice a wedge of lemon and fresh ginger.

Everything would be fine.

Russell and Colton would be fine. Faith and Miranda would be home soon.

She headed for the family room, surprised when the phone rang.

As she rushed back that way, teacup still in hand, hot water sloshed over the edges. She set her cup down and picked up the receiver on the third ring. "Hello?"

"My name is Robyn Price," a woman said, her voice quiet, cautious. "I'm trying to get a hold of Faith McMann. Do I have the right number?"

The name sounded familiar. Lilly repeated the woman's name in her mind. *Robyn Price. Robyn Price.* Where had she heard that name before?

"Are you there?"

"I'm sorry. Yes, I'm still here. Faith isn't home at the moment, but I'm expecting her anytime."

There was a long pause before the woman said, "I've been trying to track her down for a while now. It's urgent. It's about her children."

"Do you know where they are?" Lilly asked hopefully.

"No. No, of course not—nothing like that. I shouldn't have said anything. In fact, I never should have called."

"No. Please. If you have any information you think might help Faith find the kids, you must—"

Click. The line went dead.

Lilly set the receiver down. *Robyn Price.* What did the woman know about the children? Why would she call and then hang up? It made no sense.

With the wind picking up and causing a racket outside, her nerves were now shattered to hell. Her hand still trembling, she reached for her tea. She brought the fine china to her lips and savored the first sip, hoping it would calm her. Before she could take another taste, the alarm went off.

Someone was here.

She put her cup down with a clank and headed for the front entry. Before she took more than a couple of steps, the sliding glass door leading into the dining area exploded around her, glass shattering, small pieces spraying across the carpet as a man dressed all in black rolled across the floor.

Her adrenaline spiked as she held back a scream.

Another man entered behind him. His face was covered with a dark knit cap. It was pulled down past his chin with two holes where his eyes peered at her. Her gaze fell on the gun he carried.

Her feet felt as if they were glued to the floor. It took her a moment to get moving. She ran, lost both slippers on her way up the stairs. She made it to her bedroom, slammed the door shut, and locked it. She tried to push the dresser in front of the door. It was too heavy, wouldn't budge.

In a panic, she looked around, tried to think.

It would not serve her well to hide under the bed. Instead, she grabbed the Taser from the top drawer next to the bed and then ran to the bathroom. No sooner had she locked herself in than she heard shouting followed by a resounding crash as someone came through the bedroom door.

TWENTY-FIVE

Rage followed Beast into the house. Little Vinnie was stirring something in a giant pot on the stove. He looked right at her, then dropped the ladle and rushed toward them. "What happened?"

Rage and Beast had spent the second half of their day at the hospital. The cut on her chin was deeper than she'd realized and had ended up needing stitches.

Beast rubbed both hands over his head and then disappeared in the other room, leaving Rage to deal with his dad. "Something smells awful good," she said.

"Don't you dare try to skirt around this. Every time you come through that door lately, you've got a new injury. What happened?"

"I'm starved. Is that what I think it is? Homemade clam chowder?"

"Have a seat and start talking while I get you some."

She followed him into the kitchen and took a seat at the small kitchen table. "Remember Fin, the tattoo artist?" she asked. "The guy being held in Faith's garage in her Granite Bay home?"

Little Vinnie grabbed a bowl. "You were going to see if you could get him to talk. Did he get loose? Is he the one who did that to you?"

"He was definitely afraid of someone, which is why he wouldn't talk. He finally gave us two phony names, so Beast let him go and we followed him home, to an apartment building off Truxel."

Little Vinnie paled. "I saw the whole thing on the news. A bomb went off on Truxel. You were there?"

"Yeah. A little too close for comfort. Four stitches and my ears are still ringing, but I'm OK."

Beast returned from the other room with his computer. He took a seat across from her and started clicking away at the keyboard.

Rage knew him well enough to know that something else was going on inside that big head of his. Although he was a man of few words, he expressed himself in other ways. For instance, she knew something was up whenever he walked around with a permanent scowl on his face. The truth was, ever since she'd been unable to finish their morning run, he'd been acting strange. Thinking she'd been killed today seemed to have been the last straw.

"Does Faith know about any of this?" Little Vinnie asked as he set a bowl of soup and a spoon in front of Rage.

"She and Miranda went to have a look around the hotel in San Francisco," Rage told him.

"Eat," he said. "You've lost too much weight."

"That's because I'm dying. Your innards don't work the same way when you're dying. Meat and fat no longer stick to your bones."

He made a tsking sound with his tongue. "You know I don't like it when you talk like that."

When she'd first been diagnosed with stage four astrocytoma, Rage had been happy to let Beast and his father tiptoe around her, fulfill her every need, and treat her as if she were a fragile china doll, but her time on this earth was running out. She could feel it in every breath she took. Every move she made was a reminder of how sick she was. Her bones ached, her knees wobbled, and her hands trembled at times. But these two wonderful men who had taken her in when she had no one refused to believe there would come a day when she would no longer be around to argue with Beast or taste Little Vinnie's cooking and tell him what the concoction needed to make it just right.

These two big boys were in big-time denial.

Denial had been fine in the beginning, sort of a stage she figured most people went through. But lately all the things the three of them didn't say to one another were wearing her down at the seams. If she didn't get some of it out, she thought she might burst wide-open.

She reached for Little Vinnie's hand before he could head back to the stove. His fingers were like sausages, his skin weathered and dotted with age spots. "I'm dying," she said. "And the only thing I will miss, besides never getting to lay eyes on my sweet boy, is spending time with you and your son."

Beast looked up from his computer.

Little Vinnie opened his mouth to say something, but she stopped him. "Don't say it," she told him. "I'm dying. It's a fact, and you both know it. And if you don't let me say what needs to be said, then I won't be able to die peacefully when the time comes."

Neither of them said a word.

Beast couldn't seem to make eye contact, so she kept her gaze on Little Vinnie. "I love you both. You changed my life in so many ways. If Beast hadn't found me in that ditch and scooped me into his arms and brought me here, I never would have gotten the chance to appreciate the little things in life. Like the beauty of a sunflower." She looked into Little Vinnie's glistening eyes and squeezed his fingers. "Do you remember that day?"

At first he didn't move one muscle, but then he nodded. It was a subtle nod, but she saw it.

"I was mad at you about something or other, and you pulled the old truck to the side of the road. You even bothered to turn the engine off, and I can still hear it sputtering and sizzling like it does before it shuts down." She let her gaze roam over every familiar line in his face.

And then she smiled at him. "I thought you parked at the side of the road because you were going to give me one of your famous lectures, but that wasn't it at all. You sat there and waited patiently until curiosity got the better of me, and I uncurled myself from a fetal position on the backseat. When I sat up, you pointed a crooked finger at the field next to us. I looked that way, but it took a full five minutes for me to understand what you were pointing at. And when my head cleared and I saw those flowers swaying with the summer breeze, the sky as blue as ever, I cried from the sheer beauty of what you were showing me. The field was vast and never ending. I had never seen so many flowers in one place. Do you remember?"

Another nod.

"You called it a sea of sunflowers. That's right. Not a field but a sea. I'm not kidding, though. In that moment, it felt as if I'd gone through my entire life without seeing the beauty in the world. I mean, sure, I wasn't dealt the best hand when it came to families and life, but I never knew an ocean of sunflowers could be so beautiful. I thought a lot about that day since and how lucky I am to have you both in my life."

Beast pushed his chair away from the table; the legs scraped against the floor before he got up and walked back to his bedroom.

She started to get up, but Little Vinnie shook his head. "He'll be fine. He just needs a little time to himself."

Hardly two minutes passed before Beast reappeared, wearing a thick coat. He grabbed his keys from a side table and headed for the door.

"Where are you going?" Little Vinnie asked.

"I'm going to take a drive to check on Faith and her mom. The alarm is going off, but she's not answering her phone."

Rage jumped to her feet, grabbed her gun from a drawer in the kitchen, and said, "Wait for me. I'm going, too." Then she kissed Little Vinnie on the cheek and headed outside after Beast.

The ride to Loomis was quiet, and the tension between Rage and Beast was thick. It wasn't until they were approaching their destination that Rage turned her attention to the matter at hand as she realized something could be really wrong. "Faith's dad and her brother are in Mendocino. If someone has found a way into the house, we don't want them to see us coming."

"True. What do you have in mind?"

"Before you get to the driveway, there's a turnoff. We'll park there and make our way to the house by foot, through the backyard."

Beast did as she said. He made a left where she pointed, drove the truck into a clearing, and turned off the engine.

Rage examined the gun she'd brought with her and made sure it was loaded. Beast strapped a hunting knife around each leg and climbed out of the car.

The wind was strong, pushing against them as they walked. The trees creaked as they bent forward, then backward, branches swaying every which way. Rage and Beast had been to the house enough times to know which way to go, even in the dark. They came around the pond from the back, walked past the large shed they had been using as a command post since Faith's children were first taken.

Beast put a hand out to stop Rage from going any farther. The sliding glass door had been broken; shards of glass spread across the patio like crystal snow.

A high-pitched scream sent them both darting forward. Beast's long legs and sour mood powered him ahead, and he made it to the house in record time, disappearing inside. Rage rushed to keep up. A piece of glass cut through the bottom of her left shoe.

Shit!

She bent forward and was able to pull it out before it went too deep. She grabbed her cell phone, called 911, gave them the address, and told them to hurry before she hung up on the woman with all the questions.

Inside were broken chairs. Framed picture frames had fallen from the mantel and were broken on the stone hearth. The coffee table had been turned on its side. The scream had come from upstairs, where she could hear a commotion.

Beast was way ahead of her.

With a tight grip on her gun, she hurried up the stairs. Two slippers lay abandoned on the third and fourth steps. All sorts of sounds came from above. A crash, a thump, then crunching and cracking and groans and moans.

She rushed onward, praying they weren't too late.

The door to the master bedroom hung from one hinge. Splinters of wood sprinkled about the floor in the hallway. A man lay bleeding in front of the doorway. He rolled to his side, whimpering like an injured dog, his bloodied hands wrapped around his middle. Rage kept her gun pointed at his head as she stepped over him and entered the bedroom.

Beast had a hold on another man, one big arm wrapped around the guy's scrawny neck as he dragged him across the room. The man's arms and legs flailed when Beast picked him up. Beast held him straight up over his head before he tossed the man through the large-paned window. Glass shattered, and the man dropped out of sight.

"Watch out!" Rage cried as a third assailant charged from the bathroom, the blade of his knife glittering in the semidark.

Beast pivoted on his feet and tossed his hunting knife at the dark shadow as if he were playing darts, hitting a bull's-eye. The thug stumbled backward. But Beast wasn't done with him. In fact, he was just getting started.

Rage looked around the room, her heart racing as she ran to the other side of the bed, wondering why she hadn't yet seen Faith's mom. Her insides churned when she spotted Lilly Gray on the floor, half-hidden beneath the bed, her pajamas covered in blood.

It was hard to tell if she was breathing.

Rage knelt down next to her and wrapped her fingers around her frail wrist to feel for a pulse. She couldn't feel a thing. But then one of

Lilly's eyelids fluttered. At first Rage thought she'd imagined it. Then it happened again.

Rage got down lower and put her head against Lilly's chest. There it was—the faint beat of her heart. She cradled the woman's head in her lap while she gently moved the hair out of Lilly's face. "You're going to be OK." She thought of Faith and all she'd been through. "Don't even think about dying—do you hear me?" Her next thought was of Beast, and she wanted to cry.

TWENTY-SIX

Faith and Miranda arrived at the hospital a little after midnight.

Since receiving the call about her mom, Faith had barely been able to see straight. Nobody would give her a straight answer. She had no idea how badly Mom was hurt. She spotted Rage and Beast sitting in the lobby and ran that way. She grabbed hold of Beast's arm, her hands shaking. "I came as quickly as I could," she told them. "What happened?"

Rage stood. "Beast had an alert on his computer that said the alarm at your parents' house had been set off. You weren't answering your phone, so he called your mom. Since there was no answer there, either, we went to have a look around. The sliding glass door had been busted through. There was glass everywhere. Turned out there were three men inside. Beast took care of all of them, but not before they got to your mom. The police are at the house now."

"What about Mom?"

"Your sister is with her. The doctor said she's going to be OK."

About to head off to find Lilly's room, Faith stopped when Rage reached out and took hold of her arm. "You should know she's been beat up pretty bad. Her face is swollen."

Faith didn't know what to think, let alone say. It made her sick to think of what Mom had gone through. She nodded at Rage and then turned and walked toward the elevators.

"Where have you been?" Jana asked as soon as Faith entered the room.

Faith went to the bed where her mom was lying. She appeared to be asleep. Bandages and gauze covered her head around her ears and under her chin. Her eyes were tiny slits, hardly visible through the purple mass of bruises and swelling. Her left arm was in a cast, and there was a brace around her neck.

Monitors beeped all around them.

"Dad," Faith said to Jana. "Does he know what happened?"

"Steve has been trying to contact him and Colton. No luck there, but he got a hold of someone at the Mendocino County sheriff's office. They said they haven't been in contact with either of them since they first arrived. The sheriff checked the parking lot, though, and told Steve that their truck was still there."

Faith sighed. "Rage told me the doctor said Mom would be OK."

Jana frowned. "Does she look OK, Faith? So far there are no signs of internal bleeding, but they're keeping an eye on the swelling around her brain."

It was quiet for a moment before Jana cut through the tension with sharp words. "You should see the X-rays. She has a deep gash on the top of her head."

Faith slipped her hand over her mom's.

"This has to stop," Jana went on.

Faith looked at her sister. "What do you mean?"

"It's time to let it go, Faith."

Wishing Jana would go away, Faith traced a finger over Mom's fragile skin, noticing how slender and long her fingers were.

"Dad and Colton are somewhere in the mountains in freezing temperatures. Did you know they're expecting a storm in the exact area they're searching? If they don't get out of there soon, we're going to lose them."

Faith said nothing. She only wished she could trade places with her mother. She should have been there for her.

Cecelia's pale, lifeless face flashed in her mind. And the man's face, too. A stranger. Death and destruction were all around her.

"Do you hear me, Faith? We could lose them. We've already lost Craig. Bri and the kids have moved away. I love Lara and Hudson, you know I do, but I can't see how losing our entire family will bring them home or make things right. This can't go on."

Faith swallowed as she thought about what her sister was saying. She leaned close to Mom, whispered in her ear, told her everything would be all right; then she turned, lightly touched Jana's arm, and walked out of the room.

What would Jana say if she knew Faith had killed a man tonight—committed the ultimate sin? And what would her sister say if she knew Faith hadn't felt an ounce of remorse?

She had no tears left to shed.

Jana was right. She couldn't allow her family to drop like flies around her. Seeing her Mom clinging to life was the tipping point.

Back in the lobby, where Beast, Rage, and Miranda sat in plastic chairs waiting for an update, she told them it was over. No more investigative work. No more killing and bloodshed.

"No," Rage said.

Beast attempted to put an arm around Rage and pull her aside, but that did nothing to stop her from voicing her opinion. "I'm sorry about your mom. We'll have to become much more vigilant," Rage said, "but this isn't over until we find Lara and Hudson."

"I can't allow my family and all of you to continue to risk your lives. I'm going to talk to Detective Yuhasz and tell him everything I know, tell him I'm finished. I never should have dragged all of you into this mess. It's time for us to step aside and let the authorities do their jobs."

"You've got to be kidding me." Rage looked at Beast. "She's joking, right?"

Faith held her ground.

"This is bullshit," Rage said as she pulled away from Beast and lifted herself to her feet. She stepped toward Faith and went so far as to jab a finger at her chest. "Your mom, your dad, your brother—all of us—made the decision to get involved because it's not often you see one person take a stand against the scum of the earth."

Beast stood and put a hand on Rage's shoulder. "Leave her be," he told Rage. "Faith has had a rough day, and her mother was almost killed."

Rage knocked his hand off. "No. She doesn't get to change her mind because three asshole douche bags beat up her mom." Rage narrowed her eyes. "Did your mom tell you to give up? Did she?"

Faith shook her head.

"I didn't think so. Because this isn't about you, Faith. This is about your kids. Your mother's grandkids."

Faith lifted her chin as she looked at Beast. "Can you take Miranda home with you? I'm going to stay here at the hospital overnight and make sure Mom's OK."

"Not a problem." He turned toward Miranda. "Come on," he said.

Miranda wrinkled her nose. "I don't need any of your help. I'll be fine on my own."

Beast smoothed a hand over his chin, clearly frustrated with the whole lot of them. "Do me a favor, kid, and come with us. My dad makes a mean chowder soup, and he's keeping it warm on the stove."

Rage whispered a few words into Miranda's ear, then nodded at Beast.

After Beast and Miranda headed for the exit, Rage turned toward Faith once again. Her jaw was set, her spine stiff. "You can't quit. Do you hear me? Take the night to think about it, but if you do decide to stop fighting, I guarantee you'll spend the rest of your life regretting it."

TWENTY-SEVEN

From the river, Dad and Colton followed more than one trail of footprints to a small cabin half-covered in vines and weeds. It had a tin roof. Dry rot had taken its toll on the shack's eaves, and the stone chimney was cracked and crumbling.

Colton stepped up his pace, eager to see if anyone was inside. He stopped short when he noticed a bloodied hand sticking out from beneath a pile of dirt and leaves.

Dad came up from behind. "What is it?"

"It's not good whatever it is." Colton looked around for a stick and then used it to unbury a severed limb. "It looks like a forearm. Adult male."

Colton held a handkerchief over his nose and mouth. Skin and muscle were still attached in parts. The wrist bone and hand with two fingers were still intact.

"Looks as if a wild animal got to it," Dad said.

"Yeah, I would say so."

Although neither of them said the words, Colton knew his dad was thinking what he was thinking. It wasn't Hudson. Thank God.

Colton pushed himself upward, shoved his handkerchief in his back pocket, and walked toward the cabin. Pieces of the man, whoever he was, flesh and bone, were scattered about. Using the tip of his boot, he pushed open the cabin door. The inside smelled rank enough to make him wonder if he would find another corpse. He took a step back and inhaled a breath of fresh air before stepping inside. "The woodstove was used recently," Colton said loud enough for Dad to hear him.

"Could have been used by the dead man."

"True," Colton said as he walked around, his heavy boots making the old wood planks creak in protest. He examined the fish bones in the sink, where the foul smells were coming from, before opening and closing drawers. Empty cans of beans were stacked together on the floor beneath the window.

Finished with the cabin, Colton went outside again.

He found Dad near the dilapidated outhouse behind the cabin examining what looked like a small boulder on the ground. Up close, Colton saw that it was nothing of the sort. It was the head and partially eaten upper torso of a man. Not a pretty sight.

Dad gestured at the back of the head. "Looks like he was struck with an ax."

"I'll take your word for it," Colton said as he turned away, wondering if his nephew and the other boys had killed the man.

"Find anything inside the cabin?"

"Fish bones, a few empty cans of beans. Ashes in the wood-burning stove. That's about it."

"Nothing inside the outhouse, either," Dad said. "Let's go."

Without another word spoken about the dead man, they moved on.

Back at the river, it didn't take long for Dad to find the boys' trail. Embedded within layers of thick, damp leaves and soil were two pairs of small footprints. The same two boys who had taken refuge beneath the lean-to on top of the mountain had made their way to the river, maybe found the cabin and stayed there for a few nights until someone came along—that someone being the same man who had been torn into bits and pieces.

Colton held something up: a tree branch that had been turned into a makeshift spear.

His dad's eyes lit up. Colton figured it was because Dad had been the one to teach Hudson how to spear a fish in the wild. Seeing the spear gave them hope.

The boys' tracks were fairly easy to follow. Dad took the lead, but his pace had slowed since they'd first set off. He appeared flushed. "Want me to take some of that load off your back?" Colton asked.

"I'm old," Dad said over his shoulder, "but I ain't dead, kid. I can handle my own pack."

Here we go, Colton thought. He was going to get a lecture. Dad was stubborn. Always had been. And Dad never liked to be reminded that he wasn't as strong and tough as he used to be.

"Do you remember when I took you skiing for the first time?"

"Yeah, I do," Colton said. "We were at Heavenly, right?"

Dad nodded. "I bit off more than I could chew that day."

"What do you mean?"

"A storm was coming. Mom asked me, pleaded with me, in fact, not to take you up the mountain. I wouldn't listen. Not only did I take you out—I figured it was time to take you down the face of the mountain." He shook his head in remembrance. "You were freezing from the start. We barely got off the chairlift without incident. We weren't a third of the way down the mountain before you started crying. I took off one of your gloves to show you how to warm up your hands by blowing warm breath into your gloves. While I blew all the hot air I could into your small gloves, I noticed your fingers were turning blue."

"I do remember that day," Colton said, "especially being freezing cold and scared, stuck in the middle of nowhere."

"Yeah, well, in a matter of minutes, it seemed, the wind had picked up considerably. I was worried. We were too far down the mountain to head back up. And yet we still had a long way to go to get to the bottom. It was way too steep for a little boy. And to this day I don't know what made me do such a foolish thing."

"But we made it down the hill just fine," Colton reminded him.

His dad took a breath. "We made it down the hill all right. Mostly I skied with you between my legs. I took you straight to the med center inside the lodge. The doctor there thought you might lose a couple of fingers at the very least."

He'd heard the story many times before, but neither of his parents had ever told Colton how serious it had been.

"Because of the storm, Mom and I didn't want to take any chances, so we had to rush you to the closest hospital. They saved your fingers and toes, but it was a close one." He swallowed. "Your mom didn't talk to me for weeks, maybe a month."

"But everything worked out fine. Why are you telling me this, Dad?"

"Because I think you're worried about me, and worrying won't do either of us any good."

"And rightly so," Colton said sternly. "You had a stroke recently, and it's easy to see that the altitude is getting to you."

Dad placed a gloved hand on Colton's shoulder and squeezed. "I get it, son. But I want you to know two things."

Colton waited.

"We're going to find Hudson. And we're all going to get down this mountain alive. That's all that matters. Do you understand me?"

Colton peered into Dad's eyes. It wasn't just stubbornness he saw there. It was sheer will and determination. Nothing was going to stop him, not his age or his failing health, not the heavy load on his back or strong winds, and certainly not his son's worrying. Dad might have been foolish to take him up the mountain that day, but the point was he'd gotten them down the face of Heavenly Valley and when the time came he would get them down from here, too. Without looking away, Colton said, "Got it."

"Good. Let's go."

An hour later, where a fallen tree lay in their path, they stopped to have a look around. The boys' footprints continued on an uphill path, which made no sense at all.

"Maybe they were hiding from something," Colton said as he examined the tracks. "They could have been trying to lose someone."

Dad stood straight and tall, his nostrils flaring like an old English springer spaniel trying to catch a scent. "I wish I knew," he said. "Hudson has a good sense of direction. He would never have made that kind of mistake. Even if he were running from something, he would have known he needed to stay near the river in order to survive." Dad turned downhill, ignoring all the signs that pointed in the other direction.

"Dad," Colton said, straddling the fallen log. "There aren't any footprints or signs of a third party. We've been following the same tracks for a while. We can't stop now. Right or wrong, we've got to stay on their trail."

Dad looked at Colton with weary eyes, the lines in his face deeper than ever, his frustration palpable. Then he let out a ponderous sigh and led the way uphill.

———

Faith spent the night moving from a chair in her mom's room to a small couch in the hospital lobby. A nurse shook her awake to let her know Lilly was asking for her. Faith thanked her and then went to the bathroom, where she splashed cold water on her face and brushed her fingers through her tangled hair. In her mom's room she found a nurse adjusting pillows and setting up a tray of orange juice and yogurt.

When Mom saw Faith enter the room, she managed a crooked smile that revealed a chipped tooth.

"Oh, Mom," Faith said as she went to her. Faith hugged her as best she could without disturbing all the wires and tubes.

"Any news yet?" Mom asked, her voice labored.

Faith had to watch the words form on Mom's swollen lips to know what she was saying. She didn't have to ask any questions to know Mom was talking about Dad, Colton, and Hudson.

Faith shook her head.

"They'll be fine," Mom said, her voice so scratchy and small that it broke Faith's heart.

"What about you?" Faith asked. "Will you be all right?"

"Never better," she managed.

They exchanged knowing looks.

"I Tasered one of the men," she told Faith in the same proud voice Miranda had used last night. *I killed a man,* Faith thought, but didn't say.

"I would have gotten another man, too," Mom went on, "but there were three of them." She paused to catch her breath, rested a limp hand on her chest. "The third one caught me off guard."

Her voice wavered. Mom was doing her best to sound strong, but her pain was obvious. "I'm so sorry I wasn't there, Mom. If I had left well enough alone, I would have been there with you."

"Three of them, Faith. All big men. I'm glad you weren't there. I was lucky enough to get to my bedroom."

"As soon as Dad and Colton come home, I'm going to tell them it's over."

Mom scowled.

Faith threw her arms wide. "Look what they've done to you, Mom. It's all too much. No more. Enough is enough."

"Sounds like Jana talking."

Uncertainty and hopelessness weighed heavily on Faith, causing her shoulders to fall forward. "She may have been the one to open my eyes, Mom, but I'm the one putting my foot down. If not for Beast and Rage showing up, you would have been killed. We haven't heard a word from Dad and Colton."

"You can't quit now," Mom said.

Faith opened the yogurt and tried to spoon-feed her, but Mom shook her head. "I'm not hungry."

Faith set the spoon back on the tray. "From the very beginning," Faith reminded her, "you said we shouldn't get involved and that we should let the police handle this. You were right."

"Wrong. I was wrong."

Faith didn't want to hear what she had to say. She pulled out her phone. "I promised Jana I would call her once you were awake."

"They won't stop, Faith. It's too late to call a truce."

"I can bargain with them."

"How? With what?"

Money, Faith thought. She had no idea why the men had come to the house. Did they know Faith was staying there, and they wanted to shut her up once and for all? Would they have killed Mom if Beast and Rage hadn't shown up? Or maybe the attack was a warning.

Dad, Beast, and Rage were the only people who knew she had their money stashed away in the tree fort. It might be time for her to find a way to make contact. She could put a message on her website or maybe contact a local reporter. Her mind was swirling with speculation.

"Robyn Price," Mom said suddenly, her voice clearer than before.

"What did you say?"

"Before those men came crashing through the door, the phone rang. It was a woman. Robyn Price. She sounded desperate . . . said it was imperative—no, urgent—she said it was urgent. Said she needed to talk to you about the children."

Related to Richard Price? Faith wondered. The same man who had used Faith's husband's business to launder money and then, according to the FBI, was murdered?

"Did she leave a number?" Faith asked.

Mom winced as she tried to sit up in bed.

Faith helped her. "Are you OK?"

"I'm fine." She took a moment to collect herself. "The woman said she never should have called. And then the call was disconnected."

"What should I do?" Faith asked, and yet she already knew the answer. Despite what she'd just said about putting a stop to this craziness, she realized in that moment that no matter the consequences, she would never stop looking for her children.

"You need to do whatever it takes to get a hold of that woman's phone number and give her a call," Mom said.

Twenty-Eight

The minute Mom mentioned Robyn Price, Faith put off the idea of possibly sending any sort of message to the people who were doing their best to destroy her family.

By the time Jana arrived at the hospital to visit with Mom, Rage had already managed to locate a Florida address and telephone number for Robyn Price. Jana didn't say two words to Faith, and she wouldn't make eye contact. Her sister was angry, and Faith didn't have the strength to argue with her, so she said her goodbyes and left.

The first thing Faith did once she climbed into her car was pull out her cell phone and call Robyn Price. Nobody answered, so she left a message asking the woman to call her as soon as possible.

An hour later, she called again. Still no answer.

It was eating her up inside. Why had Robyn reached out to her? What did she know about Lara and Hudson? Those were the questions replaying inside her mind.

Four o'clock that same day, Faith drove to Midtown and parked in front of the offices of Kirsten Reich, a family therapist whom Jana had suggested Miranda see, even going so far as to make an appointment. Since Miranda wasn't interested, Faith decided to talk to the woman herself and see if the matter was worth pressing. According to Jana, Kirsten helped people who were struggling with a variety of challenges, including anxiety, depression, and anger.

Faith climbed out of the car. Other than the wind rattling the branches of a few trees lining J Street, it was eerily quiet. She looked across the street, up toward the higher windows, where all she could see were shadowy figures.

The feeling of being watched had not left her since she'd returned home from the hospital. Someone was watching her. She was certain of it, and yet she'd never actually seen anyone. She had no proof. Just a sense, a strange sort of energy surging through her body, making her jittery, telling her that the people who had killed Craig and taken her kids were watching her from afar, waiting to strike.

She continued down the sidewalk, her hands shoved deep into her pockets, the wind whipping her hair every which way. Relieved to reach the entrance, she checked in with the receptionist. Within a few minutes, Faith was led into an office with tranquil lighting and comfortable furniture.

Kirsten Reich greeted her with a calming smile and an outstretched hand. She was a few inches taller than Faith. She wore black slacks and a beige sweater. Her wavy blonde hair fell around her shoulders. After quick introductions were made, Kirsten gestured for her to have a seat on the couch.

Faith removed her jacket and then took a seat and rubbed some warmth into her arms as Kirsten collected pen and paper from her desk by the window. "I'm surprised to see you," Kirsten said.

"Why is that?"

"From what I've seen on television and read in the papers, you've been busy."

Faith nodded. "Yes, it's been chaotic," she said. An awkward silence filled the room as an image of her husband flashed through her mind, making her feel queasy. She rarely thought of Craig, mostly because it hurt too much. Her gaze fell on her wedding ring, and in an instant Faith was carried a million miles away, to another time, another place. She was inside a small room at the back of the church. Jana was worrying over Faith's hair, and Mom was chattering on about the flowers that had yet to be delivered. What would they do if the bouquets didn't arrive in time? Colton left the small room in a huff, mumbling something about women worrying about the silliest things.

Faith remembered her wedding day as if it had happened yesterday.

Moments before she was to walk down the aisle, her heart had been beating as fast as the thoughts running through her mind. Was she too young to be marrying? What about her plans to backpack through Europe? With a full-time job and a husband, when would she ever have time to learn to cook? She'd always planned to live in Paris for a year—that would never happen once she married.

But then the flowers arrived.

The music started.

It was time.

She peeked through the church doors and saw Craig standing by the altar, strong hands clasped in front of him. He'd looked so handsome, so relaxed.

He loved her, and she loved him.

One glimpse was all it had taken. Calmness settled over her shoulders like a warm, down-filled blanket. Backpacking through Europe and living in Paris were quickly forgotten. Her hands stopped trembling. And never once had she experienced a moment of regret after they were pronounced man and wife.

Craig was the love of her life.

And now he was gone—everything taken from her in one fell swoop.

Eyes wide-open, Faith looked around the office and wondered what the hell she was doing there. She had absolutely nothing to say to Kirsten Reich, a complete stranger. Nothing to gain by coming.

"Faith?"

Startled, Faith directed her attention to the therapist, who was now sitting across from her, legs crossed, gaze directed on her.

They both waited for the other to say something.

"Why don't you tell me what you'd like to talk about today?" Kirsten asked.

Faith had been about to get up and leave the office. Instead she remained seated. A long pause hovered between them before Faith said, "My husband was killed. I watched him die, and there was nothing I could do."

Silence.

"I loved him, and yet I haven't shed a tear for him because I'm not ready to go there yet."

The therapist jotted something on her notepad.

"My children were taken," Faith continued without emotion. "Ripped from our lives and from the only home they've ever known." A horn honked in the distance. Faith looked about, heard someone talking just outside the door. It took her a moment to regain focus. "I have reason to believe my daughter is being held captive by people waiting for the highest bidder. Whether you have children or not, I'm sure you can imagine what it might be like to lay awake every night wondering where she is and what she's doing. Is she chained to a bed? Is she alone and frightened? Are they feeding her or—"

Faith stopped midsentence, her thoughts unable to go to that darkest place. She looked at the clock on the wall and thought of Robyn Price. Why hadn't the woman called her back? More important, why was Faith sitting here wasting her time?

Rage had been right when she'd said it was too soon to quit. Faith still had work to do. Dad and Colton were risking their lives looking for Hudson, and here she was talking about what? Her fucking feelings? She couldn't cry for her dead husband because she was half-dead herself, a walking zombie. What was the point in coming here today? These men and women who took children and abused them, these horrible people whoever they were, would never stop. So why should she? She pushed herself from the couch.

"Are you leaving?"

Faith grabbed her coat. "I think so. Yes. I never should have come. I'm sorry."

"Denial. Anger. Bargaining. Depression. Acceptance."

Faith looked at Kirsten with a raised eyebrow.

"The five stages of grief," Kirsten said.

Faith slipped her coat on and tightened the sash. "Good to know."

"I might be able to help you."

"When I get to the depression stage," Faith told her, "maybe I'll give you a call."

"It's often hard to see clearly through anger."

"I know all about anger," Faith said. "It inspires aggressive feelings and behaviors. A small amount of anger is necessary for survival. But unexpressed anger can be dangerous. It can get people hurt or killed." Something she knew firsthand.

"Or thrown in jail," Kirsten added.

Faith stopped moving, exhaled. "I know. I can't end up there again. But these people must be stopped."

"I agree."

Faith inhaled as she looked at the woman more curiously than before.

"We've been following your story," Kirsten said.

"We?"

"Myself and a few friends of mine. Our group has grown over the years. We started out as a neighborhood watch. Let's just say we keep a close eye on certain people who misbehave. One of the ladies in my group has connections."

"FBI?" Faith asked.

"Something like that. Anyhow, through this connection of ours, we heard about you and your friends storming the farmhouse."

Faith didn't know where the therapist was going with all this. "And?"

"And if you ever need our help, give me a call, and I'll be happy to round up the girls."

"You're not going to try to talk me out of this craziness?"

"On the contrary."

Faith looked at Kirsten Reich in a whole new light. "Exactly what kind of help are you offering?"

"Any kind."

TWENTY-NINE

That night, as Faith drove to anger management class, she kept an eye on the car in her rearview mirror. It was a black Mercedes with tinted windows. The car had been following her for the past five miles.

Heart pounding, hands curled around the wheel in a death grip, she pulled to the side of the road and reached for the gun tucked inside her glove compartment.

The Mercedes swept by in a blur.

With a sigh of relief, she closed her eyes and rested her forehead against the steering wheel. Finally she merged back onto the main road. Ten minutes later, she pulled into the parking lot outside the building where her anger management classes were held. She spotted Rage and Beast standing at the entrance waiting for her.

"Are you still angry with me?" Faith asked Rage when she reached her side.

"Nope. Whatever you decide, I'm good."

"Liar."

Beast elbowed Rage in the side, and she shooed him away. "So what did you decide to do?" she asked Faith.

"I'm not giving up. I could never stop looking for my kids. I'd rather die." She paused for a moment before her gaze settled on the bandage covering Rage's chin. "What happened to you? And what happened with Fin? With my mom being in the hospital and everything that's been going on, I forgot to ask you and Beast about it."

"Well," Rage began, "the good news is that he's no longer in your garage."

"Where is he? Did he talk?"

"Sort of. He gave us a couple of names. But we didn't trust him, so Beast and I decided to follow him."

Faith could tell from Rage's expression that something had gone wrong. "But?"

"We followed him to an apartment building off Truxel, but he didn't stand a chance. Someone blew the tattoo man to smithereens."

"What?" Faith asked. "How?"

"After watching Fin dig around in his pocket for his keys, I set off to see if I could talk to someone in the manager's office. He couldn't have set one foot in the door before all hell broke loose. Wham bam," Rage said, using her hands for emphasis. "There was a deafening blast, crap flying every which way, and in the end, Fin was gone, as in blown to a million pieces."

Faith frowned. "Nobody else was hurt?"

"A few stitches on my chin," Rage said. "That's it." She sighed. "The bad news is that Beast had a friend check out the names Fin gave us. Dead ends. He must have pulled the names right out of his ass."

"The most important thing is that you're OK," Faith said.

"Thanks. How's your mom doing?" Rage asked as they walked inside and found a seat in the circle of folding chairs.

"She's doing better. Jana and I have been taking turns keeping her company. The doctor wants to keep an eye on her for a while. There's still a lot of swelling."

"I'm glad she's doing OK," Rage said. "Miranda is home with Little Vinnie. They've been playing a lot of card games. I think Miranda likes it there."

"Thanks for taking her in."

"Maybe when I'm gone," Rage said, "she can have my room. We're about the same size. She can have my clothes, too."

Beast let out a low growl and then got up and headed for the bathroom.

"He's in denial," Rage told Faith.

"About what?"

"About the fact that I won't be around for much longer. It's annoying."

"He cares about you," Faith said. "He's not ready to let you go."

"But if he doesn't talk about what he's feeling inside, he's going to spend the rest of his life wishing he'd said all those things he keeps bottled up."

"How about you?" Faith asked. "Have you said everything that needs to be said?"

"I try, but nobody wants to listen."

"I do."

"Really? Because I don't think you want to get me started."

"I want to hear what you have to say," Faith said. She glanced over her shoulder. The instructor was talking to a woman Faith didn't recognize in the far corner of the room.

"OK, fine. For starters," Rage said, "Beast doesn't have any idea how much I care about him because he refuses to listen to me. He's like a father, brother, and a best friend all rolled into one. He's also stubborn as an ox. I don't think he'll ever know how grateful I am for all he's done for me."

"Well, we both know he cares about you, too," Faith told her. "But he's sensitive, and he doesn't want to lose you."

Rage sighed. "And then there's the whole thing about dying. Sometimes it scares me to think about it. Does dying hurt? Am I going to linger in a hospital bed for days on end with everyone staring at me, waiting for the inevitable? And what about my little boy? When Christopher turns eighteen, will he look for his biological mother? Will he ever know how much I loved him? That I gave him up so he might have a chance at a good, decent life?"

"Maybe there's a chance we can still find Christopher."

"Beast and Little Vinnie are bounty hunters. They locate people for a living, but they haven't been able to find him. It was a closed adoption, and the people running things over there won't budge."

The instructor made his way to the center of the circle.

"Thanks for letting me vent," Rage told Faith as Beast approached and took his seat.

"You can talk to me anytime," Faith said.

"OK, people, listen up," the instructor said, putting an end to all the chatter in the room. "Tonight is a very special night. Say hello to our special guest, Julie Ryan."

"I'll be your instructor tonight," Julie said. "I'm here to show you all the proper way to throw a tantrum."

Laughter erupted.

"I know, I know," the other instructor said. "For weeks now I've been talking about how to handle your anger with breathing techniques and meditation, but tonight it's all about getting that fury, that feeding frenzy of anger out of your system."

"In constructive ways, of course," Julie added.

"What now?" Rage said under her breath.

"Maybe you've been through a divorce, or you were fired from your job," Julie said in a superpeppy voice. "Or perhaps you had one of those days. Whatever the reason may be, you're feeling stressed. Sometimes we just need to let it all out." She began shaking her body, limbs flailing. "Come on, people—join me!"

Faith rolled her eyes.

Beast crossed his arms, making it clear he would not participate.

Rage stuck her arms out like a zombie and gave her hands a shake. "Hmm. Not bad."

"If you don't want to shake your bootie," the woman said with a wide smile on her face, "then try beating your chest and crying out as if you were Tarzan."

Rage decided to give that a try, too. Her jungle cry sounded a little pitiful to Faith, but at least she was giving it a go.

"Here," Julie said, tossing Faith a pillow, seemingly unwilling to let her sit it out. "Release some of that anxiety that's been building. Put the pillow against your face and scream and wail as loud as you want. You can do it."

"For the love of God," Faith said. She was about to pass the pillow to someone else in the class when Rage stopped her.

"We're here, aren't we? Just do it."

The entire place had erupted into jarring noises and mewling cries. Off in the corner, a man holding a bat was swinging at a stuffed animal hanging from the ceiling. Another guy, Mufasa, the weirdo who had been there since day one, was screaming at the top of his lungs as he socked a punching bag.

It wasn't bad enough they made everyone use nicknames, which was why Faith had been dubbed Furious, and the same with Beast and Rage, now they had to make fools of themselves, too?

Sunshine, a hefty woman with Shirley Temple curls, was blowing up balloons and then gleefully popping them with a needle. Faith had never seen her look happier.

They were all here tonight, Butterfinger, Captain, ZZ Top, Jinx, and all the other angry people in Placer County, beating their chests or shaking their arms like crazy people. Maybe there was something to Julie Ryan's crazy idea after all.

Mufasa's screams suddenly escalated. Everyone in the room stopped to watch him. His face turned from a light shade of red to crimson right before their eyes. Instead of letting his rage out, his anger was mounting.

His ire was palpable. The moment he reached into his coat pocket, Beast shouted, "Get down!" and pulled Rage to the ground.

Mufasa fired six bullets into the punching bag and was about to reload when Julie Ryan walked right up to him and placed a hand on his shoulder. "Give me the gun," she said calmly.

Half-hidden behind a chair, Faith watched it all unfold. She knew from previous anger management classes that Mufasa's tendency to be loud and obnoxious stemmed from one incident, one moment in time. His only son had been murdered, and his son's killer would be up for parole soon. "Give me the gun," the instructor repeated as if she'd done this sort of thing a million times before. "These people are your friends, and you're scaring them."

"You don't understand."

"Yeah, I think I do. I've heard about you, Mufasa. Don't let the bastard who did this to your family bring you down with him. Don't let him win."

Reluctantly, he handed her the gun, which she promptly handed off to the other instructor. Mufasa's chin dropped downward, nearly hitting his chest.

Class was dismissed, and everyone was told to go home.

Faith looked around the room at all the people standing there, frozen in place and scared out of their wits. She knew how they felt. The world had turned on its axis, and nobody was safe.

THIRTY

Aster took his time filling the crystal vase with water. Then he carefully positioned the long-stemmed roses inside before placing the vase on the table next to the recliner where the old hag spent most of her time.

The nurse sighed. "If only all our patients were treated with such tender, loving care."

Aster smiled at the young woman with the perky breasts and slender hips. "How's Mom been?" he asked, although he couldn't care less.

The sweet little thing looked around to make sure nobody else was within earshot. "Don't tell the others," she said, "but your mother is my favorite patient. She never gets upset, and she always cleans her plate, vegetables and all."

That's because she's a fat cow, he thought. He hated his mother with a passion. The only reason she was staying in a place this nice was because of his pussy brothers. His mother's maiden name was Hall, and that was why he had all his girls branded with the letter *H*. Because, like his mother, they were all whores.

He turned to Mom then, forced himself to lean down close and plant a squishy, wet kiss on her wrinkled forehead. Then he turned back to the nurse and asked her if Mom had been taking her medication.

Looking past him, the nurse appeared suddenly concerned about something.

Aster looked back at his mom. Her eyes were bulging from their sockets as her toothless mouth flapped open and closed.

The nurse rushed forward and kneeled down so that she was eye level with Mom. "She's trying to tell us something."

Ridiculous, Aster thought. His mother hadn't said a word since falling down the stairs more than thirty years ago.

"You . . . your fault."

Son of a bitch. "I think she's trying to say she wants me to take her on a stroll," Aster said calmly.

The nurse attached an inflatable cuff to his mother's arm and took her blood pressure. "I don't think so. Her blood pressure is out of control." She stood and headed for the door. "I'm going to get the doctor. I'll be right back."

"You sneaky little bitch," he said to his mother once the nurse disappeared. He gripped the arms of her chair and peered into her eyes. "You made Dad's life a living hell, put him in an early grave with all your nagging. And now you sit here day after day staring at the wall, costing me thousands of dollars. It's going to stop. Do you hear me? Next time I come, it won't be for a visit. It'll be to take you out of this place for good. It's time for you to come live with me, your son."

Her face contorted into an ugly grimace of pain. "You . . . d-d-did this to me."

Aster took hold of Mom's hand and squeezed. When the young nurse reappeared with a doctor at her side, Aster told his mom in a loving voice that everything would be OK.

"I'm so sorry," the nurse told Aster, "but we're going to have to ask you to step out while we check her over."

"It's OK. I have errands to run." He rubbed his mom's arm and said, "Don't you worry. They'll take good care of you until I can come back and bring you home where you belong."

———

Raised voices prompted Detective Yuhasz to look up from his paperwork and see Officer Ryan O'Sullivan approaching. O'Sullivan usually knocked before entering, but not this time.

"Looks like you have a visitor," O'Sullivan told him.

And that's when Yuhasz saw his son-in-law, David Hofberg, storm past cubicles and a long row of desks, his face a brilliant mass of purples and blues from the beating he'd taken the other night.

Yuhasz got to his feet just as Hofberg came barreling through his office door, his broad shoulder knocking O'Sullivan off balance.

"You got a problem?" Yuhasz asked.

"Yeah, as a matter of fact, I do." Hofberg pointed a finger his way. "I saw you in the parking lot watching me while your dogs dragged me into the back alley. You're so fucking cocky you think you can get away with this kind of shit?"

"I have no idea what you're talking about." Yuhasz motioned for O'Sullivan to give them some time alone.

O'Sullivan hesitated before leaving and shutting the door behind him.

"You brought this upon yourself," Yuhasz told Hofberg when they were alone.

"So you're not going to deny it?"

"Deny what?"

Hofberg gestured toward his battered face. "This."

Yuhasz couldn't help but admire the work his pals had done. His aristocratic nose had been broken and now slanted to the left. His friends might have gotten a little carried away, but sometimes that sort of thing couldn't be helped.

"I didn't think so," Hofberg said when Yuhasz said nothing in response. "You're not going to get away with this. I've already put a call into the captain and assistant commissioner. I'll go all the way to the top with this if I have to."

"You need professional help," Yuhasz said matter-of-factly. "My number one priority is to protect my daughter. If you think you can settle this in a positive way and get professional help, I'm all for it, and I'll back you up one hundred percent. Otherwise, me and you have a problem, because I will protect my family any way I see fit."

Hofberg inhaled as he took careful, seemingly calculated steps toward Yuhasz. He stopped to admire his wall of framed certificates of achievements. When he got to a spot that was empty, he slammed his fist through the wall. Bits of plaster and dust fell to the floor. He then turned toward Yuhasz and said, "What are you going to do about it?"

Yuhasz took a seat and began sifting through his mail.

"A man enters your office and puts a hole in your wall, and you do absolutely nothing about it?"

When Yuhasz looked his way, the dickhead smiled at him. "I'll say it one more time, so you better listen carefully. If you have any intention of staying married to my daughter," Yuhasz said as he used a letter opener to slice open an envelope, "you need to get counseling. That's all I have to say on the matter."

"Well, here's the thing, Dad," Hofberg said with a sneer. "An old divorced dog like you shouldn't be handing out marital advice. You're way out of line. I don't know why you think you know what's best for Holly and me, considering you never could control that bitch ex-wife of yours." Hofberg brushed a hand over the top of his head in frustration. "Holy shit, man, that was painful to witness back then. All those years spent watching her trample over you, ordering you around, demanding and nagging while you ran around with your tail between your legs. Nobody, including your own daughter, could believe how long it took her to leave your sorry ass and go in search of a real man."

Yuhasz decided to let the idiot mouth off all he wanted. He would take care of him later—just not here, not now. Putting a fist into Hofberg's big mouth would only be playing right into his hands.

"You might have nothing to say, but I have plenty to say," Hofberg continued. "I'm giving you a warning. You, my friend, need to take a step back and mind your own business, because otherwise you're going to regret it. Your daughter married me. She's my wife. She hasn't been your responsibility since the day we married. She's mine now."

"Oh, really? Where is she? Because I have it on good authority that she's left town."

Hofberg's jaw twitched. "She'll be back. She always comes back to me sooner or later."

"I don't think so. Not this time. And for the record, you touch one hair on her head," Yuhasz ground out, "so much as make her cry, and it's over."

"Over?"

"Yeah, over."

Hofberg walked toward him, rested splayed hands on top of Yuhasz's desk as he leaned in close. "A man needs to take care of his household. And that includes teaching his wife to love and obey and to know her place. Holly will come back, and if she thinks she can flap her mouth whenever she feels like it and have an opinion on everything just like her goddamn mother, then she better—"

Yuhasz jumped to his feet so fast, his chair toppled over behind him. Before he could make another move, the door swung open and O'Sullivan and Hernandez stepped inside. "Everything all right?" O'Sullivan asked.

It took everything Yuhasz had not to jump over his desk and wring Hofberg's neck.

"Come on," O'Sullivan said to Hofberg, waving him toward the door. "Time for you to go."

Hofberg straightened his spine, then tucked his thumbs into his waistband and stretched a bit, letting everyone know he wasn't in a hurry and would take his sweet time before he finally headed for the door.

"She's never coming back," Yuhasz warned as Hofberg neared the door. "Next time I see you, I'll be serving you divorce papers."

"Oh, don't worry, Dad. You don't know Holly like I know her. She'll be back. Guaranteed."

———

Patrick was about to ring the doorbell when the ornate iron doors opened to a stone entry complete with a lavish chandelier and custom-painted ceiling.

Standing before him was Aster's wife. Rae's skin was flawless, her eyes like crystals, her thick auburn hair pinned up in a swirl of perfection. She wore a classic white knit sweater and white, curve-hugging slacks.

"You look beautiful."

She blushed.

Patrick looked around. "Is he gone?"

She nodded, leaving him to close the heavy iron doors behind him.

"The kids are in school," she said, her voice soft and husky.

He was facing her again, standing so close he could feel the heat from her body. Many times he'd dreamed about being alone with Aster's wife if only for a moment.

She raised one perfectly arched brow. "You needed to talk?"

No words came forth; her beauty made him speechless. He nodded instead.

"Why don't we have a seat in the other room? I'll make us tea."

Instead of heading for the main room, he followed her into the kitchen. Like the rest of the house, it was old-world architecture with thick exposed wooden beams, dark woods, and wrought iron elements throughout. While she filled the kettle and put it on the stove to heat, he admired the archways and the craftsmanship.

"Who's your designer?"

"Me," she said with a smile. "I've always wanted to be an interior designer. But then the kids came along and time got away from me. You know how that goes."

"It's never too late."

Her smile faded.

Her expression said it all. "Aster doesn't want you to work?" he asked.

"He doesn't like when I talk about those kinds of things. You know how he can be."

"Yeah, I do." He stepped close again, this time with much more confidence. He couldn't stop himself if he'd wanted to. He raised a hand to her head and gently pulled the clip from her hair, mesmerized as he watched her thick mane fall in heavy waves against her slender shoulders. He put a hand on her cheek and brushed his fingers through the silky strands. "You can talk about these things with me," he told her. "You're an amazing and talented woman," he whispered into her ear.

She rested splayed hands on his chest. "We shouldn't."

"Oh, but we should." He kissed her then, thinking she might very well push him away. Instead she kissed him back, tentatively at first and then with much more passion than he'd expected or hoped for.

They stumbled about a bit as she eagerly stripped him of his jacket and tie. She undid the front buttons of his shirt, and when she finished with that, he slipped her sweater up over her head.

Overcome with desire, they continued removing each other's clothing as if it might be their last day on this earth. When their gazes met, they smiled at each other and slowed things down a notch, took their time exploring and touching, until finally he swooped her into his arms and carried her to the living room rug.

In a frenzy of heated lust that could no longer be contained, Patrick set out to do what he'd planned from the moment Aster Williams had killed Stanton, his boss, friend, and mentor—he took Aster Williams's most coveted prize. He took every bit of her. And as she arched her hips higher, he whispered words of endearments into her ear until her cries of bliss were drowned out by the high-pitched hiss of the teakettle.

THIRTY-ONE

Dark clouds gathered overhead. The wind had picked up considerably over the past hour. While Colton relieved himself behind one of many trees, Russell Gray pulled out his cell phone on the off chance he might get reception. He wanted to talk to his wife. Needed to talk to her.

No such luck.

His days were spent thinking about finding Hudson and keeping the morale up, but his nights were all about Lilly. She was his everything, and at times like this he wished he'd expressed how he felt about her more often while he'd had the chance.

Although he talked a good talk to his son, the truth was his old bones were weary, and there were moments that he could literally feel his body shutting down. He might not make it off the mountain, but he'd be damned if he didn't find his grandson first.

Life was an amazing thing, each day an unexpected miracle— nature, the intense love he felt for his family, good food, and loyal friends—life's intricacies could be downright magnificent at times. And then there was the other side of existence, the dark side. Humans without morals who thrived on making others suffer, greed, and selfishness.

Nobody wanted to see the ugly side.

In fact, Russell always figured he'd seen enough hostility for two lifetimes, but apparently not. He'd always thought of himself as a leader and protector, but age, he realized now as he stood on top of a high mountain with vultures circling in the distance, had a way of humbling a man, bringing him down to his creaky old knees, and making him see the world for what it was—infinite and unpredictable.

"Hey, Dad," Colton said as he approached. "I think I saw something near the bottom of that ridge." He pointed down the mountain, far from the trail they had been following. "I'm going to go take a look, but it would be easier if you could stay here and I could leave my pack behind. I'll carry my pistol just to be safe."

Russell didn't like it, but they couldn't very well head on without checking it out, and if he went with his son, he'd only slow him down. Time was not on their side. "What do you think you saw? You better take the bear spray just in case."

Colton was on his knees going through his pack. He attached the spray and a walkie-talkie to his belt loop. "I thought I saw smoke," Colton said. "As if someone might have recently tamped out a campfire. I'll use the walkie-talkie to contact you if I see anything." He looked toward the sky. "Looks like more than a bucket of rain is coming our way, which means I best hurry." Colton clapped him on the back and then rushed off without another word.

Russell took a seat on the ground, then rifled through his pack for his binoculars. It took him a few minutes to adjust the focus knob to get a sharp image of the terrain and zero in on Colton. His hand trembled, and he had to concentrate on keeping a steady hand as he moved past Colton to the ridge.

He made some adjustments and used the higher magnification. The moment he located the source of the campfire, his heart rate accelerated. Small puffs of smoke came into view, and yet there was no sign of anyone close by. He set the binoculars down and used the walkie-talkie to try to contact his son. All he got was static in return.

The wind wasn't letting up.

He picked up the binoculars again, narrowed his eyes, and kept a steady gaze until he located the spot where he'd seen Colton before picking up the walkie-talkie. But Colton wasn't there any longer.

Russell took a breath to keep himself calm and steady his hands as he observed the lands and more particularly the trees, large boulders, and thick brush, places someone might be able to hide.

And that's when he spotted a man, wearing a green cap, half-hidden behind a moss-covered boulder. The bill covered most of his bearded face. His movements were quick and efficient.

What the hell was he doing?

Russell's gaze fell on the semiautomatic rifle being positioned in the man's hands.

He followed the direction the gun was pointed and saw that it was aimed at his son, who had reached the campfire and was kneeling down, checking things out.

Russell's heart jumped to his throat. He didn't hesitate. He grabbed his own rifle, got on his belly, legs spread. No time to change the caliber of the bullet. The wind would be a problem. No matter. He would make the necessary adjustments. He grabbed Colton's backpack and used it to rest the front of his rifle to make for a more stable platform. With the butt of the stock in the pocket of his shoulder, he looked down the sight of the scope.

His hands shook; his heart raced.

Although he had yet to pull the trigger, a shot was fired.

Looking through the scope, he saw his son go down. A sharp pain sliced through him. And in an instant, Russell Gray was back on the front line. The wind, the birds, the sounds of nature all but gone.

The shooter hadn't moved.

Focused, Russell opened his mouth and throat until he felt his body relax. Once again he lined up his shot, took a breath, waited for the reticle to line up over his target, and then pulled the trigger.

Bull's-eye.

Russell skidded down the mountain; he couldn't see through the spray of dirt, twigs, and pebbles. His emotions were all over the place, his heart beating so fast he thought it might explode. Before he reached the area where he'd seen Colton go down, he saw his son's head come up. His gaze appeared to lock on the man now lying on the ground. Surprise. Elation. Joy. It all hit him at once. Colton was alive.

"What the hell happened?" Colton asked when he saw him approaching. "Did you take him down from clear up there?"

Russell was having a difficult time catching his breath, but once he realized Colton wasn't hurt, he stopped, hands on hips, and bent over to take in some much-needed air. "Jesus, son," he said. "I saw you go down. I thought you were dead."

"The minute I saw his rifle, I did the only thing I could. I dropped and rolled. I didn't think I had a chance in hell of escaping a second bullet, though."

Colton got to his feet and followed Russell to where the shooter had fallen. The man had taken a clean shot through his head. Russell leaned over and took the rifle, then searched through the rest of his things. No ID.

Colton peered up the mountain toward the spot where he'd left his dad. "How did you see the guy from way up there?"

"I was watching you through the binoculars. Keeping an eye on things."

Colton shook his head. "That was some shot, Dad."

Russell wrapped an arm around his son's shoulder, didn't want to think about how close he'd come to losing him. "Come on," he said, afraid his emotions might get the better of him if they didn't get moving. "Let's go find Hudson, and go home."

Faith spent another night at the hospital, tossing and turning.

The good news was Mom was improving. The swelling had gone down, and she was no longer feeling nauseous. The bad news was nobody had heard from Dad or Colton. At times like this it felt as if time literally held still. Every minute felt like an hour, every day a week.

Detective Yuhasz had left her a voice message letting her know there was still no sign of Diane Weaver, but that they'd located her brother, Eric. He and his wife had been murdered. He hadn't given her details, only that Lara wasn't there.

Every time they got a lead in the case, any and all hope was instantly dashed.

Fin the tattoo artist was dead.

And what about the name Patrick? Right before Cecelia Doyle died, she'd said she worked for Patrick. Faith couldn't exactly track down every Patrick in the United States.

It was early in the morning as she walked down the corridor to the cafeteria to get a cup of coffee. She got in line and checked her messages—still no word from Robyn Price.

Two women ahead of her kept looking over their shoulders at Faith. They were trying to whisper, but Faith could hear every word.

"I was in my daughter's room on the second floor when I overheard the nurses talking about that McMann woman."

"I read about the attack in the paper," her friend said. "It's a miracle her mother is alive."

"I wonder if that McMann woman has any idea how lucky they are that they didn't lose her. And she's not out of the water yet. Brain injuries can lead to all kinds of problems."

A tsking noise came next. "Just last night my husband asked me what exactly the woman was trying to prove. Our taxes pay the police to investigate and protect the community for a reason."

"Exactly. When is she going to understand that those kids of hers are gone and are never coming back?"

Stunned, Faith was about to walk off when Corrie Perelman appeared from the front of the line, marched over to the two gossipers, and said, "Where do you two get off talking that way? Faith McMann is standing right behind you, for God's sakes."

"It's all right," Faith said, trying to escape without making a scene.

"No, it's not. If it weren't for Faith McMann, I never would have found my daughter. I hope neither of you ever have to be put through something as horrible as having a child taken from you. It would serve you both well to mind your own business."

Corrie took Faith by the shoulders and steered her away from the awful women. She took her to a table in the far corner of the cafeteria and then brought her a mug of hot coffee. She sat down across from Faith and told her, "Don't fret about a word they said. They're probably worried about their own sick or injured family members and taking it out on you."

"You're probably right. Thanks."

"Not a problem. If I had a nickel for every horrible thing someone said to me when Samantha was missing, I would be a rich woman."

"How's Samantha doing?"

"She's pretty messed up, actually." Corrie stirred cream and sugar into her cup, took a long swallow, and said, "But her doctor told me this morning that she'll be coming home soon." She looked heavenward. "It's not going to be easy, but nothing worth fighting for ever is."

Faith nodded in understanding.

"What's your next step?" Corrie asked.

Faith checked her phone again, then let out a long, ponderous sigh.

"What is it?"

"There's this woman. She called my mother before Mom was attacked, said she wanted to talk to me about my kids, but then she disconnected the call. I've called her at least a half-dozen times, but she won't return my calls."

"Do you know where she lives?"

"Orlando, Florida." Faith's brow furrowed. "What am I waiting for? If she won't answer her phone, then fuck it. I'll go knock on her damn door."

Corrie had pulled out her cell phone and was quick with her thumbs, tapping away. "If you hurry," Corrie said, "you can make the next flight out of Sacramento and get to Florida before dinnertime."

Faith jumped to her feet, then leaned over and hugged Corrie. "Thank you," Faith said as she pulled away. Their gazes met, and Faith thought there was something comforting about looking into the eyes of someone like Corrie, someone who knew what she was going through and maybe even knew what she was feeling: anguish, heartache, hopelessness, and hope all rolled into one.

"Good luck," Corrie called out as Faith walked away.

THIRTY-TWO

A storm brewed overhead as Miranda took a good, long look at the house at the top of the hill in Oakland, California. Gusts of wind made the long, skinny trunks and wide leaves of the palms lining the driveway sway to and fro.

Jack Byron, the man who'd paid Mother to have his way with her, lived in that house.

She'd always known she and the ugly old man would meet again; she just never thought it would happen so soon. But luck had been on her side the day she and Faith had driven to San Francisco. When Faith went to get her car, Miranda told her she needed to go to the bathroom. Instead she'd run as fast as she could back to where Cecelia Doyle had been shot down, and she'd taken the woman's wallet and cell phone. Sirens had wailed in the distance, but she'd gotten away before they arrived.

Spending time with Little Vinnie, Beast, and Rage had worked out well, too. Beast had allowed her to look over his shoulder as he used the Internet to find all sorts of information about random people. Since Miranda didn't know much about technology, she'd asked a lot of questions, including how to unlock an iPhone. A four-digit code was all she needed. Thankfully, Cecelia Doyle ended up being an easy nut to crack. It took only three tries to guess the passcode: *1-2-3-4*.

Breaking into the phone turned out to be the easy part. Looking through Cecelia's contact list took much longer. But Miranda kept at it, and right there on the calendar, on the exact date Miranda was repeatedly raped, was the name Smith/S. F. and a phone number. She'd given the number to Beast and asked him if one of his fancy Internet search engines, or whatever they were called, could figure out who the number belonged to. It had worked! Beast had pulled up an address and photos of a man named Jack Byron.

One look at his photo was all it had taken for Miranda to see that Jack Byron was the same man who had raped and sodomized her.

A part of her had wanted to stay in Roseville. Spending time with Little Vinnie, Beast, and Rage had had been cool, no doubt about it. Rage had taught Miranda how to use the Internet and YouTube, all the things she hadn't been able to do while she was hidden away at the farmhouse. What Miranda hadn't enjoyed was seeing how sick Rage was. Rage hardly ate. She pretended to, but when Little Vinnie and Beast were out of the room, she dumped her meals down the disposal.

Miranda liked Rage. She was caring and thoughtful. From little bits Faith had told her, she knew Rage had had a tough childhood. She'd hit bottom when she was forced to give up her little boy, Christopher. It sucked that the adoption agency wouldn't make an exception and tell her where her son was.

Recently Miranda had read a quote about suffering and how one's suffering could help to reveal one's true self. It was an interesting idea. It made sense that without suffering it might be difficult for some to see the true glory of a rising sun or imagine the struggles of a single blade of grass as it pushed its way through the soil.

Miranda had no idea why some people were meant to suffer more than others.

It was what it was.

And all that mattered in this moment was that Miranda's suffering had brought her here to Oakland where the ugly old man named Jack lived.

She sighed.

It was time to give the old man a taste of his own medicine, show him what it felt like to have no control over his body or situation.

After using black spray paint to cover the lens of the outside camera by the front gate, Miranda climbed over the iron fence and walked up the long drive, careful to stay low. As she approached the side yard, she could see amazing views of the Bay Area, bridges, and San Francisco. It was a nice place. The pervert didn't deserve to live here.

A gust of wind chilled her to the bone. Miranda pulled the blue knit cap lower over her ears. A bolt of lightning struck close by and lit the place up.

Startled, she took a second to calm her nerves. She'd never broken into a house before, but once again the Internet had come in handy. She'd borrowed a tension wrench from Beast's vast collection of tools and then watched a couple of YouTube videos on how to use it to get inside a locked door.

Using an online real estate site had given her access to photos of the inside. The exterior was made up of mostly stone, surrounded by perfectly manicured landscaping. Her plan was to go in through a courtyard leading into one of the smaller rooms in the house.

She made it through the side gate without a problem. No barking dogs. No alarms, at least none she could hear. She was about to enter the courtyard, a ten-by-ten area surrounded by eight-foot walls of stone, but then she saw a shadowy figure through a window.

It was him.

Although the day was gloomy with dark clouds and random bursts of lightning, there was enough daylight to see his stringy gray hair from where she stood. He walked away, disappearing to the other side of the house. She tried the closest door, surprised when it opened. Quietly, she shut the door behind her, then stood there and listened.

She was standing in a room with cedar walls. There was a steam room to her left and stacks of plush white towels in a basket. She peeked out the door and into the hallway. Stone walls and hardwood floors. She took a step back, pulled out the Taser Faith had given her when they went to San Francisco, and readied it. Then she put on her gloves and mask and stepped out into the hallway. Time to say hello to Jack Byron.

THIRTY-THREE

Once Mom fell asleep, Jana walked out of the hospital room and into the hallway to check messages on her cell phone. As usual, Faith wasn't answering her phone and had yet to return her call.

What was she up to now? Jana wondered.

Feeling the need to stretch, Jana began her daily trek to the Family Birthing Center to look at all the babies. Her phone buzzed.

It was her friend Dee Dee.

Jana pushed the "Talk" button and said, "Hello."

"You owe me big-time," Dee Dee blurted. "I have news about the boy your friend gave up for adoption."

Chills raced up Jana's spine. "I can't believe it. This is wonderful news."

"Thanks to a connection I have with the National Adoption Center and due to your friend's illness, I was able to get some information. The boy's adoptive parents' surname is Fryer. And get this—they live less than an hour away in Placerville."

"This is amazing. You're amazing. What do we do next? Do you have a number where I can reach the Fryers?"

"No, but I was given an address. I don't know the couple's first names, either. You're going to have to visit them personally and then cross your fingers and hope they haven't moved."

"Wow, this is crazy. What if they refuse to talk to me?"

"That's a chance you're going to have to take. And I'm sorry, Jana, but you can't mention my name or say anything about how you found out where they lived."

"Of course. You have my word. I've never heard of you."

"Good luck."

"Thanks, Dee Dee. You've gone above and beyond the call of duty, and no matter what happens, I'll find a way to repay you."

"No need. I was kidding about you owing me anything. I'm happy to help. Any news about your niece and nephew?"

"No. Nothing. Dad and Colton are still in Mendocino. We haven't heard a word. Mom is doing better and should be released from the hospital in the next day or two. Who knows where Faith is. She's a wreck."

"Understandably so. I can't imagine anyone taking my children. I would go berserk. Literally."

Jana rubbed her belly. She felt suddenly sheepish for telling Faith to stop searching for her children. It had been a selfish thing for her to say.

"I have to go now," Dee Dee said, "but please let me know how everything goes. I hope the little boy's mom gets to meet him before it's too late."

"I hope so, too," Jana said. "I'll let you know. Thanks again."

———

It was after five, Eastern Daylight Time, by the time Faith disconnected her call to Mom, letting her know where she was, and parked across the street from the house on Ensenada Drive in Orlando, Florida. According to Beast, Robyn Price was divorced with two grown children who lived in another state. She worked full-time as a bank manager not too far from her home.

Faith saw the silhouette of a person moving about inside. She climbed out of the rental car and crossed the street. She'd worn comfortable clothes, jeans and a T-shirt, but now she wondered if it might have benefited her to wear something nicer, something more inviting since she had no idea who Robyn Price really was and who exactly she was dealing with.

As she came up the walkway and approached the front door, she heard music playing inside. Faith took a breath and then pushed the doorbell.

The music stopped, but no one came to the door.

Faith waited another minute before ringing the bell again. She saw the curtain move.

"Who is it?" a woman's voice asked from inside the house.

"It's Faith McMann. My mother told me you called. I've been trying to reach you for a while now."

There was a long stretch of silence before she said, "You shouldn't be here."

"I was told you might know something about the whereabouts of my children."

"Go away."

"I can't. I won't. I'll stand here all night if I have to. And I think you know—"

The door opened. The woman's face was thin and pale. She had a frantic look about her, contrasting greatly with the soothing music Faith had heard only a moment ago.

With jerky motions, Robyn Price waved Faith inside, then looked around outside before she shut and locked the door behind her. "Were you followed here?"

"I don't think so."

Robyn was a tiny thing, with a pointy nose and small, round eyes. She walked to the front window, took a peek through the blinds, then put a hand to her forehead as if that might help her think of what to do next.

Faith noticed more than one piece of luggage off to the side. On the coffee table was a purse, wallet, and passport.

"You should have told me you would be paying me a visit," Robyn scolded. "I never would have allowed you to come to the house."

"If you had returned my phone calls, I wouldn't have needed to come at all. You called me for a reason," Faith said. "Tell me what you know, and I'll leave."

Robyn did not look pleased. Her shoulders fell slightly before she motioned toward the living area and told Faith to have a seat.

The walls were beige and without decoration. There was a couch and a coffee table. Nothing more. The entire house was unembellished and sparsely furnished.

As instructed, Faith took a seat and then watched Robyn disappear. The woman was going on a trip. How long, she wondered, was Robyn going to be gone? She was scared, no doubt about it. But why?

There was a knock on the door just as Robyn returned to the room carrying a three-ring binder. She looked through the peephole, then opened the door and pointed to her suitcases and bags. Through the living room window, Faith watched the driver carry her luggage to the dark sedan parked at the curb.

Robyn brought the binder to Faith and handed it to her. "Here. It's your problem now."

"You're going on a trip and you're not coming back, are you?" Faith asked.

"No. I won't be coming back."

"Who are you afraid of?"

"Everyone." She rubbed her hands together nervously.

After the driver took a second load to the car, Robyn said, "I had a moment of weakness when I called you and talked to your mother. I've regretted it ever since."

Faith started to open the binder, but Robyn stopped her. "I'd rather you look through it later, after I'm gone. I suggest you view it in the privacy of your home."

"Why—what is this?"

"Its contents are the epitome of evil and everything that's wrong with the world. I didn't return your calls for many reasons, but mostly because I was afraid for my life." She stopped to ask the driver, who had just returned, if he would mind waiting for her in the car. He nodded, tipped his head, and quickly disappeared.

Robyn paced the living room as she talked. "I grew up with two brothers," she began. "Randy and Richard, opposites in every way. Randy was a troublemaker from the start, the sort of boy who pulled girls' hair and ripped the wings from butterflies. I'll spare you the worst of it, but it came as no surprise to anyone in the family when Randy got involved with drugs and trafficking. We just never thought in a million years he'd drag his brother down with him." She shook her head. "Richard did well in school and put himself through law school. He became a public defender and spent sixty hours a week fighting for the underdogs, people who worked hard but just needed a little help."

Having confirmation that Robyn Price's brothers might have something to do with her children's abduction caused Faith's pulse to race. But she remained still. She needed to stay calm and keep the woman talking. "Do you know who killed Richard?"

"Ah," she said. "So, you've heard of my brothers?"

"Richard's name has come up, yes. I'm sorry about his death."

"He doesn't deserve your sympathy or mine. You won't be sorry once you've had a chance to take a look through that binder you're holding." She put her passport inside her purse and then grabbed her coat. "I have to go. My phone's been disconnected, so there's no reason for you to try and reach me again."

Faith stood with the binder clutched tightly in her arms. "So why all the secrecy?"

Robyn paused for a moment before she turned back to face Faith. "Because if anyone ever finds out what my brother sent me, I'm as good as dead. Someday, somehow, they will find out. And when they do, they'll come after me. And now you."

"What about your other brother, Randy? Can't he protect you?"

She laughed. "Don't be ridiculous. He's the one I'm running from."

THIRTY-FOUR

Miranda walked into a home theater, where the old man was shoving a handful of popcorn into his big mouth. His expression hardly changed when he looked up at her. He was sitting in one of four leather recliners, wearing a robe and white socks.

She didn't want to give him time to grab a weapon, didn't know if he had access to a gun or knife, but she wasn't taking any chances. She walked straight up to him and Tasered his wrinkled chest, close to his throat.

His body jolted and convulsed.

Popcorn and drool slithered out the side of his mouth.

His bowl of popcorn jiggled in his arms, his legs straight as two-by-fours. Sadly, she didn't get any pleasure out of torturing him.

She'd expected to feel something. Anything.

Revenge, she realized, wasn't all it was made out to be. She'd been fantasizing about this for weeks.

As she watched him, disappointed that it had come to this, and knowing she needed to make sure he'd never hurt anyone again, she slid the strap of the bag she'd brought off her shoulder, unzipped it, and rifled through the contents until she found what she was looking for.

Her plan had been to drag him into his bedroom, that is, if he wasn't there already, and then do all sorts of ghastly things to him. But after getting no joy out of watching him quiver and drool, she realized she wouldn't be able to go through with it. Instead she stripped his robe and socks from his body and tossed them to the side. Next she pulled out the duct tape and began wrapping it around his chest and the leather recliner. She did the same with the bottoms of his legs, making sure he was spread-eagle.

While she waited for his breathing to normalize, she walked through the house. In the master bedroom, she found many more sex toys and disgusting gadgets than she'd expected to find. She carried a box filled with his playthings back to the TV room, where she'd left him.

It was a while before he found control of his voice and could talk, but once he got started, he wouldn't stop. "Who are you? Why are you here? What do you want from me?"

"Whoa. Whoa, old man. Slow down."

"Let me go right now, and I'll pay you. Name the price."

She took a seat on the edge of the couch and then leaned forward and dragged his disgusting box of toys closer. "I came here to kill you, but now I'm not so sure I can go through with it."

He released a sigh.

"I was going to spend hours giving you a taste of your own medicine," she told him. She rifled through the bag she'd brought with her and pulled out a string of firecrackers. "Guess where these were going to go?"

"You won't get away with this, you know? Breaking into my house and making threats."

"Maybe not," she said. "But then again, maybe so."

She reached into his box of toys, picked up a double dildo with sharp spikes on both ends, and held it up.

The ugly old fuck actually blushed.

"The women I see ask for those things. They beg for it."

She pulled out a metal rod. An image of him holding it in the hotel room flashed through her mind. He'd used this very item on her. She wanted to throw up.

"They love it," he said with delight. "Every minute of it."

One of the walls in the room, she noticed, was some sort of secret wall you might see in a movie. The wall had been opened, and inside were shelves filled with DVDs. She walked that way and ran her finger over row after row of plastic covers. On closer view she noticed that every DVD had a label with handwritten dates and places.

"Hotel Durant, May 26, 2012. Lafayette Park Hotel, February 2, 2014," she said aloud. "Renaissance in Walnut Creek, October 11, 2015." She continued on for a while until she came to a DVD labeled with the hotel in San Francisco on the exact date she'd been repeatedly raped by the fucker. She pulled it from the shelf and opened the casing, then took the DVD and slipped it into the DVD player. She found the remote and returned to her seat. Ignoring his pitiful pleas to let him go, she hit "Play."

The wireless surround-sound speakers made for incredible audio quality and intense listening, drowning out anything he had to say.

Back stiff, teeth clenched, she watched her worst nightmare being replayed on the big screen. The DVD was hours long. She lasted eighteen and a half minutes before she hit "Stop."

Back on her feet, she retrieved the DVD, slid it back into its case, and put it in her bag. Then she looked about the room, feeling confused and off balance. Watching what he'd done to her on the big-screen TV, seeing the blissful expression on his face, and hearing his cackles of glee changed everything.

She grabbed the string of firecrackers and walked toward him, wrapped them tight around his head and neck.

As he shouted obscenities and demanded she stop, she pulled another roll of firecrackers from her bag, bigger and better bangers than the first round, and wrapped them around his dick and testicles and the upper part of his scrawny legs to keep them in place. When ignited, they would explode in rapid sequence.

She worked quickly until she had only two explosive devices left in her bag. She placed the quarter stick in his mouth, taped it there, then shoved the M-80 with the long fuse right up his asshole. With the help of a little lubricant from his box of goodies, it was a tight fit, but it worked.

With her backpack on and the long-reach multipurpose lighter in her right hand, ready to go, she lit the quarter stick and the M-80 first since they had longer fuses; then she lit the two rolls of firecrackers and ran from the room. She'd gotten about halfway down the hallway when she heard endless rounds of pop, pop, pop, and then a loud crack followed by a deafening bang.

THIRTY-FIVE

After dropping off the rental car and being shuttled back to the terminal at Orlando International Airport, Faith went straight to her gate since she didn't have any bags to check. She was about to remove the binder from her oversize purse when something niggled at her—something about the expression on Robyn's face and the serious tone of her voice. The woman had packed up fast. In order to escape her own brother and the people he worked with, she'd felt the need to move away, certain they would find her eventually, and just as certain they would now go after Faith, too.

These people were ruthless.

Before raiding the farmhouse, a caller had warned Faith they would come after her and her family, and that's exactly what they were doing. Crashing right through her parents' sliding glass door was proof that they meant business.

Had they been watching her parents' house? Did they know Faith's mom had been the only one home? Maybe they didn't care either way. Whether the attack on her mom was to teach Faith a lesson for causing trouble or some other reason, she didn't know.

And at the moment, the reason wasn't important. She glanced at the clock. She had less than an hour before it would be time to board. She stood, looked around, then headed for the restroom.

She went to the last stall, sat on the toilet, pulled out the binder, and flipped it open. The first few pages were assorted newspaper clippings about the attack at Faith's house in Granite Bay on Rolling Greens Lane. There were many pictures of Lara and Hudson and many articles, mostly speculation about who might have taken them and why. There was a clipping from a journal in Auburn, California, that mentioned Faith's frustration with the police and how she'd let her anger get the best of her and ended up in jail. In one of the margins was a handwritten note about Faith doing everything she could to find her children.

When someone entered the stall next to hers, Faith stopped reading. She didn't breathe until that same person washed her hands and left the room.

She turned the page. There was a handwritten note signed by Richard.

Robyn, I'm sorry for all the pain I've caused you and the family. Too many innocent people have been harmed and or killed. And for what? In the end, I got everything I thought I wanted—flashy cars, a big house, beautiful women. And yet I never felt satisfied.

The reason I'm sending you the enclosed information is because I have a meeting with an important man tomorrow. My chances of getting out of this crazy business might be fifty-fifty. Not bad odds. In case anything happens to me, though, I wanted you to have this information because you're the only one I know who might be strong enough to do the right thing.

Every john, pimp, and trafficker I ever dealt with has been included within these pages, including nicknames, addresses, and phone numbers. You'll also see articles from the local papers about what happened to Faith McMann. The hard truth is I am personally responsible for what happened to her family. I was given false information that led my men to her door. Nobody was to be harmed, but as I'm sure you know by now, since the attack on her family has made international news, that wasn't the case.

Perhaps you'll decide to hand the enclosed binder over to the police or maybe find a way to contact Faith McMann and let her handle matters as she sees fit. In the end it's your call. Burn it all if that would make you happy.

All my love, Richard

Robyn was right. Faith felt no sympathy or pity for Richard, only contempt. He'd obviously gotten what he deserved. She looked at her phone. It was time to board. She would have to look at the rest later.

THIRTY-SIX

It took Jana forty-five minutes to get from Granite Bay to Placerville. She parked her car on the street since the driveway was covered with snow and she didn't have snow chains for her tires.

The house at the end of the driveway was made of rough logs and surrounded by tall redwoods. She didn't get out of the car right away. Her eye twitched as nerves got the better of her. What if the Fryers really did live in that house and they became angry after she told them why she was here?

She didn't like conflict, never had.

Too late now, she inwardly scolded. *That's a chance I'll have to take,* she thought as she climbed out of the car and headed down the driveway, sliding most of the way, unable to get a good foothold in the snow.

Knowing she might very well be Rage's best chance at meeting her son before she passed away pushed her onward. At the door, she straightened, then quickly knocked before she lost her nerve.

A sharp kick inside her belly and then another caught her off guard. She smiled as her gaze rested on her swollen stomach. Just as she put a hand on her belly, the door opened.

The man standing before her was tall and broad-shouldered. His dirty-blond hair was on the long side. His eyes were big and round and the color of melted chocolate. He looked from Jana's belly to her car parked on the road. "Having car problems?"

"No. No, nothing like that." Her face heated. "Are you Mr. Fryer?"

He angled his head. "Who wants to know?"

"I'm sorry, yes, my name is Jana Murray. We've never met, of course, but I have an extremely delicate matter I'd like to talk to you and your wife about. Is she here?"

A little boy walked up behind his father and grabbed hold of his leg, peeking out at her with curious grayish-blue eyes—Rage's eyes. Jana couldn't take her own eyes off him. He had a thick head of hair and a mischievous expression. And then the baby kicked again, and she put a hand to her belly and laughed. "That was a big one," she said.

"Come on in," Mr. Fryer said with a sigh. "It's cold out."

"Thank you."

He introduced Jana to his wife, Sue, who was just making her way to the front entry as he shut the door. "I'm Danny," he said, "and this little guy is Callan."

"Oh," Jana said. "What a lovely name."

"Jana is here to talk to us about a very delicate matter," he told Sue.

She raised both eyebrows. "Why don't we all take a seat in the living room?"

Jana followed the three of them into the main room. *Rage would like this place,* she thought. The inside was all stone, wood, cozy furniture, and fur rugs. The dining room table was made of pine, and the side tables were beautifully refinished wine barrels. There were shelves filled with books and toys in every corner. The place was warm and comfortable.

After Danny helped her with her coat, Jana took a seat on one of two leather seats facing the couch. Callan walked over to her and handed her a toy truck. "Thank you, Callan. Such a sweet boy," she said.

"Can I get you anything to drink?" Sue asked.

"No, thank you, I'm fine. To tell you the truth, this is much more difficult than I imagined it would be."

Danny was sitting across from her. He leaned forward and said, "Why don't you go ahead and tell us why you're here."

"Well," Jana began. "There's a woman. Her name is Rage." Jana inwardly scolded herself for not finding out Rage's real name. Jana raised the palm of her hand to the side of her head. "I'm feeling odd. Maybe I should come back another time?"

"Say it," Danny said, trying to help her along. "Whatever is on your mind. Just say it."

She checked to make sure Callan wouldn't overhear, and then she looked from Danny to Sue and said, "Callan's biological mother is dying. Brain cancer. She's been given six months to live, and that was a few months ago. She's not well." Tears streamed unexpectedly down both sides of her face.

Sue looked at her husband worriedly before she said, "I can't pretend I'm not more than a little stunned by the news. We were assured this was a closed adoption, and nobody would come out of the woodwork, so to speak. We haven't yet decided what to tell Callan. He's only two."

"I'm so sorry. I understand if you want me to leave," Jana said. "Especially considering I can't tell either of you the circumstances of how I found you."

Danny Fryer frowned as he rubbed his chin and then reached over and took his wife's hand in his.

The silence was deafening.

Jana stood and wiped her tears. "I'm really sorry. For everything." She couldn't stop the tears from rolling down her face. "Oh, for God's sakes, I don't know what's wrong with me."

"Don't leave," Sue said. "I'll be fine. Despite the whole closed adoption thing, we always wondered about Callan's mom."

Danny grabbed a box of tissues and handed the box to Jana.

"Probably hormones working overtime," Sue said referring to the tears. "I'm four months along. We were told we would never have children of our own, but we've been blessed with a miracle." She looked at Callan. "Two miracles."

"That's wonderful. I'm so happy for you both." Jana couldn't stop sobbing if she wanted to.

Sue straightened. "You and this woman must be very close."

"I've only known Rage for a short time, but she's smart and sweet and very caring and loving. Her only wish before she leaves this earth is to meet her son. She gave him up because she wanted him to have the best chance at a decent life, and it's so clear to me at this moment that that's exactly what she's given him." Jana looked over at Callan and smiled at him. "The best sort of life."

Callan came up to her and rested his cheek against her leg. "Oh, my. You are so, so sweet. I hope my baby is just like you, Callan."

Danny narrowed his eyes. "Umm, so, her name is Rage?"

"Well, no, not exactly. It's a nickname she was given. It's sort of a long story."

"It's OK," Danny said. "We've got time."

"Well, I met her through my sister, Faith McMann."

"The same Faith McMann we've been seeing in the news?" Danny asked.

Jana nodded.

"I'm so sorry," Sue offered. "Not that she's your sister, of course, but you know, because of everything that's happened. Oh, my gosh, I don't know what I would do in her place." She was crying now, too.

Danny stood and transferred the box of tissue from Jana to his wife.

"I'm sorry," Sue said to her husband.

"Don't be. This is therapeutic for both of you, I'm sure," he said. "Nothing better than a good cry fest between two pregnant women."

Sue and Jana looked at each other and then began laughing instead.

Danny rolled his eyes. "So, about her name—Rage—you were saying?"

Jana got control of herself and said, "Yes, my sister, as you might have read about in the papers or seen in the news, got a little frustrated with the police and ended up in jail. The judge let her out under his orders that she would attend anger management classes. That's where she met Rage. Everyone is forced to pick a nickname because, well, I guess nobody wants to tell their stories unless it's all sort of anonymous."

"What's your sister's nickname?" Danny asked.

"Furious."

"Of course," Sue said. "That makes perfect sense. I think my name would have been Maniac."

"Or Crazy Lady," Danny offered and seemed to instantly regret it when Sue gave him the eye. "I was kidding. Just a joke," he said. "A very bad joke."

"Is Rage in the hospital?" Sue asked.

"No. She's hanging in there."

"I'm going to go out on a limb and speak for my wife, too, when I say we're not ready to make any sort of decision at this point, but what exactly did you have in mind?"

"I was hoping for a quick meeting, maybe somewhere public. I don't know, a park or one of those fun houses for kids where they serve pizza? But anything you decide would work. It's your decision."

"I'll tell you what," Danny said. "Leave us your name and number, and then Sue and I will discuss this and get back to you. Fair enough?"

"Fair enough," Jana said. "And don't worry," she said as he helped her with her coat. "If I don't hear from you, I won't be back. Nobody else knows where you live. Your secret is safe with me." Jana then bent as low as she could and said goodbye to Callan. He ran into her arms and hugged her as if they had known each other his entire life. She hugged Sue next, their bellies touching as she wished her well.

THIRTY-SEVEN

It was past eight by the time Faith got back to the Sacramento airport. She only had to wait a minute for the shuttle to pick her up and take her to the parking lot. She took a seat close to the driver. There were three other people on the shuttle by the time the doors closed. Two men and a woman. One of the men had hooded eyes and kept looking her way.

Faith pulled out her phone, turned it on, and listened to multiple messages. There was one from Rage telling her Miranda had left the house. They had spent hours looking for her, but no luck so far.

There were two messages from Jana asking Faith to call her as soon as possible. The last call from Jana was from hours ago. Faith would call her back as soon as she was inside her car. The shuttle stopped. One of the men got out. The man with hooded eyes read through some papers while the woman sat quietly staring out into the darkness.

Faith got off at the next stop. When the other two people climbed out of the shuttle after her, she thought about jumping back on and driving around for a bit, but she was tired and ready to get home. It made sense to be cautious, but she also needed to be reasonable. As she walked, she slipped her hand into her purse and pulled out her keys and a ball-point pen, since she wasn't allowed to fly with pepper spray or a Taser.

The clip-clop of heavy shoes sounded directly behind her. She kept walking, relieved to see her car up ahead. When the footsteps grew louder, she whipped about, keys jangling, pen ready. The man jumped back and then took a wide path around her.

She watched him weave through a row of cars and disappear before she hit the "Unlock" button to her car. At the same moment she opened the door, she felt a hard object jam up against the middle of her back.

"Give me your bag."

"Are you kidding me?" Faith whipped about, surprised to see the woman who'd been on the shuttle. Even more surprised to see that she was holding a gun.

Faith jabbed the pen into the side of the woman's face and then kicked her hard in the leg. The pen hardly made a dent.

The woman lunged for Faith and took her to the ground.

Faith's head hit hard.

They rolled around on the pavement, loose gravel cutting into her skin. Faith managed to grasp the woman's wrist, struggling to keep her from aiming the gun at her. It took all her strength to keep her attacker from getting a shot off.

A searing pain shot up Faith's arm. It was a losing battle. She couldn't hold her for much longer. The woman must have sensed Faith's weakness because suddenly she jerked her body, easily removing Faith's hold on her wrist. The woman was fast, and in the blink of an eye she was on top of Faith, the full weight of her body on Faith's stomach, making it difficult for Faith to breathe. Her knees kept Faith's arms pinned to the ground as she placed the barrel of the gun to Faith's forehead.

Faith tried to buck her off, but she had nothing left. She was going to die.

Wham!

The woman fell to Faith's side in a dead heap. Faith sucked air into her lungs as soon as the weight was lifted from her chest. Once she caught her breath, she found herself looking up into the hooded eyes of the same man who'd ridden on the shuttle. He was talking on the phone, his voice panicked. There was a bat tucked under his arm. He ended the call and then slid his phone into his pocket. "I called nine-one-one. Are you OK?"

She nodded as she pushed herself to one knee and finally to her feet. She saw the gun on the pavement and went over to pick it up. When she turned to face the man, her gaze settled on his bat.

"Softball," he explained. "I've been playing for years. In fact, I just returned from participating in a winter league in Florida."

Her legs wobbled. He stepped forward and reached for her elbow. "You don't seem well. Maybe you should take a seat until someone gets here."

She steadied herself. "I'll be fine." She put a hand to her head, where she could feel something wet. She was bleeding.

The guy with the bat got on a knee and felt for the woman's pulse. "Is she dead?"

"No," he said, on his feet again. "She's breathing."

Faith was relieved to hear sirens in the distance. Her gaze settled on the woman. Who was she? Faith knelt down next to her and began searching through her pockets. Faith found an envelope and handed it to the man standing there as she continued her search.

"There's five thousand dollars inside!" He dropped the envelope as if it were on fire.

Next Faith retrieved a round disc of cardboard from the women's coat pocket and pulled it out. It looked like a coaster. It was made to look like a bowling ball with the name of a bowling alley in Rocklin. She turned it over and saw a number. It was her flight number.

She shoved the coaster and the envelope back into the woman's pocket and zipped it up. She pushed herself to her feet again just as the swirling red lights of a police cruiser showed up.

In that moment, she thought of Robyn Price and wondered if the woman had gotten out of the country before it was too late.

Dillon Yuhasz had just gotten to sleep when he got the call that Faith McMann had been attacked in the parking lot at the SFO airport.

He ran out of the house and hopped in the car, wondering why he even bothered trying to get some shut-eye. He'd started his day off with the mayor of Sacramento being burglarized, followed by countless interviews of suspects and witnesses. Then the FBI had notified him that they had located Diane Weaver's brother, found him and his wife dead in a trailer home. Agent Burnett also told him they'd found evidence that Lara McMann had been living in the trailer at one time. Unfortunately, neither Diane Weaver nor Lara McMann had been found. And what about Faith's father and brother? Nobody at the Mendocino sheriff's office had gotten back to him.

At least his daughter Holly was safe. It was something.

As he zipped along the highway, lights flashing, his phone buzzed.

It was Holly. Why would she be calling him in the middle of the night?

He hit the "Talk" button on the console.

"Dad. It's me."

"What's going on? Are you all right?"

"I'm scared."

His stomach dropped. "Where's my brother? What's going on?"

"He's in San Diego. I returned home this morning."

"What the hell for? Where are the kids?"

"They're still with Uncle Bob. I'm sorry." She was crying. "David promised he would get help."

Shit. And she'd believed him. "Did that bastard hurt you?"

She was crying harder now. He could hear her sobbing and trying to catch her breath.

"Christ." He pulled the car to the side of the road. "Speak to me, Holly. Tell me what's going on. Where is David?"

"We got in a fight. Worse than usual. I fought back. He left, but he'll be back."

He could hardly make out what she was saying between the sobs.

"I'm sorry, Dad. I'm so sorry."

"I'm on my way, Holly, but I want you to get out of there now."

"He has the keys to my car."

"Then go to the neighbors until I arrive."

"OK," she said, her voice shaky. "I—I'll do that. I'll go to the—"

The call was disconnected.

Something was off.

The tone of her voice.

Her reluctance to leave the house.

The call being disconnected midsentence.

He didn't like where his thoughts were headed.

He called the station, asked for Jeffrey, and then told him what was going on. He knew they were short on men, especially at this hour, but he needed backup. He asked Jeffrey to let Detective O'Sullivan know he'd be on his own at the airport. He also told Jeffrey not to use sirens when he approached his daughter's house.

If his hunch was right, he didn't have a lot of time. He needed to hurry.

As soon as there was a lull in traffic, he climbed out of his car and rushed to the back, where he rifled through the trunk until he found what he was looking for. Back in the driver's seat, he used the navigator to help him find the quickest route to Holly's home in Folsom. He turned on the emergency lights and then merged onto the highway.

His thoughts were all over the place.

He loved his daughter and would do anything to protect her. But at the moment he couldn't help but wonder how she felt about him. They had drifted apart over the years. Deep down, he'd always blamed his ex for destroying his relationship with his daughter. But now he realized he was the one to blame. He never should have allowed Holly to push him away. He should have realized soon after she married David that something wasn't right.

The question now was did she really love her husband, or was every decision she made based off fear?

It took him twelve minutes to get to Holly's street. Once he turned on to Finchley, he gave Jeffrey another call.

"I'll be there in five," Jeffrey said, reading his mind.

Yuhasz pulled his car into the driveway next to his daughter's Honda Civic. "OK," he told Jeffrey. "I'm going in."

"Hold off for another minute just to be sure."

"If I'm right about this, I don't want to risk having your car show up and scaring anyone off. I'll see you in a few. And, Jeffrey," Yuhasz quickly added, "thanks for everything." He hung up before his friend could protest further.

He climbed out of his vehicle, slammed the door shut, and took a look around the neighborhood. Had Holly taken his advice and gone to the neighbors? Or were his instincts right on, and she was inside waiting for him?

He gave her a call. No answer.

From where he stood, nothing appeared out of the ordinary. The neighbors' lights were off. He walked across the stone path to the front door and turned the knob. Locked. The curtains were pulled tight, making it impossible to see inside. No shadowy figures running around.

He rang the bell, then rapped his knuckles hard against the door. About to head around the side of the house to find a way inside, as an afterthought he checked under the doormat, not too surprised to find a key. He opened the door and called his daughter's name. No answer.

"Holly," he said again. "It's me, Dad. Where are you?"

What sounded like a muffled voice coming from upstairs drew him that way. He took the carpeted stairs, one at a time. Just as it was the last time he was here, the place was immaculate. With two kids, there should be a few scuff marks, maybe a stain on the carpet or a couple of toys strewn about.

At the top of the landing, he stopped and listened.

First room to the right, the door was wide-open. He walked that way, stepped inside, and took a look around. The room obviously belonged to his granddaughter. All the bedding and window coverings were pink with satin bows. The bed was perfectly made. Hardly anything on the dresser. A stuffed animal sat on a rocking chair. Sadly, nothing about the house looked lived in. As far as Yuhasz was concerned, it was one more sign of a control freak demanding that everything be in perfect order at all times. Anger got the best of him as he exited the room and headed straight for the double doors at the end of the hallway. If that bastard had laid one finger on his daughter, if one hair on her head—

Both doors swung open.

"Run!" his daughter screamed.

Hofberg stood directly in front of him, his feet shoulder-width apart, knees bent, leaning slightly forward, firmly balanced and determined to hit his target.

Two shots were fired in rapid succession.

The first bullet struck Yuhasz center mass, slamming into him with as much power as Babe Ruth swinging and hitting a home run. The second shot stung like a son of a bitch. Blood splattered against the walls and speckled the perfectly white carpet, but he was still standing.

Hofberg was coming for him, eager to finish him off.

Yuhasz reached for his gun. His instincts had been right. But he'd blown it. By allowing his anger to get the best of him, he'd let his guard down just long enough to give the bastard the upper hand. His arm was deadweight, his fingers numb as he tried to grip the pistol and get off a shot. "Get down!" he shouted to his daughter when she appeared in the doorway behind Hofberg. She didn't have to be told twice. She dove out of the way, and Yuhasz fired.

The next time Yuhasz opened his eyes, he was inside an ambulance, wearing an oxygen mask, and peering up into his daughter's face. She squeezed his good hand.

Yuhasz had a quick hand. Although he hadn't counted on Hofberg getting off two shots, let alone one, he'd had the good sense to put on a vest. But even that move hadn't prevented the bastard from clipping him in the shoulder. He didn't have to be told to know that he'd lost a lot of blood, which explained the numbness he'd felt before he passed out. He couldn't remember whether or not he'd hit his target.

"Dad. I'm so sorry."

"Hofberg?" he asked, his voice gravelly.

She swallowed. "He's dead."

Butterfly stitches held together a gash on her left cheek and another cut above her right eye. There were bruises on her neck, bruises in the shape of the asshole's thumbprints.

"He made me call you," she said. "I didn't want to."

"I knew something wasn't right. The tone of your voice—the hesitation—I thought you might be trying to warn me."

She couldn't stop the tears. Her head fell forward. "You could have been killed. I'm so sorry, Dad."

"Not your fault," he said. "It was mine, all mine."

The paramedic sitting next to Holly checked his IV. "The bulletproof vest was a good call," he told Yuhasz. "You did take a hit to your shoulder, though, barely missing your subclavian artery. From what I'm hearing, your friend Jeffrey called for an ambulance before a shot was even fired. We got there a few seconds after you went down. You're a lucky man."

Yuhasz looked at his daughter. "Yes, I am." And then he closed his eyes and let the pain medication take care of the rest.

THIRTY-EIGHT

Reports were filled out, and the woman who had attacked Faith was examined by EMS, then handcuffed and taken to jail. Faith thanked the Good Samaritan with the bat for everything he'd done, including risking his own life, and then she drove straight to Sutter Medical Center.

Jana saw her in the hallway and frantically waved her arms as she rushed to meet her. "Mom filled me in. How did it go?"

As soon as Jana saw all the scratches on Faith's face and hands, she went a little crazy. "Oh, my God, what happened to you?"

"I'll tell you all about it later. What's going on? Is Mom all right?"

"She's doing fine. What I have to tell you isn't about Mom." Jana reached into her purse and handed Faith a picture she'd drawn. It was a little boy with a mop of brown hair. It was hard to tell if this was someone she was supposed to recognize. Faith looked at her sister. "Who is this?"

"His name is Callan."

Faith thought about it for a moment and then shook her head. The name meant nothing to her. Her sister had always had a talent for sketching, and as Faith continued to stare at the picture, it dawned on her who the boy might be. "Is this Rage's son?"

Eyes bright, Jana nodded proudly.

"Did you meet him?"

More nodding.

"How did you do it? How did you find him?" Beast and his dad were bounty hunters, and yet they'd had absolutely no luck when it came to locating the child.

"The friend I told you about, the woman who was adopted, was able to help me. But I'm not allowed to ever mention her name or how we got the information."

Faith nodded in understanding. She thought of Rage and how happy she would be to finally see her son. "Have you told Rage the good news?"

Jana shook her head. "Not yet. Callan's parents haven't decided what they're going to do. They have my name and number. They know all about you and how you met Rage. You would love them, Faith. Rage would love them. No matter what happens, Callan is in good hands."

Faith took Jana's hands in hers. "This is great news. You did good." Faith gestured toward Mom's room down the hallway. "Is Mom awake?"

"Yeah, she's doing well. One more question, though, before you head that way."

Faith waited.

"Do you know Rage's real name?"

"Sally," she said with a smile.

"Really? And what about Beast?"

"Charlie."

"Hmm. Never would have guessed. Charlie and Sally."

"Last names?" Jane asked.

"No idea." Faith looked at her sister. "Are you coming with me?"

"Nah. I'm going to go home to my husband for a while and maybe get a few hours of sleep. It's been a crazy day."

Yeah, she could say that again. As Faith watched her sister walk away, she hugged her bag close to her body, felt the hard corners of the binder inside. She still hadn't had a chance to look at all its contents.

After being attacked in the parking lot, she didn't feel safe looking at it in her car. She needed to check on Mom and then find a place to make copies of everything in the binder. She would have told Yuhasz about her meeting with Robyn Price, but he never showed up at the airport, and she didn't trust anyone else.

———

Early the next morning Faith knocked on the door of the house in Roseville where Beast, Rage, and Little Vinnie lived. She didn't have to wait long for Little Vinnie to open the door. Inside, she saw Beast and Rage sitting at the kitchen table eating breakfast. It was good to see all three of them. It felt as if she hadn't seen them in weeks, but it had been only a couple of days since the shooting incident at their last anger management class.

Faith was dying to blurt out to Rage that Jana had located her son, but for now she needed to keep her word and keep the news to herself. Rage looked frail. In such a short time she'd managed to lose a few more pounds. Despite the weight loss, her eyes seemed bright and her mood cheery.

Little Vinnie told Faith to take a seat at the table. He then set a plate of sausages and scrambled eggs in front of her before he joined them.

"So what's with all the scrapes and bruises?" Rage asked her.

"I went to Florida yesterday to visit Robyn Price." Since Rage was the one who had located the woman, they all knew who Robyn was, saving Faith from having to go into a lot of detail.

"You never should have gone alone," Beast said.

"You're right. It was a spur-of-the-moment idea."

He grunted.

"What was she like?" Rage asked. "Did she tell you why she didn't return your calls?"

"Robyn was extremely paranoid," Faith said. "Afraid of her own shadow. In fact, she was packed and ready to leave the country."

"Forever?" Rage asked.

Faith nodded. "She was scared out of her wits." Faith reached into her bag, pulled out the three-ring binder, and set it on the table. "Before Robyn left, she handed me this and said it was my problem now." Faith reached into her bag again and pulled out stacks of bound paper, which she handed to each of them. "I made copies for all of you."

Beast took his plate to the sink in the kitchen. "So what did Robyn have to say?"

"In summary, she grew up with two brothers, Richard and Randy. According to Robyn, Randy was bad news and Richard was his brother's opposite. It took some time, but eventually Randy pulled Richard into the trafficking business. Five years later, Richard found himself in way over his head." She stopped, swallowed, her voice pained. "Richard Price was the one who ordered his men to go to my house in Granite Bay to find the money that Joe Henderson said was hidden there."

"Who killed Richard?" Beast asked. "Did she say?"

She pointed to the stack of papers she'd given him. "There's a letter from Richard to Robyn included. If we believe what he's written, he wanted out of the business, but the boss didn't like it and most likely had him killed."

"But first he sent this information to his sister?" Rage asked. "Why would he do that? Why not send it to the police or the FBI?"

"I'm not sure, but after talking to Robyn, I think he must have thought he truly had a chance of getting out of the business. If he did get out alive, maybe he figured he could move on with his life and nobody would be the wiser. On the other hand, if he was killed, he wanted someone to know what happened. That someone ended up being Robyn."

Little Vinnie held up his copy of the files. "If Robyn was leaving the country and hadn't returned your calls, what was she planning to do with all this?"

"She said she contacted me during a moment of weakness. She wanted to do the right thing, but in the end she was too frightened to do anything. She's afraid her own brother is after her."

"I can understand why," Rage said as she jabbed a finger at the page she had turned to. "Randy Price," she read aloud. "Fifty-two years old. It says here that he was a sex-trafficking recruiter, drug dealer, and has participated in seven murders, money laundering, and extortion. Looks like he owns two properties. One in Sacramento and another in San Diego."

They took turns reading about one criminal after another.

"This is a gold mine," Little Vinnie said.

Beast nodded in agreement as he flipped through the pages.

The binder included names of johns, pimps, and what appeared to be some of the top bosses in the area.

"Do you have any idea what we have here?" Rage asked.

Faith was excited and yet worried, too. "The bad news is that someone in that list of names you have in front of you knows I went to Florida to see Robyn."

Beast groaned. "Which explains the bruises and cuts," he said.

"Who did that to you?" Rage asked.

"I was attacked in the airport parking lot before I could climb into my car. If not for a Good Samaritan, I wouldn't be here talking to you right now."

"Did your attacker get away?" Little Vinnie asked.

"No. She was arrested and taken away in the back of a cruiser. Before the police arrived I patted her down and found an envelope containing five thousand dollars and a coaster from a bowling alley in Rocklin with my flight number scrawled on the back. That's all she carried. No purse or wallet. No ID at all. My guess is she's a hired assassin."

"So it looks as if Robyn Price had good reason to be worried."

"Yeah," Faith said, "I would have to agree."

Since no one was eating, Little Vinnie stood and cleared the table. When he returned, he dropped a newspaper in front of Faith. "I realized we have a lot going on here, but I thought you might be interested to see this."

Faith looked at the paper. The headline read:

COMPUTER SYSTEMS ANALYST JACK BYRON FOUND DEAD IN OAKLAND HOME

Faith skimmed through the article. Someone had broken into the man's house. He'd been tied down and wrapped in explosives. Investigators found dozens of DVDs containing hours of various sexual acts performed by Jack Byron. Apparently he liked to pay for luxury suites in expensive hotels and then hire young girls and boys to help him play out his sick fantasies, something he wouldn't be doing any longer.

Faith looked from Rage to Beast. "Any proof she had anything to do with this?"

Beast nodded. "I'm the one who looked up the number. She did the rest. The history on my computer had it all—directions to his house in Oakland, how to find explosive devices, et cetera. I got rid of it all."

"Maybe she'll be able to find some peace now," Little Vinnie said.

"Maybe," Faith said, "although I feel as if I let her down. What if this is just the beginning? What if she goes after other men who took advantage of her?"

"I don't think she will," Rage said. "She's no killer. As far as I'm concerned, she saved future kids from becoming his victims."

"Maybe she'll come back when she's ready," Little Vinnie added. "She knows we care, and I think she knows we would welcome her back with open arms."

THIRTY-NINE

After blowing up the motherfucker and walking away, Miranda had hitchhiked her way back to Sacramento. Last night she'd slept inside the lobby of one of the shelters where she and her mom used to sometimes stay. Although she'd tried to stay off the main roads, she knew she couldn't hide forever. If the cops determined she was the one who had killed the sadistic rapist, she would be taken in, maybe locked up for the rest of her life. All in all, she didn't really care. She'd done what she felt she had to.

She wanted nothing more than to destroy the DVD she'd taken, break it into a million pieces and drop it into a dumpster, but it might be her only proof that she'd had her reasons for doing what she'd done, so she would keep it for now.

She'd spent the entire day looking for one of her mom's old friends. At the moment she was walking along the bank of the American River. It was dark, and she should be frightened, but she wasn't. This was the only home she really knew. Her mom's old friend Calvin used to spend a lot of time by the river. She wanted to ask him if he knew where her mother's body had been buried. It was time to say goodbye before she moved on.

She wasn't sure where she would go or what she would do, but she couldn't stick around here. Too many memories, good and bad.

She walked for nearly a mile before she found a group of people huddled around a campfire. She told them she was looking for any-one who knew Grace Calloway. Calvin wasn't among the small group of people huddled there, but one of the women pointed a finger at Miranda and said, "Rita Calloway! Is that you?"

Miranda hardly recognized the woman, but she hugged her all the same, then plopped down and took a seat on the ground next to her. It turned out another woman in the group remembered her mother, too. For the next hour she listened to stories about Grace Calloway and a little girl named Rita who, in her mind, had died a long time ago.

The women talked about how they all dreamed about starting a housecleaning business together, but then they would argue about who would clean the toilets, and that would be another dream of theirs shot right down the drain. And then they would laugh, a throaty laughter that made Miranda laugh, too. Neither of the women liked to talk about the time spent with Grace after her daughter disappeared, and Miranda was glad for it. She much preferred listening to their attempts to dress up and go job hunting. They said Grace was the one who always landed the jobs. And every payday, she would cash her check and divvy up her money as if they'd all worked their tails off every week.

As the people in the circle began to drift off, Miranda asked them if they knew where Grace had been buried. Surprisingly, it was an old man who had been quietly listening who had the answer to that. He said Calvin and others had signed a piece of paper saying that Grace Calloway had wanted her body to be donated for medical research. The women nodded their heads as if that made perfect sense.

Miranda thanked everyone still awake before she headed off, despite their pleas for her to stay, where she would be safe for the night.

Hudson and Joey had been walking in circles. Hudson didn't know how it had happened, but it was suddenly clear he'd lost all sense of direction. All confidence had left him, and he found himself questioning every step he took because every step in the wrong direction meant two steps back to rectify.

Twice he and Joey had headed down the mountain toward the river, and twice they'd found themselves back in the middle of tall trees and moss-covered rocks, basically nowhere. The corn nuts and sunflower seeds were long gone. All that was left was one strip of jerky and maybe four ounces of water. They were both covered with bug bites, and their legs were sore. Hudson's thoughts centered on finding food and water instead of on being reunited with his family. He was losing hope.

The worst part was that Joey wasn't getting any better. He was growing weaker by the moment, and for that reason, Hudson knew it was time to stop walking and set up camp. Once he had a warm place for Joey to get comfortable, he could take Derek's rifle and go hunting, maybe find the river or a small creek and bring water back to Joey.

He set up the tent first, then laid down a wool blanket and the warm sleeping bag inside. He helped Joey over to the tent and had to force him to climb inside and lie down.

"Don't leave me," Joey said. "I can still walk. I'll pick up the pace. I can do this."

"I know you can. It's my fault we haven't found our way to the bottom. I screwed up. I just need you to keep out of the cold for a few hours while I do some hunting, maybe find a deer, anything. Without food and water, we'll never make it."

"I'm sorry I killed him," Joey said. "I saw the look on your face. I didn't want to do it, but he was suffering. It might have taken him days to sit there and die."

Hudson closed his eyes for a moment. "He was dying. You did the right thing." Hudson didn't really know if that was true or not, but telling Joey his thoughts on the matter wouldn't help them get off this mountain, so he left it at that.

"Do you think we're going to make it?"

For days now Hudson had been trying to keep spirits up, telling Joey stories about the times he'd spent hiking and camping with his dad, uncle, and grandfather. But his thoughts had grown fuzzy, and he found himself wondering if any of those stories were even true. Maybe they were dreams, figments of his imagination. He didn't know.

"It's OK," Joey said, breaking him from a trance. "You've done everything you could. You've kept us both alive this long. I've never known anyone in my life who I considered a friend before, but you're a good guy, Hudson. And no matter what happens I want you to know I consider you to be a friend."

A bolt of lightning lit up the sky, and for a split second he saw a bit of hope in Joey's eyes. He didn't want to let him down. They'd come so far. "I'm not giving up," he told Joey. "I'm going to find us something to eat if it's the last thing I do." And then he set off into the night, one foot in front of the other, reinvigorated and more determined than ever to persevere.

———

Faith stretched her arms behind her head and yawned. She and Beast hadn't moved from the kitchen table since breakfast. It would be dinnertime soon. They had been typing names from the list in the binder into databases, trying to put faces with the names.

Little Vinnie was asleep on the couch. His head had fallen backward onto the cushion full-tilt, his mouth wide-open, his snores a long, rumbling sound followed by a little gasp. Rage was asleep, too, her body stretched out next to Little Vinnie on the couch.

"There can't possibly be too many names in the trafficking business, at least in the Sacramento area, that were left off his list," Beast said. "I wonder if the higher-ups had any idea what he was up to."

She shook her head. "I think they killed him because he wanted out. If they had any idea he'd compiled all these names," she said, sweeping her hands over the stacks of paper, "don't you think they would have somehow tracked his sister down long before this?" Faith sighed and then looked Beast in the eyes. "Everything up until today seemed so damn nebulous." She held up one of the lists, overwhelmed by what she had right in front of her—a gold mine of information. Fear mixed with excitement had been bubbling inside her all morning. "Do you realize that for the first time since Craig was killed and my children were taken I have something concrete?" She gestured toward the computer screen, where Beast had pulled up a mug shot of Randy Price. "Look at him." She pointed a finger at his picture. "He looks like a regular guy. Clean-cut and wearing a suit and tie. He could be a banker, a dentist, or a systems analyst, for God's sake." She stabbed her finger at his résumé. "But he's not. According to his brother, it says here he spent years as a drug runner, smuggling cocaine into the United States. He's killed and kidnapped, and now he's in charge of recruiting others to find vulnerable girls for the sex-trafficking trade."

"Take a breath," Beast said.

"I'll never forget Randy Price's face after today." She did as Beast said and took a moment to try to settle down, which was downright impossible. "I'm just glad I no longer have to walk around looking at every stranger, wondering if he's a friend or foe."

"The list is long, Faith. It'll take some time to get through all the names."

"That's fine with me. I'm going to memorize every face here and remember everything about these people until I know exactly who I'm dealing with."

"And then what?"

"And then I pay each and every one of them a visit."

"What about the FBI and the police?"

"I'm going to talk to Detective Yuhasz, but take a harder look at this list of johns." She grabbed a paper from the corner of the table and handed it to Beast. "We've got politicians and businessmen, people with money. As soon as one of these men gets wind of this, there's no doubt in my mind he'll find a way to put a stop to the investigation."

She paused for a minute before adding, "I won't let that happen. I've got to put some thought into this, but you know me well enough to know I can't, I won't, stand by and do nothing when we both know someone on this list could have my daughter."

"Yeah," Beast said. "I figured as much. So where do you plan to start? I mean, as far as the list of people goes?"

"With him," she said, pointing to Randy Price.

Beast frowned. "I was thinking we could start with a group of people. Maybe we pay the johns and pimps a visit first and see if anyone knows anything about Lara's whereabouts."

"Put a gun to their heads and hope we can get them to tell us if they've seen Lara or Hudson?"

Beast nodded. "Pretty much."

"It didn't work with Fin. I'm thinking we should start with the big boys—the bosses," Faith said, "and work our way down the list." She filed through a stack of papers and pulled out a sheet. "Aster Williams," she said. "He lives in El Dorado Hills. First Randy and then Aster."

He rubbed his chin, said nothing.

"No?"

"No," he stated flatly. "The problem with starting at the top is that it's more than likely that guys like Aster and Randy are the ones calling the shots, the ones with the most to lose, the guys with the security to protect their secrets and assets."

"True, but—"

"I say we check out the bowling alley in Rocklin and see what that's all about."

"We don't have a name."

"I get that. But the coaster in the woman's pocket was from there, and it had your flight number on it. I think it's a good idea if we have a look around."

"OK. Fine. We'll check it out tomorrow." Faith rubbed her chin.

"What are you thinking about?"

"I was thinking about Robyn, wondering if she made it out of Florida alive."

He said nothing in response, but instead made his way to the front door and rechecked the triple set of dead bolts he'd installed since Faith's mom was attacked. He then checked the rifles and guns sitting on the coffee table, making sure everything was loaded and ready to go.

Faith went back to work. The list of names seemed endless. It would take them days to match up faces to names.

FORTY

Faith had spent the night in Roseville. She was awoken early by her sister, who had stayed the night at the hospital with Mom. Jana called to tell her Detective Yuhasz had been shot and was at the same hospital where Mom was staying. Beast and Rage insisted on going with her. They waited in the lobby while she went to see him. None of them had liked leaving Little Vinnie home alone, especially Rage, but Faith had seen the glint in the old man's eyes, and she knew he wasn't worried. In fact, it was easy to see he looked forward to anyone who dared to come calling.

When Faith first stepped into Yuhasz's room, she thought she'd made a mistake. The upper half of Yuhasz's body was wrapped up like a mummy. He looked pale, nothing like the man she'd come to know. A young woman sat in a chair next to him. She looked up when Faith entered the room. Despite the thick bandages, Yuhasz smiled at her and then introduced Faith to his daughter Holly.

Faith gave her a sheepish look. "Sorry about bashing your dad over the head with a keyboard."

"Oh, yeah, you're the one. I read about that. Knowing my dad, I'm sure he deserved it."

When Yuhasz laughed he had to hold his side in pain.

Holly stood up, kissed her dad on the cheek, and told him she was going to grab something to eat in the cafeteria and she'd be right back.

"I like her," Faith said after she left.

"Yeah," he said. "Me, too."

"It looks like you had a pretty rough night, Detective."

"I talked to O'Sullivan," he said. "Sounds like we both had a little too much excitement last night."

"You could say that again. Not to sound braggy or anything, but I would have to say that between the both of us, you look a little worse for wear."

He grunted.

She laughed, but it was clear they were both struggling to keep things light.

"The woman who attacked you in the parking lot was found dead inside her jail cell this morning," he blurted. "She hung herself."

"Shit." Faith exhaled and then apologized for cursing. "I shouldn't be surprised, but I am. Every lead we get turns to dust."

"Welcome to my world."

Frustration took its hold on Faith, rattling her bones and threatening to conjure up all the anger she'd been working so hard to keep under control.

Yuhasz must have noticed something was wrong because he started talking. And she started listening, which took her mind off yet another dead end.

"I was on my way to the airport to see how you were doing when I got a call from my daughter," Yuhasz said matter-of-factly. "She's been having a little trouble—I guess I should say a lot of trouble—for a while now. Her husband, the same man you recognized in the picture, has been beating her. I had no idea. Needless to say, I got a taste of that anger you've been feeling lately."

She frowned. "Is he the one who did this to you?"

He nodded. "I had a hunch he might pull something like this. I wore a vest, thought I was prepared, but he was fast and he came out firing."

"Well, I hope he spends the rest of his life in jail."

"I got a shot off, too. He's dead."

She wasn't sure what to say. "So you're going to be OK?"

"Just need a few days rest and I'll be as good as new."

"There's something else I need to talk to you about."

"Does it have to do with why you were at the airport in the first place?"

"Yes. I brought something for you." She placed a hand over her bag. "What I have inside is bigger than the both of us. Hell," she said, lowering her voice, "the information in here is enough to start a small war right here in Sacramento."

"Why don't you show me what you have?"

"Before I do that I was hoping we could agree to a few things."

"For instance?"

"What I'm about to give you is for your eyes only."

He started to protest, but she held up a hand, stopping him from saying another word. "The only reason I'm sharing this with you is because you know the system better than I do. But here's the thing. Bottom line, I need to find my kids, and I wouldn't want your investigation to interfere with that." She angled her head. "I can't just hand this off to anyone. You're the only one I trust."

"Faith," he said. "You know I can't make any promises."

"If the media gets a hold of this, every drug lord and trafficking boss in the city will be coming after me and you. The men who pay to sleep with these girls are politicians and lawyers, celebrities and businessmen. What do you think they're willing to do to keep their names out of the media?"

"What exactly do you have in there?"

"Remember the name Richard Price?"

He nodded.

"Before he was killed, he sent a list of everyone he knew in the sex-trafficking business to his sister. Not just any list, either. A binder filled with names, addresses, and a long catalog of offenses."

Yuhasz glanced toward the door. "This is big."

"You won't be surprised to learn that your son-in-law is on the list. Not only was he a regular customer—it looks as if they've been paying David Hofberg off for a while now."

She saw a mixture of sadness and something else in his eyes that she couldn't quite pinpoint.

He drew in a breath and then slowly exhaled. "I've been doing a lot of thinking," he said. "And I want to apologize to you for letting you down."

Faith waved a hand through the air. "Stop it. We've already had this talk, said what needed to be said."

"No. I let you down. I can see that now. When we first met, my thoughts were all over the place. I've been, well, my life has been off balance, and I think maybe you got the short end of the stick. Bad timing perhaps but still no excuse."

"I appreciate it. But the people who took Lara and Hudson aren't exactly your average criminals. It's going to take more than you and your men to take these guys down. And believe me—I know you don't want me involved. I get it. I'm just a civilian, an elementary school teacher with no training whatsoever when it comes to dealing with traffickers and drug dealers. But I'm already in too deep to bow out now. They know that. I know that. And I'm pretty sure you know that."

"So, are you going to give me what you have in that bag of yours or not?"

She met his gaze, tried to assess whether or not she was doing the right thing.

He held out a hand. "I'll keep in mind what you've told me. And no matter what happens, Faith, I want you to know that I've got your back."

She looked out the glass window and saw his daughter walking down the corridor, heading their way. She pulled the manila folder from her bag and quickly slipped the package into the drawer of the end table next to his bed. "I'm going to go now. You take care, Detective."

"I'd tell you to do the same, but what good would it do?"

"We'll talk soon?"

"You bet."

Faith returned to the lobby, where Beast and Rage were waiting.

Always the curious one, Rage came to her feet. "How's he doing?"

"He lost a lot of blood, but he's going to make it."

"I guess he's going to miss out on all the fun when we go after these people," Rage said.

"I gave him the same information I gave you guys."

"Seriously?"

Faith nodded. "I trust him. I feel confident he won't jeopardize my kids by letting the list get into the wrong hands."

Rage didn't look happy, but she nodded.

"Bowling alley?" Beast asked.

"Someone's a little overeager to show off," Rage told Faith. "He even brought his own ball."

"It's all in the release," he said.

Faith shook her head at their shenanigans. "Let's go."

———

Patrick was not looking forward to talking to Aster Williams. The man knew how to push his buttons, every single one of them. No matter how hard he tried to ignore the asshole's barbs and stupid quips, he couldn't do it. As he followed the stone pathway leading to the front door, he saw the eye of a lens following his every move.

Was Aster watching him now? Why didn't he think of that before he came calling the other day?

Aster's wife, Rae, answered the door. Her eyes widened. "What are you doing here?"

"Just here to see the boss." And then he winked.

Her cheeks turned a shade of red before she walked off to find her husband.

Standing tall, hands clasped in front of him, Patrick admired the sway of her sweet, sweet ass as she walked off.

Rae was back within minutes. This time she refused to make eye contact. "He told me to go ahead and bring you back to his office."

"You look lovely today," he told her after she shut the door and then led him down the long, narrow hallway.

She said nothing.

"But then again, you always look like a beautiful painting that should be put behind glass and never touched."

She stopped then and turned toward him. "Please stop. What happened between us was a mistake. We must never speak of it again."

"What's going on?"

They both looked to their right, where Aster stood waiting at the end of the hall.

"If I didn't know better, I would say the two of you were having a private conversation. Mind filling me in?"

Rae's laugh came out sounding forced. "It was nothing, dear. I promise you."

"I was just commenting on the architecture and interior design. I've never seen anything like it. And Rae told me she did most of the design herself. Quite a talented wife you have."

"You and my wife are suddenly conversing on a first-name basis?" Aster asked. "I didn't realize you two had become so familiar with each other."

"Oh, please," Rae said. She swished a hand through the air and then headed back toward the front of the house, leaving them to glare at each other through a wall of tension.

Patrick was the first to relax his shoulders and head toward Aster. "I've got good news."

Aster turned away before he caught up to him, forcing him to walk behind him instead of at his side. "Shut the door," he ordered as he headed for his desk.

Patrick clenched his teeth but did as he was ordered, then waited for Aster to give him permission to take a seat.

Aster pointed at one of the chairs in front of his mahogany desk. "It better be good. I thought I made it clear that I don't like my subordinates coming to the house. If I did, I wouldn't bother meeting you and your toadies in an abandoned warehouse across town." He gazed into Patrick's eyes, unblinking. "Do we have an understanding?"

"We do."

"Well, good, then. Tell me why you're here."

"I thought you would be pleased to know that I've located Diane Weaver."

"That's it?"

Patrick felt the urge to lunge for the man. How he would love to put his fingers around his throat and squeeze the life out of him.

"So, what are you waiting for?" Aster asked, mimicking his expression. "A fucking pat on the back?"

Patrick forced a smile as he came to his feet and straightened his tie.

"It wasn't enough that you fucked my wife while I was visiting my poor, sick mother the other day? You want me to write a handwritten thank-you card for doing your fucking job?"

Patrick did his best not to show any emotion. He couldn't know. If he did, Patrick would already be dead. So he stood there silently and waited to be dismissed, dreaming of the day he would watch Aster take his last breath.

Aster sighed. "Why is it every time I tease you about my wife, you get flustered? Can you tell me that? Why don't you just admit that you want to fuck that pussy and you want it bad?"

"I want to fuck your wife's pussy," Patrick said, "and I want it bad."

The two of them stared at each other for a moment longer before Aster burst out laughing and then stood, walked over to Patrick, and clapped him hard on the back. "You're a strange one, my boy. I don't know why I like you so much, but I do. I really do."

FORTY-ONE

The first thing Faith, Rage, and Beast did upon entering the bowling alley was get their shoes. Then they found a nice, quiet middle lane where they would have a good view of everything going on inside the building.

Faith had never heard of the place, but business appeared to be good. Middle of the week and yet the place was packed with people. Birthday parties were being celebrated within private rooms. There was a kid section with an arcade and a bar for the adults.

Faith had bowled a few times in her life, but she never realized how bad she was at it until today. Beast tried to assist, helped her select the right ball with the best weight. He also showed her how to grip the ball and how to release the thumb a split second before the fingers. The whole experience was exhausting, but once she figured they all fit in, she let Rage and Beast do the bowling while she kept an eye on who was coming and going.

"See anything interesting?" Rage asked while Beast threw another strike.

"Just lots of people. Children, couples, birthday groups, business-men, a little bit of everything including—" She stopped talking when she noticed something odd.

"What is it?"

"Look at the counter where we got our shoes, but try not to be too obvious."

Rage did as she said.

"See the customer standing there?"

"The dark-haired guy with the red vest?"

"Yes. That's the guy. Watch where he goes."

Rage watched him pay the shoe guy, then walk off with a pair of bowling shoes. Only he didn't look for a ball or head for a lane. He just disappeared down a hallway. "Maybe he's going to the bathroom."

"He's the third man I've seen come in by himself, get a pair of shoes, and head that way. The first guy I saw go that way has yet to come back." Faith looked at the clock. "We've been here for nearly an hour, and I haven't seen anyone come this way. It's very odd."

"That is strange."

"Keep playing," Faith told her. "I'm just going to go check it out. See if I can find out where everyone is going."

"Maybe you should take some pepper spray just in case."

"Nah, I'll be fine. I'll be right back."

Beast called Rage over to take her turn.

"Go throw a ball," Faith told her. "If anyone's watching us and we're all staring that way, they'll get suspicious."

"I think we should talk to Beast about this first."

"Not necessary," Faith said as she walked off.

Faith pulled a few dollars from her back pocket, then went to the shoe guy and asked him for change. Next she went to the arcade and played a pinball machine. When the shoe guy bent down to spray shoes, she headed for the hallway where she'd seen three men, including the guy in the red vest, disappear.

At the end of the hallway was a door. She turned the knob and went inside, found herself in what appeared to be a dimly lit waiting area. There was a couch and a few chairs surrounding a small wooden coffee table, and a magazine rack like you would find in a dentist's or doctor's office. Only these magazines were *Hustler*, *Celebrity Nudes*, *Sexy XXX*. She could hear noises, moaning and groaning, a few whimpering cries that sent shivers through her body. Instead of another door, there was a dark curtain that hung from ceiling to floor. She peeked through the curtain and saw a long hallway, sort of like one might see on a train. Lots of small rooms, but, again, there were curtains instead of doors.

The air was heavy with the smell of vanilla-scented incense.

The third curtain on the left hadn't been pulled all the way shut. She couldn't believe what she was seeing. A girl's arms and legs were bound to four posts attached to the painted cement floor at each corner of a mattress. There was no wooden bed frame, no night table or lamp. Just one small, dimly lit wall sconce.

The woman was young, maybe eighteen or nineteen. She looked at Faith, but there was no emotion. She was high as a kite. Faith held her breath and walked on. At the end of the hallway was more of the same. Whether she went right or left, it didn't matter, just an endless hallway of rooms with dark curtains.

"Can I help you?" someone asked.

Faith gasped as she whipped about. It was the shoe guy. "I was looking for the restroom."

"That's what I thought," he said as he stepped closer and plunged a needle into her arm.

She pulled away, but it was too late. He'd done what he wanted to do. "This way," he said. But she turned and ran in the opposite direction, past the dark-curtained rooms, trying to get to the door at the end of the hallway. Every room appeared to be occupied. Every room the same, the women bound, the men doing as they pleased.

Her vision blurred. Feeling dizzy, her legs wobbled like wet noodles right before she fell to the ground. She crawled onward, determined to reach the door, but it was no use. She hung on tight to the last curtain, pulling it from the rod and feeling the dark cloth float downward over her before someone picked her up and carried her off.

———

Rage couldn't keep her eyes off the far corner of the building where she'd seen Faith disappear. Why hadn't she returned? After Beast threw another ball with perfect form and the pins exploded and dropped, Rage said, "We need to go check on Faith."

"Where is she? I thought you said she went to the bathroom."

"I lied."

"What?"

"Faith kept seeing fancy-haired guys in suits and ugly vests paying for bowling shoes and then disappearing down that hallway over there." She pointed to the hallway past the arcade room.

"And why wasn't I told?"

Rage shrugged. "I don't know, really. Faith was acting all weird. She thought we were being watched, and she didn't want anyone getting suspicious."

"God damn it, Rage."

"Don't yell at me. I was the one who wanted to tell you."

He looked around. His gaze fell on Faith's purse. He walked that way and began searching through her bag. "She didn't take any of these fancy Tasers or pepper spray?"

Rage pulled a face. "She said she was just going to take a quick look around and then come right back."

"How long has she been gone?"

"At least ten minutes now."

"Shit." He found Faith's phone, then hit one of her contact numbers.

"Who are you calling?"

"I'd like to speak to Elaine Burnett," Beast said to whoever answered the phone. "OK, when Agent Burnett is free, please tell her Faith McMann is at the Unlimited Strikes Bowling Alley on Lonetree in Rocklin, California, and we believe she's been kidnapped. Go past the arcade, where you'll find a hallway. Hopefully that's where you'll find her. I gotta go." He hung up, tossed her phone back into her purse, grabbed his bowling ball and headed for the hallway where Rage had pointed.

"Kidnapped?"

"I had to think quick," he said hurriedly. "Hopefully that will get them moving."

Rage grabbed the Taser, then looked at all the other assorted good-ies inside and took the whole damn purse before rushing to catch up with him. She never should have let Faith run off on her own. *Stupid. Stupid.* As she hurried to keep up, she tried to figure out how the Taser worked. While she'd used a gun plenty of times before, she'd never used a Taser. How hard could it be?

There was a door at the end of the hallway where Rage and Faith had seen the guy disappear.

Beast tried the doorknob, but the door was locked. "Step back," he told her. And then he swung hard, his bowling ball crashing through the door.

Rage ducked low as splinters of wood flew through the air. Beast reached his left hand inside the jagged hole in the door, unlocked it, and pushed it open.

The Taser Rage held in her hand was a hefty thing, bigger and heavier than a Glock. With Faith's purse hanging over her shoulder, she found the lever on the Taser and clicked it on as she followed Beast through a lobby filled with sexy magazines and weird smells.

When Beast pushed open the curtain, all she saw were naked men of all shapes and sizes scrambling around within the hallways, trying to get dressed. A voice came over a speaker telling everyone to get their things and take the back exit immediately. The place had to be sound-proofed because she hadn't heard a thing before Beast bashed through the door.

Rage looked inside the first room she came to and saw a woman bound, her wrists and ankles tied to posts at all four corners of an unframed mattress.

Rage's nostrils flared, and her insides exploded. She Tasered the first asshole she saw, literally. He went down. She hit another guy before she realized she had to wait a few seconds before the thing would work again. After sending a jolt of electricity through three more men, she dropped Faith's purse to the ground and shuffled around inside. Faith had smaller stun guns inside. Yellow, pink, and blue. Rage stuffed the pepper spray and a yellow stun gun in her pants pocket, then grabbed the pink and blue stun guns. She ran down the hallway and managed to stun two more guys before they could escape through a back exit.

This was complete bullshit.

She'd lost track of Beast, but she didn't care. Every room looked the same.

Where was Faith?

Disgusting pigs scrambling to escape while young women lay naked and bound. Jolting the assholes wasn't enough, she decided. She retraced her steps and started spraying them in the eyes while they were squirming on the floor, even got one man as he tried to run past her. She got nine men before the tenth guy saw what was happening and ran out the back door butt naked.

There was a lot of crashing and banging going on around the corner. By the time she found Beast, he looked as if he might rip the shoe guy in half. With his left hand, he held the little guy against the wall and was about to bash his skull in with his bowling ball.

"Don't do it," Rage shouted. "Put him down so I can Taser him."

His face was a mask of anger, his hands shaking, his eyes bulging. But he did as Rage asked. She pulled the yellow stun gun from her back pocket and jolted him good. Then she sprayed him in the eyes for good measure.

While the shoe guy cried out like the weasel he was, she looked at Beast. "We need to check this guy's pants pockets for keys so I can release these women."

Beast leaned over and ripped the pants right off the man as he writhed on the ground, then searched for the keys.

"Where's Faith?"

He gestured with a tip of his head to the back of the room.

Her heart sank when she saw Faith lying motionless, her head at an awkward angle. Rage ran to her, knelt down beside her, and felt for a pulse. She was unconscious, but she was alive.

"Is she OK?" Beast asked as he approached.

Rage pushed herself to her feet. She was about to take the keys he'd found and use them to unlock the cuffs from the other women. She'd leave Beast here to watch over Faith, but then she paused, frozen in place.

A wave of icy-cold air washed over Rage.

She'd felt it before.

Chills came next and then a feeling of déjà vu right before her thoughts began to race, ping-ponging from one side of her skull to the other.

She was having a seizure, or she would be having one soon.

She knew Beast was close by, and she reached for him. "It's coming," she said.

Her mouth twitched. Pulses of light flickered in her head as the ground beneath her feet began to rumble. She felt a tremendous pressure as if she were trapped in a car that was sinking to the bottom of the lake and there was no escape. "This is it."

She felt Beast catch her as she began falling into a black hole. She thought she saw him remove his belt. Or maybe he'd done it so many times before she wasn't seeing it at all. Maybe she just knew what would happen next.

She bit down hard, jaw clenched tight, felt the strip of leather between her teeth.

Her body twitched, and her muscles contracted.

"Breathe, Rage," he said close to her ear, his voice calm. "Just breathe."

FORTY-TWO

Diane Weaver paced the area in her motel room between the television and the bed. A reddish-brown cockroach skittered past, disappearing under the bed before she could squish it with the heel of her shoe.

Too many days had passed since Patrick had told her he'd be back with everything she needed to get out of the country. She'd left a half-dozen messages for Patrick just since yesterday, but he had yet to return her calls.

That worried her.

Patrick had changed since they first met. She usually had a good feel for these sorts of things, but when she'd seen him last, it was difficult to read his expressions. He was definitely hiding something. He knew more than he was letting on, but what? Had he helped Aster get rid of her brother and his wife? Did he know what had become of the McMann girl?

The Patrick she once knew had respected her. He never would have used his power to manipulate her into pleasuring him in that way. He wanted control; she'd seen that much in the glimmer in his eyes when he'd unzipped his pants, making it clear what he wanted without speaking a word.

He wanted to be the boss.

She looked at the few items heaped in a pile on top of the bed—a change of clothing, toiletries, and a wool coat she'd grabbed from her sister-in-law's closet.

It was too dangerous for her to stay any longer. She went to the window and peeked outside. Thunder and lightning had kept her awake most of the night. One of the biggest storms ever recorded in the region had hit Sacramento after midnight. All morning she'd been listening to the local news reporters talk about trees falling on houses and damaging cars. People were being told to stay indoors.

She moved away from the window.

As she checked her phone to see if there were any messages from Patrick, she heard a knock. Relief flooded her as she rushed to the door and opened it wide.

Aster, along with a man she'd never seen before, stepped inside. They both wore gloves and black from head to toe.

The stranger shut the door and locked it.

Diane took a few steps backward toward the bed. The emotionless look on the stranger's face sent chills skittering up her spine. Her breath caught in her throat. "What are you doing here?"

"Don't worry," Aster said. "Patrick told me everything. How frightened you were and how you felt the need to run because you were afraid I might hurt you."

Why would Patrick tell Aster they talked? It made no sense. Patrick knew Aster would punish her for running.

"All you have to do is tell me where the girl is," he said as he slowly slid off a glove, one finger at a time.

Removing his gloves was a sign that he might not harm her.

She breathed easier, although she didn't like the other man standing near the door, his arms behind his back, his expression grim. "Why did you kill my brother?" she asked. "He was all I had left in this world."

"Your brother? I didn't know you had a brother."

Confusion swept over her. Judging by the look on his face, he really had no idea. How could that be? Maybe there was still hope of finding a way out of this mess. "I left the McMann girl with my brother and his wife in Lodi. With all the media attention, I knew it was time to move the girl. I only meant to keep her safe—for you."

"Since when did you start making decisions on my behalf?" He stepped closer, his thumb rubbing against the gloves still grasped in his hands. "I take care of you. I post your bail. I do everything but wipe your ass, and this is the thanks I get? Where's the kid?"

"I don't know. I swear. I knew we might be in trouble, so I had my brother take the little whore to his place. But someone killed my brother and his wife and took the girl." She reached out for him. "Please. You have to believe me."

"You were released days ago. Why am I only hearing about this now?"

"I was going to tell you right after I found a safe place for her, but then the farmhouse was raided and I was carted off to jail before I had a chance to talk to you. After finding my brother and his wife murdered, I was scared, so I ran."

"You managed to call your brother from prison, but not me?"

She swallowed. How did he know? His cousin? Another inmate?

"How is it that Faith McMann discovered the location of the farmhouse in the first place? Can you tell me that?"

"One of the girls Mr. Smith selected escaped his suite. He's to blame. Not me."

"His name was Jack Byron," Aster said. "He's dead. His cock blown to tiny bits."

That news surprised her, but she remained silent.

"Once again," Aster went on, "I am reminded of how you took matters into your own hands instead of alerting me to her escape."

"I know how busy you are," Diane said, her voice trembling as she tried to gain his sympathy. "I thought I could handle the situation. I was shocked to see Faith McMann and her ridiculous angry mob show up at the farmhouse. I never imagined she would go so far."

"But despite being shocked, you were thinking clearly enough at the time to send the girl away?"

She swallowed.

"They easily took over your little fortress, Diane, so I guess Faith McMann and her team don't look so ridiculous now, do they?"

She lifted her chin in defiance. "Why didn't you take care of that stupid schoolteacher right from the start? I heard she was a nuisance long before she showed up at *my* door."

The scowl on his face told her she'd gone too far, but she hadn't been able to stop herself. This was Aster's fault. Not hers. The all-powerful Aster Williams had fucked up royally. "I didn't mean to imply that any of this was your doing," she said, backpedaling when she saw his expression turn dark.

"You talk too much. It's always been a flaw of yours. Talking gets people into trouble."

Her gaze darted from Aster to the other man. There was no way out. Her muscles tensed as she tried to think of what to do, where to run.

Aster walked over to the TV and turned the volume up as loud as it would go. He then signaled for the man she'd never seen before to take care of business.

Diane ran.

She darted past Aster and made it as far as the bathroom before she felt the thrust of a sharp blade cut through flesh. She fell to the floor, the left side of her face squashed against the wet, cold tiles.

There was no pain, only the mind-numbing knowledge of knowing she was dying. The beat of her heart slowed. She tried to move her hand so she could push herself from the floor, but it was no use. Was this really how she would leave this world?

She'd never imagined dying at the hands of a complete stranger. A car accident, perhaps, or by the big, strong hands of Aster Williams himself, maybe one of the many pimps she'd done business with along the way. But this?

Now that she thought about it, though, why not?

Another cockroach, or maybe the same one she'd seen earlier, crawled toward her, making her forget all else. The little bugger was fast. At closer view she could see wings and sturdy legs with claws. Cockroaches didn't die easily. He crawled up onto her hand, its body heavy against her skin as he worked his way over her wrist.

And then her killer gave the knife a good twist, causing fiery spurts of pain to rip through her body. He yanked the blade out only to plunge it into her once again, deeper this time.

Her scream came out as a piercing cry that hurtled through the air and bounced off the walls around her, sending the cockroach skittering the other way only to find itself trapped in a puddle of blood.

FORTY-THREE

"How's Rage doing?" Faith asked Beast as he entered Mom's hospital room. Jana and Faith sat on each side of Mom's bed.

"Same as always," he said. "Antsy. Ready to go home."

Faith and Rage had been taken from the bowling alley to the hospital in separate ambulances. By the time Faith had arrived at the hospital, the drugs had begun to wear off. Five hours had passed since she'd been stuck with a needle. She was still shaken, but mostly she felt exhausted. If not for Beast and Rage, there was no telling what would have happened. She kept tearing up at the thought.

Beast hovered over Mom and smiled—a crooked smile that worked its way to his eyes. Faith had never seen him smile quite like that before.

"How you doing, Mom?" he asked.

Faith looked over at Jana, and they gave each other a what-the-hell look. Since when had Beast started calling their mom "Mom"?

"I feel pretty good," she told him. "But I've been meaning to ask. Did we ever find out what happened to the guy you tossed through the window?"

He made a face. "Broken neck," Beast said. "He won't be paying you another visit."

"What about the others?" Jana asked.

"According to O'Sullivan," Faith said, "the two men who were brought into custody have been tight-lipped so far. They refuse to say who sent them to the house or why."

"I should have taken care of those thugs while I had the chance," Beast said.

"No," Jana said. "It's best that they're behind bars where they belong."

Mom nodded thoughtfully before adding, "The doctor said I could stay here another night. I think Detective Yuhasz had something to do with that."

"Everyone we know is in this damned place," Beast said with a growl.

Faith stood. "Can I go see Rage? Is she awake?"

He nodded.

"I'm going, too," Jana said. She looked at Mom. "You two visit for a bit. We'll be right back."

After they left the room, Jana said, "I talked to the sheriff in Mendocino. Still no word on Dad or Colton's whereabouts. I didn't want to bring it up in front of Mom, but it is time to hire a search team, something we should have done from the beginning."

"We have to stay calm. It's only been a few days. Dad said to give him a week before we started worrying."

Jana rubbed her belly.

"Are you feeling OK?"

"I'll be fine," Jana said. "Everything will be fine."

Faith stopped her sister and made her look into her eyes. "I hope you know I appreciate everything you've done for me, and now Rage. I love you."

Jana smiled. "I love you, too, sis."

As they neared Rage's room, Faith asked, "Are you going to tell her, or am I?"

"It's your call."

"Hey," Rage said when she saw them.

Faith didn't like seeing so much pain in Rage's eyes.

The nurse had just left her a plastic container filled with yogurt, and a fruit bowl.

"Anyone hungry?" She pushed the table away.

"You should probably eat something," Jana said.

Rage rolled her eyes as she looked at Faith. "You didn't tell me having a sister was like having another mother."

Faith smiled. "You never asked."

"Hey," Jana said. "Be nice or I'll go into labor right here, right now, and make you watch the whole sordid business."

Rage shrugged. "If you do that, I'll one-up you and die right here, right now, and make you spend the rest of your life feeling badly about being mean to me."

"Jeez," Jana said. "OK, you win."

"Well, it's good to see you two bonding," Faith said as she moved closer to the bed while Jana made herself comfortable in the chair in the corner of the room. "Do you need me to get you anything?"

"You two don't have to worry about me," Rage said. "I've been through this enough times already to know I'll be fine. As cruel as it is, I'm not done with the world yet. Speaking of which, have you talked to that FBI woman?"

"Agent Burnett?" Faith asked.

Rage nodded. "Yeah, do we know how it all ended at the bowling alley?"

"From what I heard, you made it possible for them to have their biggest john roundups ever. They're still being questioned as we speak. She said it's rare that they're able to arrest so many people in one swoop. That bowling alley appears to have been a big moneymaker and a big part of the trafficking business in Sacramento County. You and Beast did good."

"Is Beast talking to you?"

Faith nodded. "Why do you ask?"

"He was pissed off with you at the bowling alley for keeping him in the dark. You should have seen his face when he grabbed his bowling ball and took off. I was surprised he didn't kill someone."

"I guess I'll get a lecture from him later."

"What about the woman who attacked you in the parking lot?" Jana asked. "Have they questioned her?"

"She hung herself within hours of being arrested."

"Unbelievable," Rage said.

There was a long pause before Faith glanced at Jana and said, "We came to share some good news with you. I think Jana should be the one to tell you what's going on since she did all the work."

Jana sat up tall in her chair, suddenly all fidgety and nervous-looking. "Oh, well," Jana said, off to a poor start, "it's just that, umm, I had some connections with certain people, and thanks to these people, who shall remain nameless, I was able to locate your son."

Rage looked at Faith. "Is she serious?"

Faith nodded.

"I, umm, I met his adoptive parents, and they've agreed to bring Callan to meet you."

"That's his name?"

Jana nodded as she drew in a deep breath.

Rage rubbed a hand over her bald head. She'd recently decided to shave off her Mohawk. She had one of those heads that looked good without hair. She was a pretty young woman, with or without hair. Rage deserved so much more than life had given her so far. She was much too young to die.

"Wow," Rage said quietly. "This is a lot to take in." She kept her gaze on Jana. "Did you meet Callan?"

Another nod.

"I bet he's cute."

"The sweetest boy I've ever met," Jana said. "He looks just like you."

Jana reached into her purse, stood, and brought the picture she'd sketched of him. "It's not my best work, but I drew this picture of him for you soon after I met him."

Rage stared at the picture a long time before a barely audible sob escaped. She held the picture to her chest, closed her eyes, and let the tears come. Jana couldn't stop her own tears from flooding forth, so she quickly left the room.

Faith went to Rage, wrapped her arms around her, and held her close, rocking her in her arms just like she used to do with her own children.

———

Less than twenty-four hours later, Rage stood before the mirror in her bedroom looking at her reflection. Hoping to look normal when she met her son, Rage had thought it might be a good idea if she had a full head of hair. For that reason, Beast had bought her a wig.

She turned toward Beast and Little Vinnie, who were both sitting on the edge of the bed. "How do I look?"

"Beautiful," Little Vinnie said at the same time Beast said, "Not good at all."

"You two are no help." She pulled off the wig. "I don't think I can do this. You need to cancel the whole thing."

"Not a chance," Beast said. "You're going. I don't care if I have to pick you up and throw you over my shoulder."

"You wouldn't dare."

"Try me."

"The truth is, I don't want to put my little boy in danger. We've got every drug and sex trafficker in the county and beyond looking for us. This is not a good idea."

"I already told you, it'll be fine. I've got friends outside waiting to escort us all. They'll provide plenty of security while you visit with your son. Callan will be safe."

"What if he hates me?" She tossed the wig to a nearby chair. "What if he sees my bald head and gaunt face and starts crying?"

"If that happens, then you'll know how I feel every time a two-year-old sees me coming."

She laughed. She couldn't help herself.

"Just be yourself," Little Vinnie told her. "He's going to love you."

She grabbed a red bandanna from her dresser drawer and tied it around her head. "Better," she said. "Ready to go?"

"Just give us a minute," Beast said. He poked Little Vinnie in the arm. "Come on. Time to get dressed."

Ten minutes later, Rage was standing by the door waiting for them when they came out wearing suits and ties.

"Wow, don't you boys clean up nice."

Little Vinnie's eyes were glossed over as if he might lose it at any moment. He was the complete opposite of Beast. All sensitive and mushy. She wasn't sure how he'd be able to handle all the emotions when they met her little boy, but she was glad he'd agreed to come along. She went to him, reached up and cupped his head in her hands, and pulled him low enough so she could kiss his forehead. "Thanks for coming."

"I wouldn't miss it for the world. Neither of us would."

Beast led the way out the front door, where three men, each one bigger than the next, waited to escort them to the sedan with the tinted windows parked at the curb. All three of the men wore aviators along with dark-camouflage cargo pants and long-sleeved field shirts.

"Are you going to introduce us?" Rage asked Beast under her breath.

"No," he said. "It's better if they stay focused."

One of the men opened the back door. Rage slid inside. The leather was creamy and soft. Little Vinnie climbed in beside Rage, and Beast sat in the front passenger seat.

The ex-military guy shut the door, then headed to the front of the vehicle and slid in behind the wheel, while the other two men made their way to another car parked nearby.

"Your son and his parents are already in a secured building waiting for your arrival," the driver told her.

"Thank you," Rage said.

"Not a problem. Anything for a friend of Charlie's."

Charlie. Rage couldn't remember the last time she'd heard anyone call Beast by his real name. He must have thought it sounded odd himself, but she was staring directly at him and he hardly flinched. Rage watched the road as they headed off. Butterflies flittered around inside her belly at the thought of seeing her son after all this time. Beast and Little Vinnie were being nice when they said she looked beautiful. She knew the truth. She looked downright gaunt. Her skin was pale, and no amount of foundation could hide the dark shadows under her eyes. Letting her son see her like this was a bad idea. She inhaled and was about to call it off when Little Vinnie reached over and covered her hand in his. "It's going to be OK," he said. "Everything's going to be all right."

FORTY-FOUR

Aster marched across the parking area, kicking up dirt and gravel as he went along. He used a beefy fist to pound on the steel rollup door. "It's Aster. Open up!"

The door rolled open.

He growled as he passed the man standing guard and headed for the back room, where his clan of idiots stood waiting.

"Still no fucking table and chairs," he said. "Which one of you is in charge of fixing this place up?"

Nobody said a word.

"For those of you who haven't heard, they found Craig McMann's vehicle." He waved a hand through the air. "Old news, I know, but maybe at least one of you worthless pieces of shit might be interested to know they found prints all over the interior. If they get a match, it's going to lead them straight to one of Richard Price's men—one of the two goddamn men I told Price to send away. And if that happens, you better hope they keep their mouths shut."

"And you, asshole," he went on, pointing to the man he'd brought with him to the motel to take care of Diane Weaver. "The bitch is still alive. What did you do to her, slap her around a little and figure she would die from fright?"

"I quartered her insides. You saw her lying there with your own eyes. I don't get it. That woman won't die."

Aster pulled out his gun, fired one shot.

"Jesus Christ!" Patrick said, jumping out of the way as the guy crumpled to the ground.

Aster shook his gun at another man standing close by. "What's your name?"

"Harold."

"The bitch is at Sutter Medical in Roseville. Get it done, Harold."

"Yes, sir," he said before marching off.

"And you," Aster said, his attention back on Patrick. "Mr. Fucking Big Shot, coming around my house uninvited and making my wife uncomfortable, why don't you tell me why Faith McMann or anyone else in her fucking family isn't dead yet?"

"Maybe you should just let it go. Forget about the schoolteacher and her kids and move on. Going after Faith McMann so doggedly isn't helping business."

You piece of shit. He couldn't stop the fury from rising from his toes to his face. He wanted to kill every one of these men on the spot, starting with Patrick. "I'm the boss! I'm in charge! And it's my fucking reputation that's at stake!"

"Well, who the fuck hired the blonde bombshell to take McMann out at the airport?" Patrick asked. "Not me. Nobody gave me a call before hiring some two-bit assassin. At this very moment the FBI is probably getting all sorts of information out of that pussy."

"The blonde bombshell you're referring to is dead." Aster stepped closer to Patrick, the tips of their noses nearly touching. "She killed herself rather than face me. The FBI won't hear a peep out of her. But I want you to listen to me, you little smart-ass." He jabbed a finger into Patrick's chest.

Patrick's chest puffed out, and Aster waited a second to see if the kid was going to start pounding on his chest like fucking Tarzan. Instead the kid remained silent.

"I told you to keep an eye on McMann," Aster went on. "In fact, if I remember correctly, I told you to get rid of her and her nosy-ass family. But then I get a call from one of my guys, and he's wondering if I knew that Faith McMann was headed for Florida. So why don't you tell me where the hell you were when she was flying across the country?"

"I don't have my calendar in front of me. As soon as I do, I'll let you know."

In a flash Aster had a fistful of Patrick's shirt. He dragged him a few feet away and pinned him against the wall.

Patrick had the good sense to finally shut the fuck up.

"If Armageddon wasn't going on around me at the moment," Aster said through gritted teeth, "I'd have your scrawny ass taken to that dark corner over there and have your tongue cut right out of that big mouth of yours. If you don't want to be replaced by the end of the week, you better get your priorities straight. Do we understand each other?"

Patrick nodded.

"Say it so I can hear you."

"We understand each other."

He released Patrick, watched him stumble about before finding his balance.

"You've all got two days to kill Faith McMann and every friend and relative she's got. Got it?"

"The FBI is all over her ass," one of his men said, using his fingers to check off an invisible list. "They're at the hospital, parked at her parents' house, the farmhouse—you name it. They're fucking everywhere."

"I don't give a shit!" His face rattled with rage. "Kill her. Kill them all."

"What if we find the little girl—what then?"

"Kill her, too. I've had enough of this shit."

———

Patrick pulled into the garage, hit the automatic button, and waited for the door to close tight. He entered his house through the garage. Coming home to this piece-of-shit place with its cramped kitchen and mismatched furniture depressed him. His nice suits and fancy car were all a facade.

His confrontation with Aster gnawed on every nerve in his body. He knew he'd stepped over the line by being so flip with the man, but he hadn't been able to stop himself, especially after he saw a couple of Aster's thugs listening in and saw the respect in their eyes. Respect for Patrick for standing up to him, but also respect for Aster because their boss was right about one thing. Faith McMann needed to be stopped. She wasn't afraid of guys like Aster. And to men like Aster, fear equaled power.

Patrick raked his fingers through his hair. He needed to be patient. He needed to wait for the right time to make his move. Aster would make a mistake, and when he did, Patrick would be ready.

He grabbed a frozen dinner from the freezer and tossed it into the microwave. Then he poured himself a glass of five-dollar chardonnay that his neighbor had given him as a Christmas gift. At this rate he'd never be able to afford a bottle of Domaine Ramonet Montrachet Grand Cru, let alone a glass.

He'd been doing a lot of thinking lately, mostly about how he would run the business once he was the boss. That idiot Richard Price had everything, and yet he'd given it all up. For what? The guy suddenly got a conscience and wanted out? If any of his men ever told him they wanted out of the business after he was in charge, he'd have pliers ready and yank out every one of their teeth before shooting them in both kneecaps.

Richard Price had got out easy.

The microwave beeped. He scrounged around, grabbed a dishrag, then reached inside for the plastic dish and headed to the door leading downstairs to the basement. He juggled the food in one hand while he used his free hand to shuffle around inside his pants pocket, looking for the key to the door.

He shouldn't have to be doing this shit.

He should be sitting by the pool of a big mansion in El Dorado Hills waiting for his wife to bring him his slippers and a finger of expensive Scotch on the rocks.

Everything else was bullshit.

After using the tip of his toe to push the door wide open, he made his way downstairs. He stepped onto the cement landing with a thud, hoping to frighten the kid, but she always appeared to be in her own little world. Nothing seemed to bother the little girl.

As usual, she was lying on the cot he'd set up and was reading another damn book. She didn't even look his way.

"Remember that woman at the farmhouse?" he asked. "The one you were forced to call Mother?"

Nothing.

"Somebody beat her up good. She's at the hospital and might not live for long. Does that make you happy?"

Still nothing—not a goddamn peep out of her. "Answer me," he said sternly. "Does that make you happy?"

She shrugged. "I don't care."

He tossed her dinner on the table in the corner. The plastic pitcher of water was still half-full. "You must care about something."

Another shrug.

"Well, doesn't matter anyhow," he said. "Pretty soon, you and I are going to fly away, far, far away from here."

"People will recognize me," she said. "And you'll be put in jail."

That was the most she'd said to him since he'd brought her here. "They won't recognize you because we're going to play make-believe and cut your hair real short, dye it black, and make you look like a little pixie from one of those Disney movies."

"Where are we going?" she asked.

The question amused him. "I was thinking Cambodia, maybe Cuba or Malaysia."

"Oh."

"Sounds exciting, doesn't it?"

She sighed.

"You want to come upstairs and watch TV?"

"No, thanks."

"You're just going to sit here and read forever."

She nodded.

"Whatever, but you better turn off the lights before nine."

Nothing.

"Did you hear me?"

"Yeah."

He shook his head before heading back up the stairs.

———

As soon as she heard the click of the lock, Lara got up and quietly moved the cot so she could make notes. She found the nail on the floor and began scraping more words into the cement: Cuba. Malaysia. Cambodia. She wasn't sure anyone would ever see what she wrote, but she did it anyhow. It kept her busy. Gave her something to do.

There wasn't a moment that went by that she wasn't afraid, but she knew she had to work through the fear so that when the time came to escape she'd be ready. Every day she thought about how she wished she'd just jumped off the couch and run out the door of the trailer home instead of waiting for Trista to go to the bathroom. Trista was lazy. She never would have bothered running after her. If she had run after her, she would have given up before Lara reached the main road. If she'd done that, she wouldn't be sitting down here in a cold, windowless basement.

Her next thought was about Miranda. She had no idea what had happened to her. *Did she ever get away? Was she back at the farmhouse?* Lara had to admit she preferred the basement over the farmhouse. Mother was creepy and scary. Lara could still see her face in her nightmares. If what he said was true, if Mother was dying, then she'd never be able to hurt anyone again. The idea of the woman dying didn't make her feel happy or sad. She felt nothing.

Lost in thought, Lara kept digging into the cement. Her fingers were starting to cramp from holding the nail so tightly in her grasp. When she looked at her work, she was surprised to see **LARA MCMANN** written in all capital letters.

FORTY-FIVE

Faith had fallen asleep in the chair in her mom's hospital room when her phone buzzed. It was Yuhasz asking her to come see him. He told her to gather whatever she had with her since she might need to take a drive.

Mom had also fallen asleep, so she left without waking her, wondering as she walked to the detective's room why he needed to talk to her.

"What's going on?" she asked the second she entered his room and saw him looking her way.

"Maybe you should have a seat."

"No. Just tell me."

"They found Diane Weaver."

Judging by his tone, something was wrong. "And?"

"And she's been beaten up pretty badly."

"How bad?"

"Stabbed repeatedly. Since she's been admitted to this same hospital, I thought you should know. She's in critical condition and might not make it."

"What about Lara? Was she with the woman?"

He shook his head, slowly, sadly. "They found Weaver in a motel room. There was no sign of Lara."

Faith began to pace the area in front of his bed. "Tell me that your men, the FBI, someone was at least able to question her. They must know something."

"I'm sorry."

"No," she said. "Sorry doesn't cut it. That woman, my best chance at finding my daughter, was able to walk right out of prison and disappear, and now you're telling me she's not aware enough to be questioned? This is ridiculous." She yanked the strap of her bag higher on her shoulder and headed for the door.

"Where are you going?"

"I'm going to go to her room and question her myself, something you and your men should have done the moment she was apprehended."

"There's more," he said with a sigh.

She didn't like the look on his face, but she waited patiently for him to tell her the rest.

"Ryan O'Sullivan was here a few minutes ago. They need you to go to the morgue to identify a body."

Her breath caught in her throat. "Whose body?"

"A child. A young boy."

Her stomach rumbled. Her breathing hitched. "What's going on? Do my dad and brother know about this?"

He shook his head. "Nobody has been able to locate them."

"Well, I don't understand. Where did this body come from then?"

"At least a half-dozen men are still scouring the forest in Mendocino. They found two bodies. One belonged to an adult male, who has been identified as a known drug trafficker. The other body belongs to a young boy and has yet to be identified. Under the circumstances we were able to have the body brought here to the Sacramento County Coroner on Broadway."

She drew her shoulders back. "So you think it's Hudson?"

"I don't know, Faith. I only know what I just told you. I'm sorry."

This was crazy talk. There was no way Hudson was gone. Her stomach heaved at the thought. "Why would you be sorry unless you thought it was my son?" she asked, her voice shaky.

He exhaled. "I'm sorry you have to go through this, but you need to remain hopeful."

Her hands visibly shook as she searched through her bag for her car keys. She needed to hold it together. *It's not Hudson,* she kept repeating over and over again in her mind. She left his room without saying another word.

It took her thirty minutes to get to the building on Broadway. She needed to fill out some paperwork and hand over her ID. It was a while before the security guard led her through a back door, where she was handed off to a woman in uniform. She followed her down a long hallway, waited while she signed Faith in and made her sign on the dotted line before leading her through two steel doors.

The room was cold and sterile. A woman in a lab coat stood at the counter, washing her hands with her back to Faith. There was a scale near the sink area. In the middle of the room was a stainless steel table. The small body lying on top was covered with a sheet.

Faith wondered suddenly why she was here.

She never should have come. Her son wasn't dead.

She didn't need to lift the sheet to see his face because she already knew it wasn't him. Hudson was alive and well. He was only nine. Did these people realize that?

The woman at the sink put on a pair of latex gloves before she turned toward Faith. "I'm the coroner, Harriet Foster. I wish there was an easier way to tell you this, but before I lift the sheet, I need you to know there's not much left for you to view. It's not a pretty sight by any means, and if you change your mind and feel you can't go through with the viewing, I understand. We'll be able to get DNA samples and run tests that way."

Faith drew in a shaky breath. "I need to see him."

The woman nodded and then walked across the room and stopped at the table. When Faith was positioned on the other side, the coroner carefully lifted the sheet, folding it as far back as his legs.

Faith looked at the disfigured form, unblinking and thoroughly confused. Most of its head was missing. Clumps of hair remained, half a nose, bits of skin and flesh where there might have once been a face. Half the skull had been blown away. Flashes of light flickered within her brain. Why had they called her here? This thing couldn't be human. It was no boy, certainly not *her* boy.

"What is this?" Faith asked.

"What do you mean?"

"I don't understand what I'm looking at. Is this thing human?"

The woman looked across the room, perhaps searching for help. And then she took hold of the corner of the sheet and began to cover it back up.

"What are you doing?"

"I think you've seen enough."

"Leave the sheet as it is," Faith told her. She swallowed the lump caught in her throat and said, "Just tell me what I'm looking at. That's all I'm asking."

"I haven't performed an autopsy yet. The detective asked that you get a look first. Judging by the marks on the arms and legs, I would say many of the injuries were caused by more than one wild animal."

"This can't be my son."

"Does your son have any identifying marks? Moles, scars, anything at all?"

"Why would that matter? There's nothing left of him, for God's sake."

"Hair? Clothing?"

Feeling light-headed, Faith took a breath and then forced herself to look at the body again. She let her gaze roam over the small chest that was covered with a dark T-shirt she didn't recognize. Her gaze then fell on the sweatshirt that was unzipped and pushed to the side.

For a second she forgot to breathe.

And then she slowly, gently, reached for both sides of the sweatshirt and covered the boy as if she were going to zip him up and send him off to play. That's when she saw the name tag sewn near the neckline. That's when she knew exactly who the sweatshirt belonged to. That's when she knew her son was dead and that she would never see him again.

The beat of her heart was all she heard as she turned and left the room. She didn't stop when they called her name, didn't give one shit about anyone around her.

Hudson. Hudson. Hudson.

No.

This wasn't happening.

She was back home, or in the chair in her mom's hospital room, fast asleep, having a nightmare. There was no other explanation. This had to be a sick joke.

A hand touched her shoulder.

She jerked the hand off her, would have growled had they tried to touch her again, but nobody came after her. The restroom was up ahead. She opened the door, stumbled inside, and then barely made it to the toilet before she threw up everything she'd consumed over the past twenty-four hours. She couldn't breathe, didn't want to live. She couldn't do this. She wasn't a fucking superwoman. She wasn't half as strong as her friends and family liked to think. She was only human. She used to be a wife and a mother. Now she was all tendons and tissue, nothing more.

FORTY-SIX

The farther off course they got, Colton realized, the colder the temperatures. The rain was coming down hard, and the winds had picked up for the first time since Colton and his dad had begun their long journey up the mountain.

But neither of them was ready to call it quits. Never mind that they had lost the boys' trail a half mile back.

It wasn't looking good for Hudson. Hell, it wasn't looking good for Colton and his dad, either. Unless his nephew had somehow happened upon a cabin or a cave, some sort of means to keep warm, he'd never make it through an entire night in this kind of weather.

Lightning lit up the sky, and then thunder shook the earth beneath his feet. Dark clouds hovered overhead, making it appear as if it were night instead of day.

Dad's pace had slowed considerably since setting off this morning. His age, along with his deteriorating health, was showing, wearing him down.

Colton considered setting up tents right where he stood. He could leave Dad with a fire to keep warm, but he knew just by glancing over his shoulder at him that nothing was going to stop him from continuing onward. Nobody needed to say it to know that Hudson's time was running out, or that they might all be as good as dead.

The odds of Hudson surviving in the wild for so long were not good. He was a little boy. He wasn't a survivalist. He wasn't trained for this sort of thing.

What the hell had Colton been thinking leading his dad on this ridiculous path to nowhere? They hadn't run across another river or a cabin since their second day in the forest. No hints of human life. No trail markers of any kind. Why would Hudson go this way unless he was being chased?

If they continued on much farther, he'd only serve to get him and his dad killed.

And then what?

Colton turned around and walked back to his dad. He inhaled sharply. "I was wrong," he shouted so he could be heard over the rain. "You were right. It's time we headed back. I never should have—"

Gunfire rang out, the sharp retort temporarily numbing his senses.

"That way!" Dad said, pointing ahead.

Colton turned back the way he'd been headed moments before and ran as fast as his legs would carry him. The wind whipped against his face and tried to slow him; the rain blinded him as he scrambled through brush and weaved through tall trees, nearly tripping on fallen branches and pinecones.

He didn't know how far back Dad was. Couldn't worry about that now. Dad could take care of himself.

Colton ran until he was out of breath and struggling for air. But even then he didn't stop moving forward, not until he saw a circle of stones built around a small fire within a thick grove of trees. A body lay next to the fire, shreds of cloth, bits of an old tent covering everything but small boots.

Colton walked that way, still trying to catch his breath.

"Stop or I'll shoot."

The voice sounded familiar.

Colton looked past the campfire, through brush and trees, and then over his shoulder, trying to figure out where the voice had come from, but between dark clouds and myriad trees, the fire provided too little light.

Colton heard a rifle being cocked. He raised his hands in the air, praying that the voice he'd heard belonged to Hudson. "It's me. It's Colton. Don't shoot."

A small voice came through the wind. "Uncle Colton? Is that really you?"

"It's me, Hudson. Grandpa's here, too."

Through the rustling leaves and pounding rain, he heard whimpering first and then a full-blown sob, right before he saw a shadowy figure step out from behind thick brush. It was Hudson. The boy rushed toward him and circled his small arms around Colton's waist.

Colton held the boy against him, his heart pounding, tears streaming down his face. He knelt down and ran his hands over the boy's face and chest. "Are you OK? Are you hurt? Who fired that shot?"

"I did. We're out of food. I was trying to get a rabbit, but I missed."

"We?"

Hudson pointed to the form lying near the fire. "I'm OK, but my friend Joey is sick. Real sick. It's not good."

Dad cut through the brush just then, saw his grandson, and froze in place as if he couldn't quite trust his eyesight. Hudson ran to him and wrapped his skinny arms around Dad's waist.

"Thank God," Colton heard Dad say. "Thank God."

"I went the wrong way, Grandpa," Hudson cried as he held tight, his face half-buried in his grandpa's side, not ready to let go. "I messed up bad."

"You did good, boy. You did good." Dad knelt down low so he could look Hudson square in the eyes. "I've never been so proud."

Colton left them and went to see about helping the other boy. By the time Dad and Hudson joined him, Colton had already stripped off his camping gear and pulled out the first-aid kit. "He's burning up," Colton said. "And he has frostbite."

"His name is Joey," Hudson told him again.

Colton stripped off Joey's boots and wet socks. His feet were hard, and his skin up to his ankles had a waxy shine. Colton reached into his pack and pulled out chemical heating pads and a pair of wool socks. "Dad, I need fresh water and ibuprofen."

For the next fifteen minutes, Colton and Dad made plans while Colton worked on warming Joey up and Dad worked on Hudson. Both boys had blue fingers and yellowish skin. He wasn't sure if Joey would make it unless they got his temperature down and got him help right away. "We need to get this boy help."

Hudson shivered uncontrollably while Dad unwrapped more heating pads and replaced Hudson's wet clothes with warm ones.

It didn't help matters that his dad was weak, his movements slow. He was worse off than Colton had first thought.

"Dad," Colton said. "We need to leave as much gear behind as possible so we have a better chance of reaching the bottom of this mountain as quickly as possible."

Dad didn't have it in him to argue.

There was no time to question Hudson about his ordeal, either. If they wanted to save both boys, they needed to hurry.

By the time they were ready to go, Colton's pack, along with anything he didn't need for the trek downhill, including his tent, were left at the base of the tree close to Hudson's campfire.

Colton would be carrying Joey and therefore needed to lighten his load. They had talked about making a stretcher, but it would only slow them down. And besides, Colton was just as worried about Dad as he was about the two boys.

"Ready?" Colton asked.

"Let's do this," Dad said.

The fire was out, and all three of them, Hudson, Colton, and Dad, had headlamps attached by Velcro straps around their heads in case they didn't make it to the bottom before dark. They were all armed, and they were dressed for warmth, their ears and most of their faces protected from the cold wind.

They started off single file.

With Joey cocooned in a blanket and partially slung over his shoulder, Colton led the way. Hudson followed closed behind, with Dad trailing in the back.

The ground was muddy, and the leaves were slick, making for a slow and slippery pace. With each step Colton thought of Faith and how much she'd suffered these past few months. She'd become nearly unrecognizable.

But they had found her boy.

It was a miracle—a glorious miracle.

If he didn't get them off the mountain sooner rather than later, all would be for nothing. Colton spared a quick glance over his shoulder. Hudson kept his gaze on the ground, making sure not to slip. The expression on Dad's face was one of courage and determination. Nothing was going to stop any of them from reaching the bottom as quickly as possible.

And when he turned back to watch his own footing, he thought of Craig and all that had happened to bring them to this place, this moment, and he cried, couldn't stop the tears from streaming down his face, blending in with the rain and trickling down his chin and neck. He cried for the loss of his brother-in-law, he cried for his own daughters having to witness such tragedy at such a young age, he cried for his family and for all the girls and boys who never stood a chance.

FORTY-SEVEN

Rage thought it felt strange being escorted by three men with biceps bigger than Beast's, but she had to admit she felt safe. She also knew Beast and Little Vinnie were close behind. In fact, it wasn't often that she didn't sense Beast watching over her. She'd told him many times to stop hovering, that she needed her space, but that was a lie. She'd grown accustomed to Beast. Everything about him was huge, including his heart. She wouldn't know what to do if she ever glanced over her shoulder and he wasn't there.

Her legs felt a bit weak after yesterday's episode, but at the moment, excitement and nerves overrode all else.

Callan. She liked that name. It fit somehow. For two years now she'd begun to think her little boy might be a figment of her imagination.

But he was a real boy.

And today she would see him for the first time since she'd made the decision to give him up for adoption.

The nameless ex-military guy who had driven them here stopped at the door, his hand wrapped around the handle. His aviators rested on top of his head. When he looked at Rage, she saw kind blue eyes. "Are you ready?" he asked.

Rage looked over her shoulder at Little Vinnie and then at Beast, who gave her a reassuring nod. She went to Beast and threw herself into his arms. "I don't know if I can do this."

"I know you can," Beast said. "You gave him life. You gave me life, too. You can do this."

"What if he doesn't like me?"

"He's going to love you. How could he not?"

She wiped her eyes and then nodded at Beast before turning back toward the door. After taking a breath, she looked at the man in camouflage and said, "I'm ready."

"We'll all be waiting right here when you're done," Little Vinnie told her.

"You can take as much time as you feel you need," Beast added. "His parents, Danny and Sue, are eager for Callan to meet you."

She opened the door.

Danny and Sue jumped up from their seats, both seemingly as nervous as she was. Danny shook her hand, and then his wife did the same. Sue was pregnant. Nobody had told her.

"Boy or girl?" Rage asked nervously before wondering if that was a rude question.

"Girl. We just found out yesterday."

"Callan's going to have a little sister," Danny said proudly.

They both nodded in unison—a perfectly adorable couple. They reminded her of Roger and Anita from the Disney movie *101 Dalmatians*.

"Go ahead and say hello to Callan if you'd like. He loves to play with his trucks."

Rage had never been so nervous in her life. "Does he know anything about me?"

"We discussed that recently," Sue said, "and ended up telling him he was going to meet our good friend Auntie Sally. I hope that's OK."

"Jana was right. Callan couldn't be luckier. Auntie Sally is perfect. Thank you."

Rage looked over her shoulder at Callan and then headed that way.

He was a tiny person. An adorable boy, just as Jana said. His hair was light brown and soft and wispy-looking. He had cute, chubby cheeks. She got down on her knees and asked him if she could play trucks with him. He handed her a fire truck, and she felt an instant connection as they zoomed around the room. She laughed at all the cute sounds he made, and he laughed when she played peekaboo with him and then a game of tag.

After an hour of playing with him, she asked his parents if it would be OK for her two friends to meet Callan.

Little Vinnie was nervous. He patted the boy on the head, but he had a twinkle in his eye as he watched Beast, Rage, and Callan play with wooden blocks, making towering buildings and then laughing when the blocks fell.

Minutes turned to hours, and Rage could see that Callan was getting tired. She left Beast and Callan alone and went to talk to Sue. Rage reached into her bag and held up a gift she'd brought for Callan. "Can I give him a present? It's a book. *Goodnight Moon*. He might already have it, but I wrote a note in the back of the book and signed it. I hope that's OK."

"That's fine," Danny said.

"It's his favorite book," Sue said.

Rage smiled. "It was mine, too."

Beast and Little Vinnie said goodbye to Callan and his parents and headed out of the room. Callan left his toys and eagerly came over to sit down next to Rage so he could open his gift. "Moon!" he said when the book was revealed.

"Want me to read it to you?"

He nodded and scooted closer.

She read it twice, and both times he was able to say many of the words and read along with her. He was a smart boy. And she was surprised by all the emotions she was feeling. When he grew tired, he grabbed his tattered blanket and laid his head down on top of it on the floor in the middle of the room. "Looks like I wore him out," Rage said to Danny and Sue.

They had both busied themselves with checking messages, or pretending to, on their phones. Sue picked up a book of her own and joined Rage and Callan on the floor. Callan stirred, but he was already half-asleep when Sue opened a photo book, revealing pictures of Callan's life from the first day they brought him home all the way up until a week or so ago.

"Thanks for sharing this day with me," Rage said. "It has meant everything to me."

Sue hugged her tight.

Danny helped them both up and then gave Rage a photo book for her to keep, filled with dozens of pictures of Callan at different stages in his life. During the visit, when she wasn't looking, Danny had taken pictures and printed them off on the gadget she'd noticed on the table earlier, and those pictures were included on the last page.

Rage gave Danny a hug, too.

"We hope this won't be the last time we see you," Sue said.

Rage smiled, but she knew chances were slim that they would meet again. She didn't want Callan to ever see her in a hospital bed, sick and dying. She'd prefer he remember this day. The day they played with trucks and read *Goodnight Moon*. She didn't ever want to risk ruining this perfect day. "Do you mind if I say goodbye?"

Of course they didn't mind at all.

Rage got down on her knees, kissed his chubby cheek, and said, "Good night, Moon. Good night, my sweet Callan."

FORTY-EIGHT

Faith walked briskly down the corridor of the morgue, each step echoing off solid, heavy walls on either side of her.

Someone called her name as she exited the building.

She kept walking, marching onward. The dark clouds hovering overhead were reminders of every gray and somber moment of the last months since her husband was killed before her eyes and her children were ripped from their home.

Fucking bastards, every single one of them.

She climbed into her car, started the engine, and then input the destination as Sutter Medical on East Roseville Parkway into the navigation system. Diane Weaver was in a warm bed in a hospital room not too far from where her mother and Detective Yuhasz were.

Diane Weaver was alive and breathing. Her son was dead, but that woman was alive. Faith wished her dead, but her need to talk to her about Lara's whereabouts overrode any deep-seated desire she might have to kill her with her own bare hands. She would go see the woman, and she would make her talk.

She drove a few miles over the speed limit.

Her phone vibrated. Caller ID: Detective Yuhasz.

She ignored the call.

By the time she found a parking spot, the phone was buzzing again. She didn't bother checking to see who was calling. In fact, she left the phone in the car, her focus on Diane. This was her chance.

She felt dead inside as she walked toward the hospital entrance.

They had killed her husband. They killed her son. They took Lara. Bri had moved away, and Miranda was missing. She had no idea what had become of Dad and Colton. The bastards had fucked with every member of her family, every fiber of her being.

An ambulance sounded in the distance. More than one.

She was about to walk past the ER entrance and enter through the main entrance, when she noticed hospital staff running around inside. Something was going on. The door to the ER was wide-open, so she headed through it.

She knew Diane Weaver was on the fifth floor, but she didn't know which room.

The ER was chaos. Something big had happened. Doctors and nurses rushed about, everyone dishing out orders at once. From what she gathered as she walked through the main area, there had been an accident involving a city bus and a semi. At least forty people injured—a sharp curve and speed being factors.

Faith continued on to the elevators, hit the top button, and waited for the doors to open. She stepped inside. When she stepped out again, it was as if she were invisible as she walked past the nurses' station. Nobody looked her way or asked for her ID. Three nurses were huddled together, talking about the accident, which apparently happened only ten minutes ago on Sunrise Boulevard, not too far from there.

Faith's heart beat in perfect rhythm with the sound of her rubber soles flapping against the tile floor. She didn't care what Diane Weaver's situation was. She'd threaten to pull the plug if that's what it would take to make the woman tell her where Lara was. Enough was enough. *Talk or you die*, she thought. *Talk or you die.*

With her gaze fixed straight ahead, she figured she would look in every room until she found the woman. Up ahead, first room to the left, an odd-looking man wearing blue scrubs made a hurried exit. His wild eyes, wide and alert, darted around. Their gazes met just before he walked past her.

Something wasn't right.

Faith turned and watched him disappear into the same elevator she'd ridden to this floor.

Suddenly a high-pitched alarm went off. Two nurses darted past her and ran into the same room Faith had just watched the man exit. What was going on?

Faith stopped at the doorway, where she could see both nurses working valiantly to save Diane Weaver's life. The same woman who had demanded that Miranda, Samantha, Lara, and so many others call her Mother was struggling to hang on.

Don't you dare die on me now, Faith thought. *Don't even think about it.*

The machines, the pandemonium, it all brought her back to her recent stay in intensive care. It seemed like yesterday and years ago at the same time.

When the machine flatlined, Faith stood there in disbelief. The seconds ticked slowly by. Her shoulders stiffened, and her hands curled into fists at her sides.

Diane Weaver was dead.

As she turned slowly away, she thought of the man she'd seen exit the room and all the names and faces collected from Richard Price's binder. *Which one,* she wondered, *had ordered Diane's death?*

Diane Weaver was gone, taking everything she knew about Lara's whereabouts along with her.

Pressure built. Lights flickered. Tiny, devilish eyes opened and closed. Sharp nails clawed. Her anger was back, red and raw, fiery hot, ready to destroy anything in her path.

It wasn't over.

Not even close. "Nobody fucks with my family," Faith said under her breath as she headed back toward the elevators.

More hospital staff rushed past her, heading in the opposite direction. Faith stepped into the elevator, watched the doors close, then hit "L" for lobby. She didn't go to see Mom or Detective Yuhasz. Instead she headed for the parking lot.

For now she just needed to be alone. As she walked onward, the people, the noise, it all disappeared. She stepped outside. A chill breeze swept over her. She welcomed the cold, felt a tremendous desire to lay down right there in the middle of nowhere and let Mother Nature's cold, icy fingers do their worst.

But she thought of Hudson then, and she kept walking, trying to conjure her son's beautiful, boyish face, trying to remember the last words they'd said to each other, recalling his expression in the rearview mirror as he sang along with his sister.

Her heart twisted and broke, fell like a rock to the pit of her stomach.

Her pain was no longer a flickering, quivering, throbbing ache. Her pain was now a part of her—a limb, an organ.

Every movement felt robotic as she walked across the parking lot. She opened the door to her car, slid onto the driver's seat, closed her eyes, and did nothing but breathe.

Once again her cell phone buzzed. She leaned over the console, found her phone, and picked up the call.

"Faith, it's me. I have someone right here next to me who wants to talk to you."

"Dad?" Faith asked, dazed and in shock, thankful he was alive but having a difficult time pulling her thoughts away from Hudson. Unable to comprehend that he was gone. She did think of Mom then, battered and bruised. Did Dad have any idea of what had happened while he was away?

"Mom. Mom, are you there?"

That voice gave her a jolt. She had to be hearing things.

That voice, that familiar voice, was the sweetest voice she'd ever heard. That voice belonged to the same little boy she'd rocked in her arms too many times to count.

But how could that be? She was about to toss the phone, angry with herself for letting her imagination get the best of her, when she heard it again.

"Mom, it's me, Hudson."

She needed air. She opened the door. "Hudson," she said breathlessly as she stumbled out of the car and fell to her knees. Her hands shook as she held the phone to her ear. "Is it really you?"

He was crying.

She was crying.

"It's me, Mom," he managed. "Grandpa and Colton found me. Have you found Lara? Is Dad there with you?"

The questions were fired at her like darts. Her heart broke for him.

She felt a tickle as something squeaky and weak climbed its way up her throat, defying gravity, trying to find the right words to say before it reached the top.

But nothing came.

He was alive. Her son was alive.

"Mom," he said again. "I'm coming home."

Acknowledgments

Some books are more difficult to write than others. The Faith McMann trilogy is a good example. I thought writing about serial killers was tough until I started to research human trafficking. Writing about this subject has opened my eyes to a reality I really didn't want to believe existed. Human trafficking is growing every day. It's happening right here in the United States. We need to help get the word out in hopes that someday modern-day slavery will become a thing of the past.

There are so many people to thank when it comes to the making of a novel—my editor, JoVon Sotak, for working so hard to make the Faith McMann trilogy a success. Your support is appreciated, and I feel lucky to have the opportunity to work with you. Thanks to Charlotte Herscher for her keen eye and for pushing me to squeeze out every bit of emotion I could possibly summon. And to the Thomas & Mercer Author Team, thanks for always being responsive and helpful.

Special thanks to my sister and friend Cathy Katz for being my first reader and editor for more than twenty years and for encouraging me to follow my passion, my heart, and my dreams.

I want to thank my husband and kids, Joe, Jesse, Joey, Morgan, and Brittany. You guys are my true inspiration. Not a day goes by that I don't think of each and every one of you and feel grateful to have you in my life.

And last but never least, my readers. Without you none of this would be possible. Thank you!

ABOUT THE AUTHOR

Photo © 2014 Morgan Ragan

New York Times and *USA Today* bestselling author T.R. Ragan (Theresa Ragan) and her husband, Joe, have four children and live in Sacramento, California. Since publishing her first book in 2011, she has sold two million books and has been mentioned in the *Wall Street Journal*, the *Los Angeles Times*, *PC Magazine*, *Huffington Post*, and *Publishers Weekly*. Besides writing thrillers under the name T.R. Ragan (including the Lizzy Gardner novels *Abducted*, *Dead Weight*, *A Dark Mind*, *Obsessed*, *Almost Dead*, and *Evil Never Dies*), she also writes medieval time-travel tales, contemporary romance, and romantic suspense as Theresa Ragan. *Outrage* is the second novel in her Faith McMann suspense trilogy, following *Furious*. To learn more about Theresa, visit her website at www.theresaragan.com.